"I think you should continue the class."

"I don't see a lot of point in taking it."

"I'll..."

Molly's voice trailed off and Finn's expression shifted. "What, Molly?" One corner of his perfect mouth curved into a wry expression that was somehow both cold and amused. "Be gentle with me?"

The way he said it brought more color to her cheeks. "Yes. I will."

"Thanks for the offer, but no."

"I'll...help you." What on earth was she saying?

"No. Thank you."

He pulled the truck door open and Molly heard the word "Chicken?" emerge from her lips. Finn stopped dead and turned back.

Had she really just said that?

Dear Reader,

Molly's Mr. Wrong is all about trying to get life right. During high school, Molly Adamson was a shy, bookish teen with a raging crush on one of the high school elite. You know how that usually works out, right?

Right...

Well, in Molly's case, she got a (mercy) date with her dream guy—Finn Culver—who then brought her home early from the homecoming dance and went out with another woman. Ouch. But those are the kinds of moments in life that inspire people to change, and that was when Molly decided to reinvent herself.

Fast-forward a decade and Molly is a successful college English teacher. She knows what she wants in life and she also knows what she doesn't want. Top of the list for Doesn't Want? Finn Culver blasting back into her life. But Finn is now one of her students, and Molly finds that while she knows exactly what she's looking for in her Mr. Right, she keeps feeling a tug toward Mr. Wrong.

Is she ever going to get life right?

This was a fun book to write because once upon a time I was Molly. I didn't have her homecoming experience, but I did have a couple of cringe-worthy high school moments. But don't we all? I hope you enjoy *Molly's Mr. Wrong*.

Happy reading,

Jeannie Watt

NOV 2 9 2016

JEANNIE WATT

Molly's Mr. Wrong

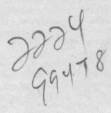

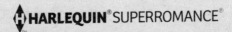

Recycling programs
for this product may
not exist in your area.

ISBN-13: 978-0-373-64009-6

Molly's Mr. Wrong

Printed in U.S.A.

Jeannie Watt splits her time between her homes in rural northern Nevada and western Montana. In Nevada, she enjoys the quiet life living off the grid, and in Montana she and her husband help with the family cattle ranch. Jeannie enjoys riding, hiking, sewing and making mosaic mirrors. She also enjoys adding to her small menagerie and has her eye on a baby goat. Shh—don't tell her husband. Check out Jeannie's website, jeanniewatt.com, for more information.

Books by Jeannie Watt

HARLEQUIN SUPERROMANCE

The Brodys of Lightning Creek

To Tempt a Cowgirl
To Kiss a Cowgirl
To Court a Cowgirl

The Montana Way

Once a Champion
Cowgirl in High Heels
All for a Cowboy

Too Many Cooks?

The Baby Truce
Undercover Cook
Just Desserts

Crossing Nevada
Maddie Inherits a Cowboy
Once and for All
Always a Temp
Cowboy Comes Back
A Cowboy's Redemption
Cop on Loan
The Brother Returns
The Horseman's Secret
A Difficult Woman

HARLEQUIN WESTERN ROMANCE

Montana Bull Riders

The Bull Rider Meets His Match
The Bull Rider's Homecoming

Visit the Author Profile page at Harlequin.com for more titles.

This book is dedicated to the Mathews Clan.
You guys are the best!

CHAPTER ONE

"Be careful of that box," Lola Martinez called from behind the cash register as Finn Culver came in through the front door of the feed store. "It's full of pottery."

"Right." Finn sidestepped the box blocking the aisle and barely kept from shaking his head as he crossed the store to his grandfather's office. Two weeks had passed since he'd returned from overseas deployment, and he was still having trouble wrapping his mind around the changes that had occurred here during the year he'd been gone.

He'd left a dusty space containing the bare essentials for serious ranching and farming and come back to a full-blown Western gift boutique and coffee corner—thanks to his cousin's new fiancée, Jolie Brody. The crazy thing was that his grandfather, Mike, who'd taught him his frugal ways, was good with it. No, he was *great* with it—because his friends hung around the store now, and he didn't have to wait for Thursday-night poker to be with the guys. Business was booming, despite competition from chain ranch stores, and how strange was that when a year ago he could have fired a cannonball through the store and not come close to hitting someone?

"Hey, Finn." Karl Evans, one of Mike's best friends, hailed him from inside the office, where two of the three chairs that usually sat side by side in front of the small television had been swung around to face Finn's desk. "We need an opinion."

Finn gamely made his way to stand behind the chairs. He'd given a lot of opinions and settled a lot of bets since returning home. Debating and small-time wagering were a way of life for his granddad and his friends Karl and Cal Sawyer.

Karl looked over his shoulder at him. "We're thinking of introducing Cal into the wonderful world of online dating. Which photo?"

On the desk were printouts of three hilariously unflattering photos of the missing member of the geriatric trio.

Finn's face grudgingly split into a smile as he picked up the photo that made it appear as if Cal's eyes had rolled back into his head. "You guys wouldn't."

"We're just going to mess with his head," Karl said with a laugh. "Teach him that it's danger-ous to miss buddy time."

Finn pointed at the photo he'd just set down. "That one. Definitely."

He left the two guys cackling and typing up Cal's bogus profile.

"I have the grain order ready for approval," Lola said as he came out of the office. She was an easygoing woman in her midforties who used to live next door to Mike. She was there temporarily until his cousin Dylan and his fiancée, Jolie, returned from Colorado, where Dylan was training in forensic biology. But with the way business was going, they could probably keep her on. He went to the counter and pulled the papers closer, reading through them slowly and making a checkmark by each item as he approved it.

"You okay?" Lola asked.

Finn glanced up in surprise. "Yeah. Why?"

"You seem…preoccupied?"

He jerked his head at the office door. "Just concerned that I might be the next guy in their sights for a prank."

"Yeah. That wouldn't be good. Those guys… they have too much time on their hands."

"That's what I'm afraid of."

"THIS IS A CUTE HOUSE and all, Molly, but what's with these closets?"

Molly Adamson's younger sister, Georgina,

stood in front of the pint-size closet, holding a fistful of hangers and looking perplexed. At nineteen, she was a year older than Molly had been when the family moved from Eagle Valley, Montana, to Darby, Illinois, where her father had been tasked with reviving yet another failing store. Moving every year or two, depending on how long it took her father to work his magic or declare the store a bust, had been a fact of Adamson family life. But Molly had been lucky that the family had stayed in the Eagle Valley for three whole years, allowing her to finish high school there. It'd been the longest she'd ever lived in one place and probably the reason she was back. Eagle Valley was the closest thing to a hometown that she had.

Georgina set the hangers on the dresser and propped a hand on her hip as she regarded the space. "Didn't people hang up clothing in the 1940s?"

"They probably didn't own as much clothing as you do."

"Point taken, but seriously, look at the size of this thing."

Molly had to agree it was small, but other than the tiny closets, the house was perfect. Situated on the edge of town with a creek on the other side of the backyard fence and beyond that fields and mountains... It was more than she'd hoped for after making the decision to return. Housing options were limited in the Eagle Valley, unless you were rolling in money, which Molly definitely was not. *Thank you, Blake.* Her ill-fated relationship with an almost-pro ballplayer had played hell with both her finances and later her self-esteem, but it had also helped her to grow a backbone.

"I would have loved this closet when I was eight," Georgina said. "Kid-size." She tapped a finger on her chin. "Maybe I could build something. You know, shelving and stuff."

Molly had seen that light in her sister's eyes before. "Uh…give me a heads-up before you start knocking out walls, okay?"

Georgina flashed a smile. "I'll probably be too busy with classes to do any serious renovation, but at semester break…don't worry," she said with a laugh. "I'll have a plan in place."

"Yes, I'd appreciate a plan." Then it wouldn't be like the time her sister had taken it upon herself to join her room to Molly's by knocking out a space between wall studs with a hammer. Both girls had gotten a lesson in drywall installation and repair shortly thereafter, with Molly handling the brunt of the work, since she was six teen and Georgina had been six. Their brother David, who perfectly split their age span, was five years older than Georgina younger than Molly, had enjoyed himself immensely, since for once he wasn't the Adamson in deep trouble.

Molly walked down the hall to the kitchen, which was crammed with unopened boxes. She leaned against the door frame, letting her glasses slide down her nose as she regarded the room. Yes, she would make order of chaos, but she didn't have much time, because her new job started in less than a week. Feeling a surge of adrenaline at the thought, she pushed off the door frame and opened the box closest to her and starting unwrapping her grandmother's china and loading it carefully into the cupboards. Rain beat on the roof as she worked, a sound she hadn't heard all that often in Phoenix, where she'd recently finished up her degree. Now it was a sound she'd been hearing for the past twelve hours.

"Need some help?" Georgina, apparently having given up on closet plans for the time being, drifted into the room. She opened a box without waiting for an answer and began unpacking kitchen utensils.

Finally, at nine o'clock, Georgina straightened from where she'd been kneeling next to the linen drawer and pushed her long dark hair away from her face. "Maybe I should go get us some take-
~~ ~~nething."

"I don't know how much takeout you're going to find here. Maybe we should hit a grocery store instead."

"Are you sure they're open this late?" Georgina asked with a tiny smirk. "And that the sidewalks are still down, for that matter?"

"Hey, you're the one who wanted to move with me to a small town," Molly said as she looked around for her purse. Although Eagle Valley was bigger than it had been when she left a decade ago.

"I'm all over this small-town thing." Georgina lifted a piece of packing material and handed Molly her simple brown leather purse. "But I was eight when we moved. There's a lot I don't remember." And a lot that she did. She'd talked about it on the drive from Arizona to Montana, wondering what had changed and who still lived there.

Molly had been surprised when newly graduated Georgina had decided to move back to Montana with her and start postsecondary at Eagle Valley Community College. She'd also been glad for the company. She'd spent a lot of solitary hours while Blake had been on the road, blithely unaware that he wasn't as alone as she was, so being alone felt different now. It reminded her of how stupid she'd been.

Georgina rolled up the rickety metal garage

door, putting up her hand as a blast of water blew in. "You know, I used to like the rain."

Half an hour later they were back with a carload of groceries. Georgina rolled down the garage door while Molly gathered as many bags as she could carry in one trip. She was starving, and the sooner the frozen pizza was in the oven, the better. She started for the steps leading up to the kitchen door only to stop dead as she came around the front of the car.

"What?" Georgina asked as she almost ran into her from behind.

"That." Molly pointed to the far wall where water was starting to seep across the garage from under the edge of the door that opened to the yard.

Her cute house had a problem more pressing than closet space. Her cute house was flooding.

"Did the creek overflow?" Georgina asked.

"I don't think so. It seemed pretty low yesterday." Molly quickly climbed the steps and unlocked the kitchen door, set down the groceries and headed out to the back deck. The creek was still in its banks, but something was making the garage flood.

Using the small flashlight on her key chain, Molly walked around the edge of the house and shone the light on the concrete garage entryway, which was lower than the surrounding landscape and created the perfect place for runoff to flow. Water lapped against the bottom of the door.

"Damn. That's at least three inches deep."

"Poor design for sure," Georgina muttered. "What do we do?"

Molly pushed her wet hair back. "We get out of the rain and cook our pizza."

"Seriously?"

Molly shrugged as she led the way back to the deck. "We have nothing in the garage other than the car. The house sits a couple feet higher than the garage, so we ignore it until morning."

When she and the real estate agent were going to have a chat.

But it turned out that the agent was on vacation for the next week and a half.

"I have half an inch of water in my garage from the storm last night and I want something done about it."

"We're a real estate office," the woman on the other end said irritably. "You need a plumber."

No. She needed to know why this situation wasn't mentioned when she specifically asked about flooding and plumbing problems and was told there were none. "Have Mr. Hettle call me when he gets back, please."

There was a hearty sigh on the other end of the line and Molly forced herself to stay silent. Not to apologize. It was hard to break that habit, but hitting her breaking point with Blake had changed her, helped her find her backbone, and people with backbones didn't apologize so that other people would play nice with them.

"I'll connect you to his voice mail." Molly was abruptly switched over and after the greeting, she left a short message. One problem not solved. She glanced at her watch, then went to the closet to grab her dark blue blazer. Even though her job didn't start for another week, she had to attend orientation meetings over the next several days. "Hey, George! I've got to go."

"See ya." Her sister's voice drifted down the hall from her room, followed by the sound of hammering.

Hoping all the walls would be in place when she got home, Molly backed her car out of the still-damp garage, then stopped when she noticed the older man next door digging around his rosebushes. Molly rolled down her window.

"Excuse me," she called. The man looked up, then set down his shovel and crossed his yard to the fence. "My garage flooded last night during the rainstorm... Do you know if the people who owned this place before me had the same problem?"

The man shook his head. "Flooded, you say."

"Water filled up the entry leading to the side garage door. It's receding, but if we get rain again…"

"Ah. There's a drain in the bottom of that concrete slab. Yours must be clogged."

A clogged drain. Easy fix. Suddenly the world seemed brighter and Molly smiled at him. "Could you recommend a good plumber?"

"If you don't mind waiting. They're building more houses on that hill near the lake and the guy I know is pretty busy, but he'll get to you. Eventually."

"Is there anyone else?"

"Probably not anyone you want to hire." The old man cocked his head. "How 'bout I send my grandson around? He's pretty good with that stuff and he'd fix you up for free."

Molly started shaking her head, then again stopped. Small town. Helpful neighbors…why say no to that? "If he doesn't mind. I'd prefer to pay him, though. I'd feel more comfortable that way."

"Well, I don't know if he'd take money, but I can ask him to stop by tonight after he gets off work and he can see what's what. Does six o'clock work for you?"

"Yes. It does." And she needed to get moving. "I have to get to a meeting, but thank you. I really appreciate your help."

The guy raised a dismissive hand. "Not a problem. We're neighbors. Mike Culver, by the way."

"Molly Adamson. Glad to meet you, Mike." She put the car in Reverse, waved to her neighbor, and backed out onto the street. If Mike's grandson could help her out with this problem, then her biggest dilemma would be closet space. After the trauma of the past few years, she could live with that.

FINN HAD A BAD FEELING about this. Mike was a totally capable plumber, a master of the drain snake, so why had he asked Finn to take care of his neighbor's problem? He assumed it was because she was female. Finn had no trouble meeting women, but the kind of women he dated weren't generally the settle-down kind. Mike wanted him settled—not that he was actively matchmaking. No, he'd just been dropping heavy hints for the past two years.

Finn also suspected that Mike considered himself the mastermind behind his cousin Dylan hooking up with Jolie Brody, who'd worked at the store. Maybe now that he'd tasted success, he was moving on to his next targets—him and Cal.

The thought made Finn's blood run a little cold.

The lights were off in Mike's house when Finn parked in the driveway. Maybe his grandfather really was busy and didn't have time to help the lady. Feeling slightly better, he started up the neighbor's walk. The door opened before he reached the low porch, and a slim woman with straight honey-colored hair that fell just past her shoulders and heavy black glasses that gave her a sexy secretary look stepped out the door to meet him.

"Hi," she said as she closed the door. "You must be…" Her eyes widened as her voice trailed off and Finn had to stop himself from looking over his shoulder to see what had frozen her expression. "Finn Culver."

She said his name as if it was an accusation and he had the distinct feeling that he had just crossed that line into the twilight zone.

"I am." He ran his gaze over her, looking for a clue. He sure as hell wasn't wearing a name badge, so he had to know her from somewhere. Mike said she was new in town, but there was something about her that niggled at his brain.

"You don't remember me." The words were spoken in the same flat tone as his name.

Angular face, hazel eyes, really nice mouth, kind of wide and full. A few freckles. Big glasses. He was drawing a blank. "You seem familiar." No lie there.

"It was a long time ago," she said.

"What was?"

She folded her arms over her chest. "The mercy date."

CHAPTER TWO

MOLLY FELT LIKE smacking her forehead as she ran her eyes over the man standing in front of her, looking self-confident to the point of cockiness.

Okay—that had been stupid of her, not cluing in on the fact that her neighbor's last name was Culver. But she hadn't thought about Finn Culver in a long time. She had fresher humiliations to think about, like her ex-fiancé spreading the love as he traveled with his ball team. Finn Culver hadn't even been a blip on her radar—or at least not until he appeared at her door just now, looking even better than he had in high school. Of course he couldn't be one of those guys who started to thicken up in their early thirties. If anything, he was more muscular, his face more sculpted. And the little lines at the corners of his eyes added to the package. She hated the fact that the package still looked so good.

"Mercy date?" Finn repeated. Then an expression of dawning understanding crossed his handsome features and his face split into a grin. "Wow. That was a long time ago."

And that grin pissed her off.

"Yes." But not so long that she'd forgotten any of it. First there'd been the embarrassment of their mothers arranging the date so that Molly could attend the homecoming dance. To this day Molly didn't know if her mother had been aware of the fact that she'd had a wild crush on Finn, who'd been two years older than her. She'd approached the date with anticipation and terror.

When the big day had finally arrived, she'd gone to the game with one of her friends since Finn was playing, hooked up with him afterward for the dance, thought they were having a good time, and then he took her home as soon as the last song had ended. No kiss at the door. Nothing. Oh well, she'd told herself. So he wasn't a guy who pushed.

It turned out that he wasn't a guy who pushed *her*.

After dropping her off, he'd gone to a party where he'd scored with one of the high school's socially elite. Molly knew because the girl had wondered aloud in the locker room if she was going to get pregnant because she and Finn had "forgotten" to use protection. And then in a nightmare moment, the girl seemed to remember (a) that Molly was standing at a locker a few feet away and (b) that she'd also been with Finn that night, though not in nearly such an intimate way.

Heat rose in Molly's cheeks at the memory. Everyone in school had soon known that Finn had ditched her to spend the rest of the evening with someone more in his league. And they'd sure had a great time.

She realized then that even though she hadn't thought about it in a long time, she hadn't forgotten the searing humiliation of the homecoming episode—she'd buried it and stacked rocks on top. But the feelings were pushing their way to the surface, and Molly discovered that those feelings were still just a bit raw. She didn't have to put up with guys like Finn or Blake anymore. Not for one lousy second.

"You know," she finally said, hoping he didn't notice her overly pink cheeks, but needing closure on this matter, "I can understand how being saddled with a date our mothers cooked up might not have been the greatest, but did you really have to nail Sheena that same night?"

"Shayna."

"I stand corrected."

Finn shifted his weight uncomfortably. Good. "I didn't intend to humiliate you."

"Well, you did."

"Obviously you're still angry about it." He

quickly held up a hand. "Not that you don't have cause. You do."

"I'm not angry." Molly drew in a breath. "But you know, honestly? I'll be more comfortable calling a professional for this job." She'd made her point and now she wanted him gone.

Finn rubbed the back of his neck as if his muscles had gone tight, then met her gaze, and she was irritated to discover that she still thought he had pretty amazing eyes. "Let me look at the problem. I owe you."

"You owe me?" She spoke on an incredulous note.

"I showed poor judgment."

"You were monumentally insensitive."

"I was a horny teenage boy."

"Who didn't make one move on me." The words blurted out and Molly was surprised to find that she didn't regret them. Not one bit.

A look of surprise crossed his face. "You were so…"

He stopped before he got himself into trouble, but Molly was not letting him off the hook. Her eyebrows lifted coolly. "Please. Finish your thought."

"Mousy."

Molly's eyes went shut for a fraction of a second as her lips thinned. Yes, she'd been mousy. Which was worse than being invisible, which is what she'd thought she'd been. She opened her eyes again and fixed her gaze over his head at his Mustang as her economical self battled with her pride. On the one hand, the incident had occurred a long time ago. His grandfather was her neighbor. On the other, he'd taken her out on a date, dumped her and screwed another woman that same night.

"Tell your grandfather thanks for sending you." She started to cross her arms over her chest, then stopped abruptly. No more drawing into herself. "I appreciate you taking the time to stop by. I'll reimburse you for your gas."

"Forget the gas," he said. "And for what it's worth, I apologize for what I did."

"Accepted." Molly meant what she said—even as she wondered if he did—because she was not going to let ancient history weigh on her. But she also wasn't having the guy work on her drain. Wouldn't be beholden to him in any way, shape or form. "Now, if you don't mind…I have more unpacking to do."

"You're back already?" Mike looked over his glasses at Finn.

"Your neighbor—" for the life of him he couldn't remember her last name "—wants to hire a professional."

"Are you sure it's not a case of her feeling uncomfortable about taking up your time and getting help for free? I mean, she wasn't just being nice, was she?"

"Trust me. She wasn't being nice." She was totally pissed over an incident that he'd long forgotten. He doubted very much that she'd walked around regularly stewing about the incident for the past dozen years, but there'd been no question that once she'd been reminded, she still harbored resentment.

"Meaning?"

"She didn't want me to do it. Maybe she took one look at me and decided I was incompetent." Or an asshole. Actually, there was no maybe about that. He was not on her A-list.

Mike studied Finn for a long moment, his gray eyebrows coming close together, making Finn feel very much as he had when he'd been guilty of some kid crime and Mike had wanted him to fess up on his own. Finn always had, but today he didn't think that Mike needed to know all the details of what had gone down between him and Molly whose-last-name-escaped-him.

"Is something weighing on you?" Mike finally asked. "You haven't been yourself lately."

Finn gave a snort. "I'm good."

"You seem unsettled."

Finn almost said something about the military changing a man, but he didn't want his grandfather to latch on to the notion that he was suffering from PTSD. He wasn't. He forced a smile. "Maybe I grew up a little while I was overseas. I'm fine. Anything else?"

His grandfather took a few seconds before shaking his head in a way that told Finn that the matter was not yet considered finished. "Nope." Mike focused back on the ledger in front of him and Finn left the office.

Until now, he'd thought he'd done a pretty good job of hiding the fact that he no longer wanted to spend his life selling grain and Western doodads. He wanted to do something that spoke to him, that *meant* something. It wasn't sales and it wasn't mechanics, which had been his specialty in the service.

Finn had always been woefully bad about choosing the right path, unlike his cousin Dylan, who'd managed the store while he was overseas. He and Dylan had grown up together, sons of brothers, but Dylan's father had been terminally ill during their teen years, so his cousin had been all about school and academics and doing well so that his father would be proud. Finn had been all about good times. Academics had never interested him. He excelled at sports, so that was what he'd pursued. After graduating from high school, he slid into the family business, apprenticing under Mike before taking it over when Mike semiretired.

The business had done all right under his watch, but it hadn't thrived as it had under Dylan's—or rather his fiancée Jolie's—and Finn knew that was because managing the store was not what he wanted to do. It was what had been *easy* to do. His real life had started after closing, but that life—hitting the bars, playing sports, watching games—no longer called to him, either.

During the service a crazy thing had happened—he'd discovered that he enjoyed teaching new recruits the ins and outs of mechanics and enjoyed working with people in a way that didn't involve ringing up a sale or loading a bag of grain. Teaching made him feel...valuable... in a way he'd never felt before, and on the flight back to the States, he'd come to the conclusion that he wanted to teach industrial arts, to show kids how to work with their hands. He had a feeling he'd be good at it, that it would give him satisfaction, but he didn't know how his grandfather was going to take his abandoning the store.

Mike was getting older, had retired once, and there would come a time when he would retire again. Who would manage the place then? Because both he and Mike felt strongly about having a family member present in the family business.

Maybe Jolie when she and Dylan returned? That would be a perfect solution.

One that he was going to discuss with his cousin as soon as he got a chance.

As soon as the water had gone down, Molly took the top off the drain and shone a flashlight down the drainpipe, but she couldn't see any obvious obstructions. She then pulled up a video on YouTube about snaking drains and watched it with Georgina looking on over her shoulder.

"Where are we going to get one of those things?" Georgina asked, pointing at the reel holding the industrial-size snake.

"I don't think we are." Not unless she could find a place that rented the equipment. She doubted that Finn had the equipment necessary to handle the problem either...unless of course he was a plumber. Which was totally possible, so she paid close attention to the last names of the plumbing experts she found online before choosing one to call. She wasn't about to ask Mike Culver for his recommendation again, because she didn't want to explain why she'd sent his grandson packing. She hoped to stay friendly with her neighbors.

Plumbers in the area were busier than she'd anticipated, working on the new houses going in around the lake. But the forecast was clear and sunny for the next seven days, so Molly didn't panic when she couldn't get an immediate appointment without paying an emergency fee. She took the first regular appointment, two weeks away, and told Georgina that they wouldn't be storing anything that wasn't waterproof in the garage for a while.

"Maybe you should have let the hot prom guy handle it."

"Homecoming, not prom. And I'd rather sing opera naked in the park."

"YOU SURE YOU don't want to watch the game with us at McElroy's Bar?" Karl asked as Finn got ready to leave the store for the evening. "We three could attract the girls and maybe one of them would feel sorry for you."

"Hard to turn down an offer like that," Finn said with a grin. "But I've got some stuff to catch up on at home."

From the way Karl and Cal exchanged glances, Finn gathered that Mike had shared his concerns with the boys. Finn had to admit that he'd never turned down an offer to go out in favor of kicking around his house before he'd gone overseas, but he hadn't had a focus or direction then, either.

"Give me a rain check," he said. "The guy who sublet my place while I was gone let a few things go to hell, and if I don't take care of things now, I'll regret it later."

"We understand," Cal said, stepping forward to clap Finn on the upper arm, as if he were about to embark on a perilous journey and making Finn wonder if he'd be better off going with the guys to McElroy's and letting them attract women for him. It'd get these two off his back, but the truth of the matter was that he wanted to register for classes and before he did that, he wanted to give his cousin Dylan a call.

"Thanks for understanding," Finn said with a grave nod. He'd have to go out and disgrace himself one of these days to keep Mike from worrying about him.

He grabbed his coat off the peg by the door and headed toward the side exit. Behind him he heard Karl, Cal and Mike shutting down the office in preparation for dinner out followed by the evening game. He was glad his grandfather had good friends, because it was going to make it easier when Finn informed him that he wasn't going to be with the store forever.

After returning home, Finn signed into his newly created account at Eagle Valley Community College and registered for two evening classes, figuring that would allow him to ease back into school without affecting management of the store. He finished his registration, then got to his feet, feeling a surge of energy. No, make that energy coupled with unexpected anxiety.

What in the hell had he just done?

When he'd walked across the stage wearing his mortarboard twelve years ago, he'd sworn that he'd never subject himself to anything close to a formal classroom again. Yet here he was, wading in.

For a good reason.

He opened a beer, turned on the game and tried to focus, but even though the score was close, he kept going over the pros and cons of his plans for his future. Maybe he should have used the money he had coming due to his military service to dive in with both feet and do a four-year college program instead of a couple of courses at the local community college. That would show commitment. Was signing up for only two classes a wishy-washy approach to his new life?

Finn didn't do wishy-washy. But on the other hand, he couldn't just abandon his grandfather on short notice…although he had a feeling that if he did, Mike would wish him Godspeed and hire someone to do his job at a lower salary.

He leaned his head back and closed his eyes. Action erupted on the screen in front of him, the announcers went crazy, and Finn opened his eyes again. His team had pulled ahead. Cool.

Karl was probably going nuts because he hated Finn's team. Finn smiled faintly and took a long drink, wishing he was enjoying the moment more.

Finally he reached for the phone and dialed his cousin's number. Dylan answered on the first ring.

"I'm going back to school," he blurted as soon as his cousin had said hello.

"No kidding." Dylan sounded stunned at his announcement and he didn't blame him.

"Yeah. I am. I want to become an industrial arts teacher with an emphasis in automotives." There was a long stretch of silence. "Hello?" Finn finally said.

"Yeah. I'm here. I just thought I heard you say you wanted to be a teacher."

"Not a real teacher. A shop teacher."

"Last time I heard, they were real teachers."

"What I meant was that I want to teach hands-on skills that kids who don't go to college can use in life."

"You want to be a teacher."

"Strange, huh?"

"I gotta say that I never saw this coming. What does Mike think?"

"I haven't told him yet."

"Why not?"

"I…don't know." Fear of failure maybe?

"What school are you going to?"

"The community college let me in. I got official notice last week. I'm only taking two classes. I thought it best to start slow."

"Definitely. Especially after…uh…" Dylan gave a discreet cough and Finn filled in the blank for him.

"I did crappy in high school?"

"Yeah. Something like that."

"I had no reason to do well. Now I do." And his grades hadn't been that bad. He'd graduated with a high-C average. He'd actually excelled in math, the only class he'd truly enjoyed. The rest had been more a chore than anything, but again, now that he had a reason to learn, he'd do better.

"I think this is a good idea, Finn."

That was what Finn had been waiting to hear. Dylan knew school. He knew academics. He knew Finn.

"Maybe I'll tell Mike, then. I can take math and English in the evening and still work full-time. After that, then we'll have to work something out."

"After that, Jolie and I will be back and she can take over your job." Just the words Finn had hoped to hear.

They talked for a few more minutes about

life in Colorado, then Finn hung up feeling a lot more certain about his course of action.

Hell, he was actually kind of excited.

"I KNOW THIS is a full schedule," Mary Jean Flannigan, the curriculum director, passed a printout of Molly's new classes across the desk to her, "but with funding cuts, we've all had to pull extra duty."

"I'm okay with it." As a new instructor to this school, she'd be stupid not to be okay with it, but the truth of the matter was that she didn't mind being overloaded, and this schedule didn't seem that bad. The only addition to the mock-up she'd received the week before was an evening basics class and a composition class run in conjunction with the local high school, which gave the high school participants college credit. Molly was well familiar with the program. She'd had nine college credits by the time she'd graduated from high school, but had never dreamed she'd one day be teaching in the program.

"Let's see…" Mary Jean flipped through some papers on her desk, then squinted up at the computer screen. "Looks like you're set. You'll share an office with Kelsey Cunningham and you have a key to that, so…any questions?"

"Class lists?"

"Will be loaded by the end of the day."

Molly smiled. "I'm set."

She walked out of the director's office and started down the hall to her office, only to slow her steps as she caught sight of a guy walking ahead of her who looked an awful lot like Finn Culver from the back.

Finn was a student?

He certainly hadn't been one in high school. Rumor had it that the only reason he made grades was because the coaches needed him to be eligible to play.

It couldn't be him.

But when the man turned down another hallway, Molly caught his profile and her stomach twisted a little. Yep. Finn.

She put her head down and continued to her office at a brisk pace. So what? He was probably there for the diesel mechanics course. Or maybe welding. Even if he was in one of her courses—so what? What had happened between them was history—and more importantly, it truly *felt* like history now that she had gotten her chance to address the matter with him. That had been satisfying, even if she hadn't gotten her drain fixed for free.

Mousy.

Pfft.

The one thing she was never going to be again was mousy.

FINN HAD NO IDEA what to expect his first night of class. His schedule was simple—an hour-long English class on Monday and Wednesday and an hour-long math class on Tuesday and Thursday. Classes started midweek due to Labor Day, so he only had one of each that week. And thankfully, the classes started late enough that they didn't interfere with work, meaning he didn't have to tell his grandfather what he was doing just yet. He preferred to test the waters before making any big announcements and now, as he was getting out of his car in front of the community college, he was glad he'd kept his plans to himself.

Registering for the courses had felt surreal, but now that he was in the building, looking for his classroom, well, surrealism was replaced by good old-fashioned nerves.

Which was stupid. He'd seen action in the Middle East; he shouldn't be intimidated by an English class. But his gut twisted as he recognized his room number. The two middle-aged women walking ahead of him went into the room. Cool. They didn't look at all intimidating. They looked like normal people. Like him.

Drawing in a breath, he walked into the room, automatically searching for a chair in the back.

"I'd like all the students to sit in the first two rows, please."

Finn froze at the oddly familiar voice, then slowly turned his head to meet Molly whatever-her-last-name-was's rather grim gaze. Then he looked down at the schedule he still held in his hand as if it were a ticket to get into the room. M. Adamson.

Adamson. Her last name was Adamson. Bringing his eyes back up to hers, he tried to decide if the night could get any worse. Maybe if his car caught fire or something. Forcing a smile, he made his way to the second row and sat one desk away from one of the women he'd followed into the room. She smiled at him in a motherly way and he smiled back as he checked out Molly from the corner of his eye. She was welcoming another student, guiding her to the front of the room.

Son of a bitch. What were the chances?

He drew in a breath. He could do this. A woman he'd humiliated twelve years ago was now his teacher, but surely she'd treat the situation professionally and not find small ways to torture him. Because if she was going to do that...

What?

He was going to quit?

He didn't think so. He centered his notepad on his desk, pulled a pencil out of his pocket and readied himself for battle. From the look Molly gave him before she turned to write something on the whiteboard, she was doing the same.

Let the game begin.

MOLLY HAD LEARNED that Finn was one of her students early that morning when the class lists finally posted—late because of a computer error. So she'd been ready for this moment. He hadn't had a clue that she was his instructor, and she had to admit to feeling a certain satisfaction at the flash of the deer-in-the-headlights look he'd given her when he'd realized who his instructor was. Yes. That had been one small bright spot in what was no doubt going to be a series of long, self-conscious evenings.

Even now he was sitting with his feet stretched out in front of him, a half smile playing on his lips, looking way too sexy and comfortable. Making her feel less than comfortable. It was almost as if the air was snapping with small sparks now that he was in the room.

She started to speak, but had to stop and clear her throat. "Welcome to English Basic Comp. I'm Molly Adamson…"

She explained her grading procedures, her class expectations and what her objectives were for the course. She handed out the syllabus, gave a brief overview, then leaned back against her desk and asked if anyone had questions before they began the night's work. Several hands went up, but Molly was expecting that. She'd taught classes specifically for older adults at college in Arizona while she'd worked on her degree and knew that nontraditional students liked to ask questions. They wanted some bang for their buck.

Finn had no questions and when she chanced a look straight at him, instead of letting her gaze skim past him as she'd been doing, she saw that his expression had shifted from cavalier to something bordering on serious.

She swallowed and called on the lady next to him—Debra—who had a lot of questions. When the students were finished grilling her, Molly handed out a paper.

"What you're getting is your first assignment. A writing assessment to let me know where you are as a writer. The topic is simple—describe a moment in which your life changed forever. I'd like at least one page. No more than two."

Finn was once again wearing his half smirk, but Molly ignored it.

"The computers are behind you. When you're done, please hit Print, then place your papers in the in-box on my desk. I'll have them back with comments and suggestions next week."

Debra raised her hand. "Will this grade count?"

Shades of high school. Molly smiled. "I'll put

a grade on the paper, so you get an idea of where I think you are, but no. The first paper is for me to figure out what each of you need. Then I'll do my best to give it to you."

And damned if her gaze didn't stray back to Finn, who met her look dead-on as the last words came out of her mouth.

CHAPTER THREE

FINN LEFT THE EVCC campus feeling drained and in deep need of a beer. No wonder there was so much drinking on college campuses. Although he wondered if regular students found sitting through a basic English comp class as challenging as he had. He'd sweated over that damned essay, typing a single sentence while Debra, at the computer next to him, seemed to be blasting out pages.

At least he could type, but he wasn't fast. It'd been so long since he'd put thoughts down on paper that the whole process seemed foreign to him. But he'd done okay in the end, talking about how his parents' divorce had affected him as a teen and managed a page and half. Hopefully Molly would go easy on him, realizing he hadn't been in the classroom for a while. Hopefully...

Once he was on his way home, his tight muscles started to give. He rolled his neck and shoulders, told himself that the hard part was over. He'd sat through one class; Molly hadn't embarrassed him, or even looked at him more than a couple of times…although that last look she gave him had him shifting in his seat.

Molly Adamson—he wouldn't forget her last name again after tonight—didn't look mousy anymore. A couple of times as she was answering student questions she'd become animated and he'd been surprised to see dimples appear at the corners of her mouth. She'd smiled and gestured, and then seemed to remember that he was in the room and instantly became the English Teacher.

She clearly was aware of him and probably still thought he was the king of assholes, but he felt better about the course walking out than he had walking in. He was also now less intimidated by his math class on Thursday. As long as it wasn't taught by someone he'd once screwed over, he should be good.

MOLLY BIT THE END of her pencil as she read through Finn's essay for the second time. The first time she'd thought he'd been putting her on, playing with her, so she'd skimmed over it, expecting to find some kind of punch line at the end. There was no punch line, so she'd turned back to the first page and started reading again. He hadn't written about a moment, but rather a summer. His parents had divorced and he'd gone to live with his grandfather, Mike, while they sorted things out. It was the first time he hadn't played summer ball because he'd been too ripped up inside, but he'd pretended to his friends that he had a shoulder injury.

Molly had had no idea that might Finn Culver's life had been anything other than perfect during high school. He never showed a sign. But it wasn't the experience she was grading. It was the writing, which wasn't good.

His sentences were short and to the point, but more often than not, he used clauses instead of sentences…and sadly, the sentences/clauses were the strongest part of his writing. As far as structuring meaningful paragraphs, it was as if someone had fired a shotgun of disjointed thoughts at the page—and there were a lot of thoughts, since he'd dealt with a season—summer—rather than a moment as assigned.

Molly leaned back and tapped the pencil on her teeth. He couldn't be serious. Could he?

She had to assume he was. He was paying for the course.

Finn, the sports hero, had obviously not spent much time in English class and now he was suffering the consequences. That piper, which people spoke of paying, was now making an appearance in Mr. Culver's life, and she was in the unhappy position of having to point this fact out to him.

She marked his paper, the last of the evening, and slipped her grading folders into her bag as the phone rang. *Please, don't be the plumber canceling...*

"Molly? Hey." She froze at the rich deep tones of her ex's voice. "Molly?" he repeated.

"Yes."

"How're you doing in Big Sky Country?"

"I'm doing well, thank you." If she didn't make small talk, he'd get to his point and they could end this conversation all the sooner.

"I'm doing pretty good down here in Arizona, too, thanks for asking."

She drew in a breath, but kept her mouth shut. "The season is winding down, but it's been a good one."

"What do you need, Blake?"

"I need the sale of the house to hurry along so I have some money to live on during the winter." Twice the small house they'd shared had been in escrow and twice it had fallen through as the market fluctuated.

"And I'm supposed to do that how?"

"Would you let me borrow some money against the sale?"

"Are you kidding?" She used to be nicer about this. So much nicer.

"I need it." His voice went flat.

"No." Blake was still having trouble getting it through his head that she wasn't in the make-Blake's-life-easier club anymore. When he hit a wall, the first person he'd turn to, if he didn't have a current girlfriend, was her. For old time's sake. Because he'd made mistakes. Because he'd always loved her best.

Because he was a narcissist and she'd been stupid.

"Molly, I don't have the resources to get through the winter."

"Get a job." She ended the call, then scrolled through her menus and blocked his number. There. Problem solved.

She should have done that the second time he'd called for a date. But no. She'd been blinded by his beauty, in awe of the fact that the gorgeous guy who sat next to her in English 405—an athlete, for Pete's sake—wanted to go out with her. And he'd continued to go out with her. At first she thought he'd wanted help with his studies, but he did all right in his classes without her. That was when she'd given herself a good hard look in the mirror and realized that she really wasn't that different from other women her age—she only perceived herself as different. As lacking in areas that other woman took for granted. Blake had even seemed charmed by her awkwardness and because of that, it had started to fade.

Her gift from Blake—a jump start to her self-confidence.

If she owed him for anything it was that, but not enough to lend him money. Especially when his behavior at the end of their short marriage had knocked her newfound self-confidence sideways.

She was still getting over a few of the knocks.

Molly pushed the thought aside. She'd moved back to the Eagle Valley because she'd been happy here. There'd been the usual high school traumas—*cough*, homecoming with Finn, *cough*—but in general she'd been a happily invisible nerd, with happily invisible nerdy friends. In Eagle Valley she'd found a sense of peace she'd never gotten anywhere else.

And it was a thousand miles away from Blake.

Yet still he called her to make things better.

She walked down the hall to her bedroom, glancing into Georgina's room as she went by. One wall was stacked high with clear plastic bins that had become the temporary wardrobe solution. One bin sat on the floor next to her bed, which was scattered with the clothes she'd tried on before deciding on the perfect thing to wear for a Friday night out. Being as outgoing as Molly had been shy at the same age, she already had a circle of friends she'd met the first week of classes and had connected with two people she'd known when she'd attended third grade at Eagle Valley Elementary. Molly was in awe. To be born with confidence…what a gift.

But maybe if one had to fight to develop confidence, one appreciated it more.

And maybe they always had that tiny niggling fear that if they didn't hold on to it with an iron grasp, it might just slip away.

FINN FOUND WALKING into English class the second time a lot easier than it had been the first. He held the door open for Debra and her friend Sharla, smiled back at them when they thanked him, and took the same seat he'd sat in the week before. Molly was busy talking to a student, but she glanced over at him as he sat and he nodded at her. Last week had been stressful. This week he was ready to light this candle.

Debra sat up a little straighter when Molly announced she was going to hand back last week's papers.

"If your grade isn't what you expected, don't worry. The purpose of this class is to identify trouble areas and learn what to do about them. If you got over a 90 percent, you really don't belong here."

Debra leaned forward as Molly set her paper

facedown on her desk, then eagerly flipped it over. Finn shot a quick look at the grade—85 percent. Debra beamed and started reading comments.

A 70 percent. That was all he wanted. Average. Nothing wrong with average.

Molly glided by his desk, set the paper facedown. Finn flipped it over. Then he almost flipped it back.

His gaze shot up to Molly, who happened to shift her gaze toward him just then. She gave him an unreadable look and walked toward the front of the class.

"As you can see we have some work ahead of us, but again, let me emphasize that this is a starting point."

Finn's starting point was almost at ground zero.

Okay, he had some problems putting words down, but…this grade smacked more of payback than it did of assessment.

"What did you get?" Debra whispered. Finn automatically shifted his paper, planning to say something along the lines of "not as good as I'd hoped," but she caught a glimpse of the percentage before he'd managed to hide it. "Oh."

Yes. *Oh.* He smiled gamely at the older woman. "It's been a while since I've written anything."

"That's what this course is about. Getting

comfortable with writing again." She gave him an encouraging nod, then fixed her attention back on Molly, who explained that they'd start with sentence structure.

The sentence structure made sense as Finn listened. And he knew he was doing exactly what she was talking about, although according to Molly's comments, he wasn't. The remainder of the class was spent on simple exercises. Molly circled the room while Finn stared at his paper, a slow burn building into a flame. He didn't get much done by the time class had ended, and Molly had avoided coming his way. He left the class with everyone else, but lingered in the hall until he was certain the last person, who seemed bent on telling her life story to Molly, had finally left. The hall, and probably the entire building, was empty when he walked back into the room. Molly did not look surprised to see him.

"Finn." She held her folders to her chest as if they were a shield. "I assume you want to talk about your grade?"

"You assume correctly. What gives?" He set the paper down on the table. "If this had any more red, the white wouldn't show." He leveled a long, hard look at her. "Is this because of what happened back when we were *kids*?" Like an eon ago.

"This is because it's that bad."

He stilled for a moment. "That's hard to believe because this is basic English, pretty much the equivalent of high school English, and I got straight Cs in high school English. I couldn't have forgotten that much."

"And I don't think your grades in high school reflected your abilities."

His gaze snapped up to hers. "What the hell does that mean?"

Molly let out a sigh. "You were an athlete…? A good one…?"

"You're saying my grades were fixed?"

"I admit I have no way of knowing that, but this paper—" she pointed at the bloodbath sitting on the empty desk next to her "—is not C work in high school. Or here at EVCC."

"According to you, it's not even D work."

"I have to be honest."

He stared at her, at an uncharacteristic loss for words, then when nothing brilliant popped into his head, he snatched the essay off the desk and headed for the door.

"We can fix this, Finn."

Like hell. As soon as he was out of her line of sight, he crumpled the paper, tossed it into the nearest trash can and headed out the door.

FINN HADN'T DROPPED the class. Molly couldn't say why that was important to her, but she scanned the class lists on Tuesday and Wednesday, fully expecting to see his name missing. It wasn't, but he didn't show up for the Wednesday class, either. As she started the lesson, she saw Debra glance over at his empty chair and give her head a sad shake.

Molly didn't feel sad. Reality was reality, and Finn couldn't write. He could tackle the matter and try to improve himself, or he could ignore it. It appeared he'd chosen to ignore it. His choice. There was no reason that the class should feel empty without him.

Empty and a lot more comfortable. The nervous edge Molly had felt during the first two classes was gone and she traveled around the room, answering questions, offering suggestions as her class worked on skill-building exercises, feeling very much at ease. Therefore, she had no reason to look up Finn's address and drive by on her way home—just to see if he was there. He lived just past the city limits, so it wasn't as if she could tell herself she was taking a different route to her place. Nope. She went well out of her way to discover that Finn's house was well lit and there was a truck and a car parked in front of the garage.

Finn was home. He just hadn't come to class.

Molly drove on by, wondering why she had a sinking feeling. Finn had made the choice to screw up his high school education. Now he was living with the consequences. She'd only told the truth.

Maybe it was remembering the stunned look on his face as she'd told him that truth. The complete shock to discover that she wasn't indulging in petty payback. She was doing her job. She let out an audible sigh that made her shoulders drop as she looked for a place to turn around so that she could drive back home. Too softhearted. That's what she was. That was why Blake had been able to play her.

When she drove back by Finn's house, she kept her gaze straight ahead. Right where it should be. If Finn chose to drop her class, it was none of her concern.

So why did it feel as if it was?

CHAPTER FOUR

FINN WASN'T A guy who backed away from trouble—if anything, according to his dad, anyway, he ran forward and embraced it—however, academic trouble was foreign territory. And apparently he was traveling that territory with an expired visa. So what was he going to do? Quit school? Tough it out? Risk flunking?

After glancing around to make certain that no customers had wandered into the warehouse, he peeled out of his T-shirt and shook out the grain dust. The stuff made him itch like crazy and he had to wear a paper face mask when moving the bags, which put up dust every time he set down a pallet a little too hard. He was tired of itching.

Mike loved his business, and until he returned from the service, Finn had been perfectly fine working there, too. Now he needed more. When he'd gone overseas, he'd discovered what it felt like to be part of something important. To make a difference. It didn't help that he was becoming more and more convinced that the store no longer needed him. Before he'd left, he'd essentially been the only employee with the exception of the bookkeeper. The place had been dusty and lonely and he hadn't cared as long as he could hook up with his friends after work, or go home and work on his cars and trucks.

Those things were no longer enough. He wanted to teach automotives and shop and, as he saw it, he didn't need stellar English scores to teach hands-on courses, but he did have to pass the class to get a degree. Molly Adamson was standing in his way and he still believed that their past was firmly tied to the score she gave him.

Finn pulled his T-shirt back on, grimacing as he tugged it into place. Still uncomfortable, but not as bad. He walked across the warehouse to the small dust-covered fridge on the opposite wall and pulled out a water. He fumbled the plastic top after opening the bottle and it fell, rolling across the floor. A split second later, Marcel, the cat that had adopted the place as a scraggly kitten years ago, shot out from behind the pallet and attacked. After whacking the cap into submission, the cat stared at it as if daring it to move, then hit it with his paw, causing it to slide across the floor like a hockey puck.

"Good one, Marcel."

The cat gave him a golden-eyed blink, then disappeared back behind the pallets. The cat was

certainly a whole lot tamer than he'd been before
Finn had gone overseas, but actually, so was he.

He finished the water, dropped the bottle in
the recycling container that Lola had put next to
the fridge, then started across the concrete floor
to the forklift. Before he could fire it up, Lola
announced over the intercom that a customer
needed loading. Eighteen bags of alfalfa pellets.

Codie James. It was her usual order.

Finn smiled a little. He and Codie had had
some good times, and maybe that was what
he needed. To go out with someone like Codie
who enjoyed life and seemed to know what she
wanted.

When he emerged from the warehouse and
approached her big red Dodge, though, she was
talking to a guy who nodded and then headed
for the store proper, and as she handed him the
load ticket, he noted a big rock on her left hand.

"Hey," he said. "Congratulations."

Codie beamed. "I know… I said I was never
settling down, but I met this guy…" She rolled
her eyes toward the sky and gave a goofy smile,
which made Finn smile in return.

"Must be some guy."

"He is. Hang around and you can meet him."

Finn glanced at the ticket, then gave her a
quick nod. "I'll get this loaded for you."

"Thanks, Finn." She reached out to run her

hand over his shoulder and down his arm. "Good to have you back."

"Good to be back."

After Codie and her beau, Colin, who did seem really decent, left, Finn disappeared back into the warehouse, even though he didn't have that much to do. Chase would arrive soon and then he was free to do…whatever. Everyone, it seemed, was moving on, and it aggravated him that he'd barely started his own moving-on process before hitting a major roadblock named Molly. Maybe he deserved some comeuppance, because he'd been a jerk with that whole homecoming dance thing, but he'd been a self-centered, hormone-driven teenager at the time.

And she'd been an insecure, quiet girl whose feelings you didn't give much thought to.

Finn snorted. Well, now she'd gotten a few licks in of her own.

A vehicle pulled into the lot as Finn reached the warehouse door. He didn't have to look back to know it was Chase—the loud 427 under the hood told the tale. The kid really needed to get a tune-up and he probably couldn't afford one.

Chase disappeared into the store and Finn walked into the warehouse, where he stood for a few seconds, watching the dust motes drift about in the sunlight filtering in through the fiberglass roofing. The obvious solution, the one

in which he didn't cut and run, was to change
English instructors and see if someone new,
someone without an ax to grind, had the same
opinion as Molly.

But what if that instructor told him he was
incompetent, too?

He was no coward, but after what Molly had
done...yeah, kind of hard to face the prospect
of someone else announcing via red pen bloodbath that he was stupid. And he'd yet to discover
what the math teacher was going to do to him.

But he would. This was just a bump in the
road. He'd overcome it, because if he didn't go
to school, then that meant he was stuck here in
the family business, or in some similar occupation. The life that had seemed so comfortable
before going overseas no longer fit him.

He needed a way out, and Molly Adamson
was not going to stop him.

SHE'D DONE THE right thing. No question about
it. She had to be honest. *Right?* She'd been no
harsher on Finn than she would have been on
anyone else. It wasn't as if she'd written insults
in the margins. She'd even tapered off marking
it up toward the end, when it became apparent
that he wasn't joking—that he was actually trying to write an essay.

Unfortunately, there was a lot of red ink on

the paper by that time, and…well, maybe she had felt a certain level of glee during the first couple comments. And usually she read through the entire essay without writing anything, but with Finn she'd started marking as soon as she saw something to mark, which had been in the first sentence.

Not good, that.

And then he'd reacted just as Blake would have—with extreme outrage that someone had dared point out his faults.

Well, the faults are real, buddy. There was probably a root cause that could be addressed, but he'd left before she could speak to him about it and then failed to show up at the next class.

Typical spoiled-jock behavior.

Molly gathered the grammar pretests she'd given her freshmen into a neat stack and put them into the wire basket on the edge of her desk. Actually, she was kind of surprised that Finn was in school at all. From what she'd gathered, he'd followed the classic peak-in-high-school path and joined the family business. Nothing wrong with that, but it wasn't exactly ambitious. Molly liked guys who were open to new adventures—as long as they were safe and well-thought-out.

And she shouldn't be spending so much time thinking about one student whom she'd probably never see again when she had so many who needed her attention.

Some of her students had some serious deficits in their English educations, which was something she had to address and remedy over the course of the next semester. But right now she needed to head home and remember that thing about not burying herself in work. Georgina was supposed to be cooking an actual meal and she was looking forward to food that wasn't thawed or microwaved.

A muffled *thud* from the other side of the wall brought her head up. For the past thirty minutes or so, there'd been a lot of noise come from the art studio room next door—tables scraping along the floor and the odd *thump.*

Once upon a time, Molly probably would have ignored the noise, at least until she was more secure in her surroundings, but those days were gone. No more safe route. She needed to meet people before they sought her out. She needed to forget shyness and uncertainty and put herself out there, which was why she left her office and poked her head into the room next door on the way out of the building for the two-hour break between her afternoon class and evening class.

"Hello," she called to the woman crouched next to a large cardboard box on the opposite side of the long room. The woman hadn't been to any of the faculty meetings, and while the old shy Molly might have waited until the two of them had bumped into each other in the hall to introduce herself, the new Molly pushed herself to make first contact. She had no trouble addressing a roomful of students, but one-on-one always froze her up. She was working on it, though, so she smiled when the woman looked up, startled.

"Hi." She got to her feet, pushing back the long blond hair that had fallen into her face while she'd been crouched over, and sidestepped a few boxes before starting across the room.

"I'm Molly Adamson, your next-door neighbor."

"Allie Brody, and you'll only be my neighbor one night a week. I'm teaching a community art class on Wednesday evenings."

"Community, as in—"

"Regular Joes," Allie said with a half smile. "Nonstudents. People who want to expand their horizons and get out of the house one night a week."

"Sounds like fun."

"It's my first time teaching at the community college. I'm a little nervous." She wiped her hands down the sides of her pants. "What do you teach?"

"English comp. Technical writing. One literature class."

"Sounds like a lot of work."

"I'm not going to lie. It is. Fortunately, I love what I do."

Allie cocked her head. "You look familiar. Do we know each other from somewhere?"

"I don't think we do…but I did graduate from high school here."

"Me, too," Allie said. "Born here, graduated here, engaged, married and divorced here. I'm a lifer, it seems."

Molly laughed. "I've spent my life moving, but I hope to settle for a while." The five o'clock bell chimed and she said, "I need to get going." Georgina had texted her that she'd started dinner a few minutes ago. "But I'm sure we'll run into each other again."

"Do you have a class tomorrow?"

"No. But I'll probably be here. I promise myself every year that I won't work late and usually that promise lasts until the first big batch of grading lands on my desk."

"Well, if you are here, I wouldn't mind some backup if my class gets rowdy. I'll just knock on the wall and you can come and save me."

Molly laughed. "I'll be happy to oblige."

She continued on out of the building, glad that she stopped by, but feeling a little off center, as she always did on first meeting people. She'd love to be more like Georgina, who never met a stranger. Or her brother, David, who didn't care what people thought about him. But she wasn't like her siblings. Or her parents. She'd been the nose-in-the-book nerd who had a difficult time leaving her comfort zone. Not that she didn't want to…it was just that the fear factor had been so strong. Then Blake had come along and drawn her out of her shell.

It wasn't until she'd discovered that he was a serial cheater while on the road that she realized that Blake took after his father…and that she closely resembled his stay-at-home mother who'd turned a blind eye to her husband's indiscretions and made life as easy as possible for Blake, his father and his two brothers.

Well, that wasn't what Molly had signed on for. She'd refused to give Blake another chance, even though he'd worked up a few man tears, and she'd insisted that they put the house they'd purchased together—*stupid, stupid, stupid*—on the market, then packed up and left. After getting a new place to live and a new wardrobe, so she could give away all the clothing that reminded her of Blake, she'd buried herself in her work until she felt as if she could face the world again.

Being cheated on hurt like hell. And trust…

what was that? Not anything that Molly believed in anymore.

But trust issues or not, she was going to put herself out there. Step out of her comfort zone socially. She owed it to herself not to let what had happened with Blake ruin her future…she just wasn't going to get herself into any kind of an emotional bind with any kind of flashy too-good-to-be-true guy again. From now on she was dating her own species—as in guys who were reliable, honest, predictable. She couldn't live with lack of trust.

When Molly pulled into her driveway, Georgina was not tending to dinner—she was in Mike Culver's yard crouched next to a flower bed. She waved and got to her feet as Molly walked to the fence that separated the properties.

"Mike is teaching me about fall bulbs," she said happily. "If we put them in now, we'll have flowers next year."

"I'd like that." Just as she was going to like living in the same place come spring that she was in now. Molly had never lived anywhere long enough to get too deeply into yard beautification, and in Arizona, her house had been xeriscaped in a minimalist way, as was common in the desert. No spring flowers except for yucca, which were pretty, but not in the traditional way.

"The people who lived here before weren't

much for flowers, but I always thought that some tulips around the trees and maybe some narcissi or daffodils in front of the lilacs would be pretty."

"There are lilacs?" Georgina's eyes widened.

"Those bushes over there are lilacs," Mike said, pointing to the hedge at the edge of their lawn. "The heavy flowering kind."

"I love the smell of lilacs. I haven't smelled them since we lived in Iowa. Remember, Molly?"

Molly remembered, but she was surprised that Georgina did; she'd been so young then. "Didn't we have lilacs when we lived here?" she asked her sister, who gave an emphatic shake of her head in reply. "Nope. We had those big yellow bushes—"

"Forsythia, probably," Mike said.

Georgina looked impressed at the off-the-cuff identification. "And those pink roses that had no scent. We didn't have lilacs."

Molly smiled a little. She didn't remember much about the flowers. "I'll take your word for it."

Mike leaned his arms on the top of the chain-link fencing. "I was telling Georgina that I can put together a mix of bulbs from the store and bring them home or I can get you a catalog."

"You probably know what grows best." And she would pay for said mixture of bulbs, of course, but it didn't seem like the time to make that point.

"That's what I thought," Georgina said. "And I love surprises."

"Then I'll fix you up." Mike smiled at Georgina, then shifted his attention to Molly, and she saw that his eyes were the same color as Finn's. A deep, rich hazel. More green than brown. Why had she noticed that? A trickle of annoyance went through her. "Got that drain fixed yet?"

"I have a call in to a plumber. He's working me in this weekend." Mike had been right about all the locals being contracted to the construction companies. The Eagle Valley was experiencing a mini housing boom. "I called four before I got one. O'Malley's Plumbing and Heating? He promised Saturday and said he wouldn't charge weekend rates, since it's a simple job."

Mike didn't look as if he fully believed the guy would honor his word. "Crazy, all this rain," he said. "We had floods a little over a year ago, then this summer was so dry that there were bad fires."

"I heard," Molly said. "Some people lost homes."

Mike gave a nod. "My nephew Dylan's fiancée lost her ranch house in the fire."

"That's terrible." Molly remembered Dylan. She'd liked him. He'd been a year ahead of her, quiet and studious. Invisible in a way. Like she had been, except that he could have been as popular as Finn, had he chosen to be. Somehow she didn't think that popularity was one of her options. "Who is his fiancée?"

"Jolie Brody."

Brody. Of course. Allie Brody looked just like Jolie Brody, whom she'd graduated from high school with.

"Does she have an older sister?"

"Three sisters."

"I just met an Allie Brody at the college."

"She's the oldest. She's teaching a night class at the school. Painting or something."

Small world…but maybe not. It was a small town, so ending up with a class next to Finn's cousin's fiancée's sister wasn't that unexpected. And the connection to Finn was a bit distant. Still, she was going to watch what she said around Allie about certain people.

Molly frowned as a memory crept into her brain. "Wait a minute…didn't Jolie used to…" Mike waited for her to finish and Molly, who wished she'd kept her mouth shut, searched for a tactful word. "Bother Dylan?" *Torture* would have been a better word, but she was being polite. The strained and somewhat adversarial relationship between wild-child Jolie and quiet

Dylan had been legendary in Eagle Valley High School, now that she thought about it.

Mike laughed. "Yes, she did. She and Dylan worked things out."

"I guess so."

Georgina was following the conversation with interest and Mike glanced over at her and laughed again. "I'll get you that mixture of bulbs and maybe we can put them in this weekend."

"We?" Molly asked on a note of amusement.

"If you needed help, that is."

"I think we'll need a lot of help," Molly said with a smile. If he wanted to help, she wasn't going to stop him.

They talked for a few more minutes about colors, and then Mike's phone rang from inside his house and he excused himself.

"I like him," Georgina said as she and Molly walked to their back door. She shot Molly a look. "You're going to fill in the gaps about this Dylan guy and his fiancée. Right?"

"I don't know a lot," Molly said as she opened the front door. "Dylan was really quiet and hardworking and Jolie was outgoing. Kind of a live-for-today girl."

"Just like you?" Georgina asked with mock innocence.

"Exactly," Molly replied. Because she was going to be more like that. Work in progress, et cetera. "All I remember is that they somehow drifted into nemesis territory due to being partnered up in some class and her not taking it seriously enough and him being worried about his GPA."

"And now they're getting married."

"Yes." Molly headed for the fridge. So very romantic. She wished them well, but hearts-and-flowers romance had been stomped out of her by the lights of reality being snapped on in her own relationship, brilliantly exposing the truth that lay before her and leaving her blinking.

She was still blinking a little. Blake had not only robbed her of most of her savings, he'd robbed her of her hard-won self-confidence. She'd fought to rebuild it little by little, but she hadn't been able to let go of her resentment. It'd be a while before she could.

"I thought we'd microwave lasagna tonight." The microwave was truly their best friend with their crammed schedules—which was why having a two-hour break to eat an actual dinner between her afternoon and evening classes was gold. "I made a salad."

Molly drifted over to the counter and pulled a small tomato out of the mixture of greens and popped it into her mouth. She'd skipped lunch and was famished. "Sounds good."

Georgina pulled the aluminum tray out of

the freezer. "This Dylan is hot prom guy's cousin, right?"

"Homecoming guy. He is."

"But you liked him better."

He didn't screw me over, so yes. "He's a nice guy. How were your classes today?"

The corners of her sister's eyes crinkled as Molly firmly redirected the conversation away from "hot prom guy." "Excellent. How was your day?"

"Excellent." Molly used the hand-carved wooden tongs she and Blake had bought on a Mexican vacation to lift salad into a bowl. She'd gotten rid of most of her past, but some things stayed, for practical purposes. "They're always excellent in the beginning. You know—when everyone has high expectations for themselves and not too much reality has set in."

Except for in Finn's case. She'd slammed that reality home there.

She'd address that tonight. She wasn't exactly going to apologize, but she was going to explain what she thought might be going on. Not a conversation she was looking forward to, but one they needed to have. If he showed up to class.

FINN DID NOT show up for class.

Molly found her head coming up every time she heard the door to the main entrance, only a few yards down the hall from her classroom, open and close again. Finally she closed the door to her room so that she focused only on her class and not on the reasons Finn wasn't there.

She knew why Finn wasn't there. But she didn't know what she was going to do about it.

What could she do?

Relax and enjoy teaching.

Not having Finn there made her feel as if she owned her classroom again—which was annoying. Of course she owned her classroom, but when Finn was there…she felt as if she were being judged. It made her thoughts trip over themselves, which wasn't conducive to great lesson delivery.

Tonight her lecture flowed. She gave amusing sentence examples, had the class engaged for the entire fifty minutes. No stumbling about for explanations, no quick glances to a specific area of a classroom just to check whether or not one specific student was smirking a little.

After class ended, she explained a few finer points of the essay assignment with Debra and Mr. Reed, a sweet man in his late sixties, listened to Denny's take on higher education, then turned off the lights and locked up the room, telling herself she should feel great. Class had gone very, very well.

But you're tougher than this. You should be

able to teach regardless of who's sitting in the back row, history or no history.

Molly hated it when the nagging little voice in the back of her mind pointed out things she didn't want to hear. She'd returned to the Eagle Valley because she'd wanted a nice, stable, un-surprising life in a nice, stable community. Getting the position at the community college had been a godsend. She'd been so very happy with how well things were working out, so determined to do the best job she could teaching her new students—right up until Finn had appeared in her life again and she'd indulged in her red pen revenge.

That wasn't what a good teacher did, and beyond that, driving students away wouldn't do her professional reputation any good. This job was important to her. She didn't want to jeopardize it.

THE CLOCK SAID English class was halfway over and Finn felt nothing but relief at the fact that he wasn't there.

Liar.

Okay, part of him felt relief that he wasn't there and the other part thought he should have sucked it up and gone. He'd never quit anything in his life, and not going to class bordered on cowardly behavior. But what was the point, when he was going to drop the class anyway?

The point was that Molly was going to think she'd won.

Finn flipped through the channels a couple dozen more times, then got to his feet and grabbed his jacket so he could head to McElroy's Bar. There probably wouldn't be many people there on a weeknight, but Finn needed to do something other than sit in front of the TV and feel like he'd let himself down.

The lot was almost empty when Finn parked, but he figured he'd have one beer, talk to Jim McElroy and then head home again. He enjoyed getting out, being around people, but when he pulled open the heavy wooden bar door, the usual pleasant anticipation for the evening ahead was replaced with the feeling that he was avoiding the real issue in his life. Probably because he was. He didn't really want to go to McElroy's. He just didn't want to be alone with his annoying thoughts.

Finn walked into the bar and paused just inside the door. The place was relatively empty, as he'd suspected. Wyatt Bauer was there leaning on the bar, staring at the sports news that played over Jim McElroy's head. His eyes were glazed over and Finn wondered if the guy was even aware of what was happening on the screen, or if he was asleep with his eyes open.

"Hey, Wyatt," he said as he walked by. Wyatt grunted in return. He was awake.

"Usual?" Jim asked.

"Sure."

Jim poured a dark beer and set it in front of the stool Finn had settled on. "Haven't seen you much since you got back," he commented.

Finn gave a casual shrug. "Readjusting." Which was true. He hadn't seen action overseas, but the experience had changed him in ways he hadn't expected. For instance, he knew now, more than ever, that he did not want to end up like Wyatt—a walking cautionary tale staring glassily at the television screen.

Jim gave a casual nod, then glanced up as the door opened again.

"Look who's here," a familiar voice said from behind Finn.

"We thought you were missing in action!" an almost identical voice chimed in.

Finn turned on his stool as the Tyrone brothers came in. "Just lying low," he said. "You know… avoiding people such as yourselves."

"I assume you're buying after insulting us," Terry, the older of the two brothers, said as he clapped a heavy hand on Finn's back.

"I hadn't really considered it."

"Best reconsider," Lowell said.

Finn signaled Jim, who nodded before turning

to the taps. Terry and Lowell pulled up stools and after Jim set the drafts in front of them, they commenced catching Finn up on who had done what during the time he'd been gone. Not that long of a time really, but it seemed as if there'd been a lot of marriages and breakups and job changes while he'd been away.

Terry glanced at his watch when Jim asked if he wanted another beer, then practically jumped off his seat. "Gotta go. I promised Janice I'd be home ten minutes ago."

"Trouble?" Finn asked. Terry had never been all that concerned about getting home before, but then Janice was usually there with him.

"There have been some new developments on the home front," Terry said with a half smile before downing the last gulp of beer and setting the mug back on the bar. "I'm going to be a dad in three months. Got to start setting a good example for my kids."

"Plural?"

"Twins."

"Unfortunately, his newfound Mr. Mom status is screwing with my social life," Lowell muttered. "We never go out and when we do, we have to be home at nine. How am I supposed to meet women?"

"Go without your brother?" Finn said.

"I need a wingman."

Sadly true. Lowell never did anything alone. "Do not look at me," Finn said.

"What? You have something better to do?"

"Maybe I'm getting old." He drained the last of his beer, then looked up to find the brothers staring at him. "It happens to the best of us."

Finn lingered after the Tyrone brothers left. He could talk to Jim.

"So what are you doing now that you're back?" Jim asked as he wiped the immaculate bar yet another time. He tossed the bar towel into the bin under the bar, then waited for Finn to answer.

"Working at the store."

"Taking it over again?"

"For the time being."

"It's changed," Jim said. "All those gifts and things."

"It used to be a lot quieter," Finn agreed. "It's more pleasant now in a lot of ways, and Mike's really happy, but I don't know. I guess I'm not used to it yet."

"Not the place you left."

"Not even close."

Jim smiled a little. "Time marches on."

Finn nodded in agreement. He pulled out his wallet and found a ten.

"Come back on Saturday," Jim suggested as

Finn headed to the door. "I have a band coming in."

Finn raised a hand in acknowledgment, then pushed his way out the heavy wooden door and stepped into the chilly night air, knowing full well he wouldn't be back. A cloud moved over the moon as he walked to his truck, but the sky was relatively clear. The predicted rain had apparently bypassed them and he was okay with that. He had to replace one of the haystack tarps that had a rip.

There was nothing wrong with tightening and replacing tarps on haystacks. Not one thing. But it wasn't what he wanted to do anymore.

CHAPTER FIVE

AFTER SKIPPING ENGLISH, Finn told himself he had to go to math—even if it meant receiving another red-ink-bleeding paper. How else would he find out if math was another area in which he'd been fooling himself into thinking he had basic skills? Was it possible that his high school As in the subject had been the gift of teachers who were concerned with the school's sports success?

Recalling Mrs. Birdie's stern face, he thought not. The woman had been out for him, calling him on every infraction of the rules, then grudgingly giving him decent marks on his work. Mrs. Birdie hadn't been a sports fan or a Finn Culver fan. Yet he'd gotten an A in the class.

Finn drove into the lot and, seeing Molly's small car, parked next to it. He wasn't certain exactly what his objective was—it was more of a go-with-his-gut moment. He walked into class a few minutes late, but congratulated himself on being there at all, and then found a seat in the back and waited to get his assessment paper back. The instructor smiled at him as she set down the paper and moved on. Annoyed that his heart was beating faster—it was only a math paper, for Pete's sake—Finn flipped the paper over, then fought a smile as the taut muscles in his shoulders relaxed.

The only ink on the paper was turquoise, rather than killer red, a brief note asking him to show more of his work. He could do that—although he wasn't all that good at laying out the steps in his head on paper in a way that others could easily follow. He knew that because it had driven Mrs. Birdie nuts. And many times he tackled things in a roundabout way that made sense to him, but wasn't the prescribed method for solving the problem. But what did it matter as long as he came up with the proper solution?

Bottom line—this paper showed that he wasn't deluding himself. He could do math. Did he need English at all?

Well…yes—if he was going to get a degree. But he didn't need English right now. This semester he'd focus on his math class, learn to follow the prescribed steps and how to show his work. By the end of the semester, he'd be more comfortable in an academic environment and have a better idea of how to tackle learning without feeling intimidated. And he wasn't going to give Molly another shot at eviscerating him.

And maybe tonight was the time to tell her that. Nicely, of course.

TRUE TO FORM, Molly was already breaking her promise to herself not to stay late on campus working. But the grading was piling up and if she didn't keep on top of it, she'd get buried. Besides, Allie Brody might need to knock on the wall.

She set down her pen, pulled her glasses off and pressed the heels of her hands to her tired eyes.

"Hey…"

Molly jumped a mile at the unexpected male voice, automatically reached for her glasses and instead hit them with the back of her hand, sending them skittering onto the floor. Finn bent down to pick them up and solemnly handed them back to her. Molly set the heavy dark brown frames back on the desk. Having Finn a little out of focus wasn't necessarily a bad thing.

"You missed class yesterday."

Finn leaned carelessly against the door frame, the picture of the who-gives-a-damn jock he'd been in high school. "I'm going to drop it. I thought I'd give you official notice."

Molly looked down at the papers in front of her. There were remarks written on the top one, but nothing like what she'd done to Finn.

"But you haven't dropped it yet?" When she looked back up at him, she saw him watching her carefully.

"Tomorrow. Just thought I'd let you know." He smiled tightly and then pushed off the door frame and walked back down the hall, leaving Molly staring at the empty space he'd just filled. For a moment she sat stone still, then she jumped to her feet, grabbed her glasses so she didn't trip over anything and started after Finn. He was already on his way out the main exit, so she hurried her steps, finally giving up and calling his name after pushing through the glass-and-steel doors.

He slowed down, then stopped and turned. Now she'd done it. She'd engaged and she had to follow through.

Drawing in a deep breath that wasn't nearly as calming as she'd hoped it would be, she started toward him. "I think we should talk about this."

"No offense, Molly, but there's not a lot to say."

Molly stopped a few feet away from him. "I want you to know that I wasn't engaging in some sort of petty revenge when I marked your paper."

He said nothing as he studied her with those striking hazel eyes, but if he hoped to fluster her, it wasn't going to work. Much.

All right. It wasn't going to work in any way that showed.

"I didn't say one thing on your paper that wasn't true, but... I was a bit overzealous with my pen."

"Yet there was no petty revenge involved." Finn sauntered forward as he spoke. A slow, almost predatory movement, as if he were a big cat moving in on his prey. Molly's prey days were over, so she took a step forward, too. A brisk no-nonsense step that brought them almost chest to chest. Miscalculation on her part, but she wasn't going to have him in the power role.

And she wasn't going to react to the heat coming off his body or the fact that his scent now seemed to surround her and certain parts of her body were taking notice. That was what the Finns of the world, the Blakes of the world, banked on.

"Perhaps a little." She'd almost stuttered. Damn. The old Molly was starting to take over now that they were so close, and she would not have that. She pushed her glasses up a little higher, straightened her back. Finn's gaze narrowed, as if he was wondering what she was doing.

"And you have me pegged as a dumb athlete who was handed a diploma he didn't deserve."

"I didn't say that."

"I'm not talking about what you said, Molly. I'm asking about what you think." His voice went down a notch. "*Is* that what you think?"

Molly couldn't help it—she glanced down, her gaze fixing on the gray cotton T-shirt that covered his flat abs…he'd been an athlete and it looked as if he still was—then forced her chin back up, meeting his eyes. "The idea had crossed my mind."

"Points for honesty."

She pulled in a breath. Big mistake. The heady scent of the man about two inches away from her once again filled her nostrils and she felt herself leaning forward, even closer to him, which was nuts, since she was already way too close for comfort.

"But I don't think that's the problem."

She felt him go still, she was that close.

"What," he asked softly, "do you think the problem is?"

She raised her chin, shaking back her hair in the process. "Have you ever been checked for dyslexia?"

"Dyslexia?" He frowned. "I don't turn letters around."

"It's more than that."

"Yeah? What else is it?" Finn took a step back, finally freeing up the space around her, and folded his arms over his chest.

"It has to do with organizing thoughts and finding the right word and translating what happens inside your brain onto paper."

"I see."

He was now officially closed off, his expression stony, his eyes narrowed as he regarded her.

"There's a lot of information about it, if you look into it."

"Yes…but will I be able to read it?" He was being sarcastic. Before she could answer, he said, "Thank you for the helpful suggestion, Molly. And the diagnosis."

"I'm not diagnosing you. I'm offering up a suggestion as to what you might look into to—"

"Explain my shortcomings?" he asked mildly.

"If you want to put it that way."

He put his hand on the truck's door handle. "Well…your duty is done. Thank you."

"I think you should continue the class."

"I don't see a lot of point in taking it."

"I'll…"

Molly's voice trailed off and Finn's expression shifted. "What, Molly?" One corner of his perfect mouth curved into a wry expression that was somehow both cold and amused. "Be gentle with me?"

The way he said it brought more color to her cheeks. "Yes. I will."

"Thanks for the offer, but no."

"I'll…help you." What on earth was she saying? "No. Thank you."

He pulled the truck door open and Molly heard the word, "Chicken?" emerge from her lips. Finn stopped dead and turned back.

Had she really just said that?

For a moment she thought he was going to address the remark, but instead he shook his head as if she were beyond help and got into the truck, closing the door and leaving Molly feeling worse than when she'd left her office. She turned and started back across the parking lot as students began to leave the building in small groups. Art class was over. Behind her, Finn's truck fired up. There was nothing to do but close up her office, get into her car, curse the fates for the fact that she lived next to his grandfather and plot how never to see him again.

He'd been the jerk in high school, but she'd been the jerk just now.

OKAY. MOLLY HAD surprised him. Finn was going to give her points for that, even if she had pissed him off. And she wasn't exactly the meek girl he'd taken on the mercy date at the behest of his mom ten or so years ago. She'd just freaking called him a chicken.

And dyslexia?

Yeah, right.

Finn's mouth tightened as he wheeled out of the parking lot. He'd decided to try a few classes to better his life, not to make it worse. The satisfaction he got from finding out he could still do math—that he really liked to do math—was deeply overshadowed by the fact that he sucked at English. That he'd been passed along by his teachers. No…that wasn't what bothered him most. It was the fact that it had been so clear to Molly that had happened. And meanwhile the thought had never crossed his mind.

When Finn got home, he paced through the house. Normally, in his old life, he would have gone to McElroy's, but after last night, he didn't think that strategy was going to work like it used to. The last thing he wanted was to become a bar fixture like Wyatt. Times had changed. Everything around him seemed to have changed.

And his house was ridiculously empty when he walked inside and let the door swing shut behind him.

Son of a bitch. He was losing it. That was what was happening. He needed to get a grip and make some decisions here.

He'd make decisions in the morning.

Finn put on a pot of coffee and headed out the side door of the house and followed the packed dirt path to the shop. He snapped on the lights and then slowly walked around the 1972 Ford three-quarter-ton he'd bought at an auction before heading off overseas, his steps echoing as he paced the concrete in the metal building. There was a skittering sound in one corner of the room and he figured that if there were mice in the corners, then there were mice in his truck. He'd have to do something about that.

He walked over to the arc welder, which he hadn't touched since coming back, the sheet metal leaning against the wall. The hammers and anvils and forms his father had left when he'd moved south to live in a condo on a golf course—his lifelong dream finally achieved. Finn closed his eyes, drew in a deep breath that wasn't tainted with grain dust. Just the good smell of grease and oil and metal. He'd done a couple quick walk-throughs after returning home, but he hadn't actually put his hand to anything. Now the big question was...where to start?

GEORGINA GOT HOME a little after midnight—kind of late, since she had classes the next morning, but Molly reminded herself that just because she hadn't gone out and done college stuff until she'd hooked up with Blake, it didn't mean that Georgina couldn't. And shouldn't.

But still...she had an eight o'clock class the next morning.

"So much fun," Georgina said as she dumped

her purse and denim jacket on the chair and settled in next to Molly. "Chips?" She nodded at the
half-full bowl, a sure sign that Molly was dealing
with some kind of stress. "I thought you were
all caught up on your schoolwork." Her expression hardened before Molly could answer. "Did
Blake call?"

"I'm happy to say that hasn't happened."

"Then…?"

Molly gave a dismissive shrug. "Sometimes
I just like chips." Too bad this wasn't one of
those times. But at least Blake wasn't behind this
stress—just someone kind of like Blake. Great-
looking. Confident. Astounded at the idea that
he wasn't perfect.

"You need to come to this place," Georgina
said as she kicked off her shoes. She stretched
out her legs and slumped back into the cushions,
closing her eyes.

"Once I get my feet under me job-wise, maybe
I will."

"Promise?" Georgina asked.

"No."

"Stick-in-the-mud."

"That's me." Molly took another chip and
nibbled the edge. She knew better than to keep
chips in the house during potential times of
stress, but at least she hadn't gotten out the
French onion dip.

Georgina yawned and got back to her feet. "Staying up?"

"For a while."

Georgina started for the bathroom. "Don't stay up too late," she admonished.

Molly didn't bother to answer. She got to her feet and took the chips into the kitchen, where she dumped the remainder of the bowl into the trash. Finn wasn't going to push her back into old habits.

CHAPTER SIX

Dys...lex...ia.

Finn typed the word into the search engine. He'd held off for three days, working on his truck as soon as he got home and avoiding his computer. But Molly had planted a seed that refused to die and now he figured if nothing else, he could prove her wrong. He clicked the first site that wasn't trying to sell him something.

Take this quiz.

All right...

Finn took the quiz, which had to do with how well he remembered and organized and spelled. He spelled okay—he'd spelled *dyslexia* correctly after only one misfire. Obviously he was poor at organizing written work, but that was probably because he'd never paid much attention in English class—which explained a hell of a lot, really. He did have trouble with left and right— hated it when he had to come up with a direction quickly off the top of his head, but that didn't prove anything. Pronunciation? Well, if he didn't know a word, he didn't say it. Slow reader? Not really…hmm…maybe…

He gave a small snort.

Define slow.

After finishing the quiz, he took another. By the time he finished the third, he had to admit that some of the symptoms seemed familiar.

Finn leaned back in his chair and laced his fingers behind his head as he studied the screen with his score. Maybe he was talking himself into having the symptoms.

Or maybe he needed to face the fact that he might actually be dyslexic.

But what were the chances of Molly picking up on it, while none of his English teachers had?

Probably pretty good if he was being passed along, as Molly had suggested. He'd had no aspirations for college. He'd made that clear to anyone who listened, so why not give him those inflated grades when the school's reputation in sports needed to be upheld?

Finn didn't like that possibility. He'd been happy with his Cs in English that he'd barely worked for, but had never questioned whether or not they had been a gift. Back then his biggest concern had been the next sporting event, the next party, the next anything-that-didn't-have-to-do-with-school. He'd done his schoolwork, because his parents would have had his hide if he hadn't, but he never considered the fact that maybe not everyone had the difficulty he had with some classes. School was supposed to be hard—and it was.

But maybe it shouldn't have been as difficult as it'd been for him.

Finn got to his feet and paced through the house, then went back to the computer and started typing into the search engine box.

Professional dyslexia diagnosis...

Strategies to overcome dyslexia symptoms...

Famous people with dyslexia...

Athletes with dyslexia...

Smart people with dyslexia...

Finally, almost an hour later, he turned his computer off and headed for the kitchen, where he poured a glass of water and then took a couple aspirin for the headache that had started beating against his temples.

If he was dyslexic, then he had to deal with it, and from what he'd gleaned, a formal diagnosis wasn't going to get him anywhere, because there was no cure or medication or anything. Just strategies to overcome symptoms.

Well, his first strategy was going to be to go to bed and deal with this tomorrow. Or the next day. He'd lived his life just fine until now, never dreamed anything was holding him back. He'd continue to live it just fine. He just might have to come up with a different career goal.

Or, hell, he might just tighten tarps and schlep grain and find satisfaction in other areas of his life.

But even as the thoughts passed through his head, he knew he wasn't going to do that. He was going to come up with a way to deal with this and continue toward his goal.

MIKE TURNED AWAY from the rain-splattered window and shook his head gravely. "I'll bet you anything that plumber never showed. You know how Neil O'Malley is."

Actually, Finn had no idea how Neil O'Malley was, but obviously Mike did, since he'd paced to the front of the store about eight times to stare out into the driving rain and wonder aloud if his neighbors were dealing with a flood.

"Not our problem."

Mike's eyebrows shot up. "Those girls are my neighbors."

"They have neighbors on the other side."

"What is it with you and them?"

"Molly wanted to handle this on her own. If she didn't, then I'm pretty sure she would have called."

Mike gave his head another shake, then started for his office. Finn had a bad feeling about the gleam of grim determination he'd seen in his grandfather's eye, so he followed. By the time he got to the office, Mike was already dialing the phone.

"Hi. Georgina? It's Mike... I'm fine." He cleared his throat. "How are you two faring in this rain?" He listened for a moment, his expression becoming more concerned by the second, then he turned toward Finn with an I-told-you-so look.

Hey, Finn felt like saying, *I'm not the bad guy here.* It wasn't as if he'd kept Molly and her sister from phoning for help. As he'd told Mike, Molly had made it quite clear the first time Mike offered assistance that she didn't want it.

"No plumber, and he won't answer his phone." Mike shot another look at Finn. "How bad is it? Uh-huh... Well, we can't have that. Ask your sister if she's good with someone coming over to help." Mike laughed then. "Command decision, you say? Well, don't worry. We're on our way."

We? Our?

Mike hung up the phone, then jerked his head toward the door. "You best get Chase and the snake and head on over."

"What?"

"My bursitis is acting up with the weather."

Finn simply stared at his grandfather. "I don't

want to just show up if Molly doesn't know I'm coming." Not after the parking lot encounter.

"She'll get over it."

Finn knew from experience that when Mike was in one of these stern parental moods, he may as well do as he was told. It didn't matter if he was thirteen or thirty. "If she kicks me out, you owe me a beer."

"If she kicks you out instead of thanking you for saving her garage from flooding…well, then I've read her all wrong."

Finn thought that was extremely possible as he shrugged into his raincoat, then dashed out the side door and through the deluge. Lola had called Chase on the intercom and he was in the process of loading the drain snake.

"What's going on?" he asked once they were both safely inside the vehicle.

Finn wiped the rainwater off his face with one hand. "Rescue mission. I think you're coming along so the lady of the house doesn't do me harm."

"Why would she do that?" Chase asked in a mystified voice.

"Just kidding." He hoped. He wouldn't know for certain until they got there.

THE RAIN CAME DOWN in buckets and the plumber was a no-show. Molly dialed his number for the ninth time after trying every other plumber number in the book. Nobody seemed to work on Saturday. Either that or they were all out dealing with other people's emergencies.

Molly tossed the phone onto the sofa and marched through the kitchen door into the garage and stood beside Georgina. Water was inching its way across the garage toward the kitchen and they pretty much had to act. Now.

"Do you know anything about sandbags?" she asked, only half joking. They had to do something before the water hit the kitchen.

"Mike's on his way. He called a few minutes ago and I told him to come on over."

"Thank goodness." The only reason she'd turned Mike down the first time he'd offered was because she had this thing about being beholden to people.

Well…that and the fact that he was related to Finn.

The teakettle whistled—emergencies in the Adamson house often called for strong tea—just as they heard a vehicle pull up in front of the house. Molly went to tend to the tea while Georgina went into the living room.

"It's not Mike," Georgina called. "It's Hot Guy."

Of course it was.

Molly glanced down at her old comfy T-shirt

and oversize work jeans with the paint on them that barely hung on her hips, then snapped off the burner under the kettle. She was at a disadvantage, but that was okay. She could deal. Besides, she had some things she wanted to say to Finn, and now he was here. *Thank you, flood.*

"And he brought someone with him."

"Mike?"

"Not Mike," Georgina said. She gave a soft cough. "Definitely not Mike."

Molly couldn't help herself. She went to the window and peered out over her sister's shoulder. Finn and a guy who looked to be in his very early twenties strode up the walk and out of sight of the window as they climbed the porch steps. Georgina was on the way to the door before they knocked.

"Hi," she said, stepping back so that Finn and his friend could step inside. They were both bareheaded, their hair soaked, even though they'd only walked a few yards through the rain from the truck to the house. "Thanks for coming!"

"Not a problem." Finn smiled at Georgina. "This is Chase. He works with me."

"I'm Georgina," she said, the dimple appearing next to her mouth. "That's my sister, Molly." Both Chase and Finn turned toward Molly, and while she understood Finn's cool expression, she was a touch puzzled by the odd look Chase was giving her.

Finn jerked his head in the direction of the garage. "If you would open the garage door, we'll bring the snake in that way. So we won't have to lug it through the house."

"Right." Molly headed for the kitchen, where she hit the garage switch. Finn followed her, opening the door leading from the kitchen to the garage. He let out a low whistle, then looked over his shoulder at Molly.

"If you had waited much longer, it would have been in the house."

There was a note of accusation in his voice, as if she should have called him earlier but hadn't out of sheer stubbornness. Well, he hadn't been on her call radar.

"I phoned every plumber in the book. Nothing." Molly cleared her throat. "I really appreciate you coming." Totally true, even though she felt uncomfortable with it. He turned, cocked an eyebrow at her.

"I bet." His voice was low. Halfway ironic. An unexpected quiver of…something…traveled through her. Molly abruptly jerked her chin toward the water. "What can I do to help?"

"Got it covered." He glanced toward the living room. "Chase!"

Chase came into the kitchen, the remnants of

a smile still playing on his lips. From behind him Georgina lifted her eyes upward in a way that clearly conveyed her interest in the guy.

Great. But young lust could wait until after the flood.

"Whoa, shit," the kid said when he saw the water. He glanced at Molly. "Sorry."

"Don't worry about it. This is a whoa-shit situation." Molly stepped back to allow him to move past her. Georgina shrugged into the coat she carried in one hand and followed the guys outside. Molly stayed right where she was. In the kitchen with her thoughts. It wasn't like she could do anything out in the cold and wet to help the situation, and she had no desire to be a cheerleader.

A good twenty minutes later Chase and Finn tramped back into the kitchen, their jeans soaked from the knees down. "We got it," Chase told Molly, a smile on his handsome face. He glanced over at Georgina, who smiled back at him.

"I videoed it," Georgina said, holding up her phone, "so we can do it ourselves if we need to later."

"Good thinking." She glanced casually up at Finn. "I made coffee and we have hot water for tea. You guys have got to be cold." And Finn probably wanted to get out of those wet jeans.

She understood that, but she did want to talk to him and had no idea if she'd get another chance.

"We should get back to the store," Finn said as Chase headed out to load the snake in the truck.

Georgina put her hands on her hips and cocked her head at Finn. "Have a cup of coffee. It'll warm you up."

Molly had a feeling that Finn knew as well as she did that Georgina wasn't so much concerned about warming their rescuers as keeping them around a little longer. He met her gaze, then gave a quick nod. "Thanks."

The furnace came on then, filling the kitchen with a blast of warmth—the house seemed to have only two temperatures, almost too cold and almost too hot—making Molly suddenly feel overly warm, but she had a mission and she was going to accomplish it. She went to the cupboard for cups while Georgina found a bag of Oreos.

Georgina poured two cups and took them into the living room, leaving Molly to follow with Finn. Only she and Finn didn't follow.

"I want to talk to you," she said as soon as her sister was out of hearing range.

Chase came in the front door then, but didn't come close to making it into the kitchen. He saw Georgina and the coffee and took an instant detour.

Finn ignored the coffee and leaned back

against the counter. "If this is about school, this isn't the place."

"Where is the place?"

"There isn't one."

Molly jammed her hands in the back pockets of her loose pants, shifting them down a half inch or so, exposing skin below her shortish T-shirt. Finn's eyes followed the motion and she assumed he couldn't help himself. He was a guy, after all, and while she might not be his usual type of woman, she was a woman.

"You haven't dropped my class yet."

"Haven't had time."

"Don't drop it." She couldn't read the expression that crossed his face, so she forged on. "You looked up dyslexia, didn't you?"

"I did."

"What do you think?"

"That this is none of your business."

Unfortunately, he had a point. It wasn't her business—except for the part where she felt guilty about driving him away from a class that could have helped him. So…maybe the full truth was in order.

"I feel bad about what happened."

"Guess you'll have to live with that." He spoke matter-of-factly, rather than bitterly, which gave her the impetus to move forward, both mentally and physically. She took a step toward him, lowering her voice as she said, "I'm sorry I called you chicken. I was trying to keep you from quitting."

"What made you think that would work?"

"Gut instinct, I guess."

He gave her a long, appraising look and Molly did her best not to swallow drily. He was so damned good-looking and this was not the time to be noticing that. "That kind of stuff works on a playground."

"I've found it works elsewhere, too."

"Have you?"

Molly crossed her arms over her chest. Mistake, because the hem of her shirt rose higher and Finn's gaze again dropped lower, his eyes widening when he saw that Molly wore navel jewelry. Somehow she managed to keep from tugging her shirt down, but it was perhaps one of the most difficult things she'd done in the past week or so.

"If you take the class, I can help you work on organization. Adjust assignments."

Finn tore his eyes away from the simple bar that adorned her midsection. "Isn't that cheating?"

"Differentiating."

"Will I know what I'm supposed to know when I get done with the class? Or will you just pass me along?"

Molly ignored the jab. "You'll have more skills than when you started."

"That might be handy."

"What degree are you considering?"

"Why does that matter?"

"Some degrees take more than basic English."

"Degrees I will probably avoid."

The sound of laughter filtered in from the living room and Molly took a step back. When had she gotten so close?

"Continue in the class," she said in a low voice.

Finn dropped his gaze, toward the floor this time, instead of to her belly button, a deep frown drawing his dark eyebrows together, and Molly found herself thinking, *Come on. Don't be such a guy about this.*

When he finally raised his gaze, she saw a glimmer of determination there. *Yes.*

"You want me to continue in the class to soothe your conscience."

"I can also help you."

"And soothe your conscience."

"Come on, Finn. I don't have all that much to feel guilty about." He raised an eyebrow and she said, "I feel bad, but I was doing my job. I'm not losing sleep."

"We're in the same boat."

Now it was her turn to frown. "Meaning…?"

"I feel the need to soothe my conscience, too."

Molly's heartbeat stuttered. He couldn't mean...

The look on his face told her he did. But she waited for him to say the actual words before beginning her protest.

"I want a chance to make up for the shitty homecoming date."

"No, you don't." The words blurted out instantly.

"Yes. I do."

The furnace blasted on and Molly stepped over to the thermostat and turned it off. There was more than enough heat in the kitchen, thank you very much. When she turned back to Finn, she expected to see a challenging smirk on his face. There wasn't one.

"You're serious."

"Totally."

"Then it would have to be after semester, because I can't go out with a student."

"Not even an old friend?"

"We were never friends."

"We might have been if I'd known about the belly ring."

Oh, thank goodness. They were back on solid ground. This Finn she could deal with. "That date is ancient history. You don't have anything to make up for."

"Here's the deal. I'll stay in English and you'll let me make up for that lousy night."

Molly opened her mouth to argue, then thought better of it. If she said yes, she had a good three months to get out of allowing him to make up for anything.

"You drive a hard bargain."

"So do you."

She held his gaze as if afraid that looking away would give him time to think up another twist on the deal. "I agree," she finally said. "If you show up for the next class."

"I'll be there." Another burst of laughter came from the direction of the living room and Finn fought a weary smile. "We need to get back to the store."

"I need to pay you."

"We'll bill you," he said in such a matter-of-fact tone that Molly believed him. He pushed off the counter, leaving his full cup of coffee sitting next to Molly's full cup of coffee, and said, "Come on, Chase. We gotta get going before Mike calls looking for us."

Oh, yeah. He needed to go.

And Molly felt as if she needed a shot of whiskey. Straight up.

CHAPTER SEVEN

BILL HER.

Finn shook his head as he walked head down through the rain to the truck. Oh yeah, Mike would love that. His nerves were still humming a little as he got into the truck. Chase had been all stony-faced when they'd walked out into the rain, but Finn glanced over at him and caught a sappy smile playing on the kid's face. Molly's cute little sister had had an effect.

Chase noticed Finn looking at him and his expression went double serious. He cleared his throat, then stared out through the rainy wind-shield. Finn shifted his full attention back to the road. No sense giving the kid shit if Chase could turn around and give it back.

Molly had a belly ring.

What other secrets was she hiding?

And why had she made such an effort to talk him back into class? She said that it wasn't guilt, but he didn't know if he believed her. It wasn't as if she were comfortable around him. He made her edgy, but she was starting to make him feel edgy, too.

And when had he started to find glasses so sexy?

He smiled as he thought of her reaction to the date do-over, then remembered Chase and blanked out his expression. The offer had been pure knee-jerk response on his part, an attempt to get the upper hand in a situation where Molly had the definite advantage.

He didn't want to go back to English. Hated feeling stupid, but he'd said he'd try again and he would. That didn't mean he couldn't allow himself to be distracted by the teacher…or for him to distract her.

Thanks to the coffee, which he hadn't touched, they'd get back to the store later than he'd hoped, but he doubted there'd be too many customers on a soggy day like this.

Chase was once again smiling to himself as he watched the road and Finn half wondered if that was the outcome Mike had anticipated when he insisted that Chase accompany him on the snake mission. Was his grandfather trying his hand at matchmaking after the deal with Jolie and Dylan falling for each other at the feed store?

If so…well, he'd have to watch himself, and definitely never let him know about the infor-mal deal he and Molly had hammered out in her kitchen. Yes, he'd step out of his comfort zone and try to improve his writing skills—for a while anyway—but she was going to step out of hers, too.

"Everything go okay?" Mike looked up from his computer as Finn came into the office ten minutes later, carrying his dripping wet coat.

"We got the drain unplugged." He wasn't going to say a word about the way that Chase and Georgina had hit it off.

"We should have taken care of matters the first time," Mike said.

"She didn't want us to, and it isn't like you can force a drain-snaking on someone."

"We could have sneaked over after dark."

Mike had changed. As the store had become busier and more vibrant, so had he. It was as if he were ten years younger than he'd been when Finn had been deployed. And now he was suggesting late-night plumbing raids.

Mike logged into the computer and started scrolling through his email as Finn hung up his coat next to the heater. It'd taken a bit to get his uncle to embrace the computer age, but once he'd gotten the hang of it, there was no turning back.

"Son of a bitch."

Mike rarely cursed, so the muttered words stopped Finn in his tracks. When he looked back at his uncle, Mike was shaking his head grimly.

"What?"

"I have a date."

"Congratulations."

"No."

"No?" Finn moved around behind Mike to see the screen, where there was a forwarded message from his friend Cal—the one Mike and Karl had put on the matchmaking site. The message was from a woman who'd agreed to a time and place for their first date. Only the date wasn't with Cal. It was with Mike.

"He pretended to be me and set this whole thing up."

Finn did his best not to laugh, because Mike was obviously upset. "Well…" he said slowly "…you've got to kind of admire his strategy."

Mike grunted and then shook his head. "This won't do."

Finn didn't bother mentioning that Mike had brought this upon himself. He figured that Mike was well aware of that. "I gotta get going." His grandfather needed privacy as he came to terms with this unexpected turn of events.

Mike waved at him, still staring at the monitor. Finn headed out the door, almost bumping into Lola, who was sweeping dried mud near the side exit.

"What's up?" she asked, motioning toward the office with her broom.

"The roosters have come home to roost." She frowned. "Cal got the better of him. For now, anyway."

"I don't want to know." Lola focused on the floor once again.

"You don't," Finn agreed. The store was quiet and Chase was in the warehouse inventorying stock. "If you don't need me, I'm going to clock out."

Lola waved a hand, very much as Mike had done, and Finn headed back out into the weather. Fifteen minutes later he parked as close to the house as he could get and dashed through the rain to his front porch. He shoved the key in the lock and had just turned it when he heard the noise. A faint mewling.

He cocked his head and held still, wondering if he'd imagined the sound.

Nothing.

He opened the door and then heard it again. A faint thread of sound winding its way through the pounding rain.

Finn stood, half in and half out of the house, listening. Then he scuffed a foot over the porch and the soft cry sounded again. A baby...something.

He pulled his ball cap down tighter, stepped out into the rain and walked about the porch to crouch at the side opening to see if he could find anything. No, but he could hear the sound more clearly. Hoping against hope that he wasn't about to rescue a small skunk, he got down onto the wet grass and eased himself under the porch on his side. He stopped halfway in, his legs still sticking out in the rain, and waited a moment to get his bearings. The baby had gone silent, so he rolled over onto his belly to get a better view. There, in the far corner where the ground sloped up toward the foundation making the space between ground and porch way too tight for him, was a small gray kitten.

Oh man.

He scooted farther under the porch. "Come here, baby."

The kitten hunched back into the corner, so Finn continued to inch forward, until his back hit the joists above him and then he reached his arm out as far as it would go. The kitten shrank back again, but he managed to get hold of the nape of its neck with two fingers and drag it toward him. The baby let out a distress howl that would certainly have brought a mother to the rescue, if one was in the vicinity. Finn had a bad feeling that she was not.

Slowly he pushed his way backward out from under the porch and into the soaking-wet grass. Once he was able to sit upright he put the kitten to his chest, where it immediately stuck its tiny claws into his coat, clinging like a cockle-bur. Finn put a hand over the small animal and got to his feet.

"So where's your mama, little guy?"

The kitten pressed against him as Finn walked up the steps and in through the door he'd left open. The furnace was blasting away in re-sponse to the cold air that had come into the liv-ing room while he'd been belly-crawling under the porch. Finn shut the door behind him then went into the bathroom for a hand towel, which he used to rub the shivering kitten.

His best guess was that if the little guy had a mother, she would have been there with him dur-ing the deluge, keeping him warm. Finn held the kitten up in front of him. His eyes were mostly open, which made him around two weeks old and nowhere near weaned. The kitten opened his mouth as if to cry, but nothing came out, so Finn curled the little guy up under his chin, tilt-ing his head to make him a warm pocket, then reached for his phone.

"Hey," he said when Mike answered. "We have kitten milk replacer, right?"

"I think so."

"Would you look?" Otherwise he was going to have to start calling the larger ranch supply stores or see if he could find a vet.

"Yeah. We do," Mike said when he came back on the line.

"I have an orphan kitten. He's skin and bones. Barely two weeks old."

"I'll be right over."

"I can come to your place. Or the store."

"Naw. Wait there. I wouldn't mind an excuse to escape. Cal's here."

"Enough said. Could you round up a feeding bottle and an eyedropper?"

"You bet."

Finn hung up the phone and closed his eyes as the baby snuggled into him, his little nose poking at Finn's neck. "Hang tough, buddy. Mike's on the way with the grub."

When Mike got there, he agreed with that the kitten was probably an orphan. "Look how skinny he is."

Finn handed the kitten over to Mike, who cupped him in one large palm, then read the directions on the milk replacer package.

"You'll need a hot-water bottle or something to keep him warm."

"I have a heating pad. I'll put it under a towel." Finn heated the water, whisked in the milk replacer. "Mom did this once," he said. "Remember? Raised a whole litter."

Mike smiled a little. "Yeah. I do."

Between the two of them, they managed to get

most of a feeding into the kitten, instead of onto him. Even though he sputtered and protested the strange delivery method, he soon got the hang of the bottle and pushed his little paws against Mike's hand as he fed him.

"Going to name him?"

"I'm going to call around to the vets on Monday and see if they know of any mama cats who might take him."

"You sure about that?" Finn frowned at Mike, who grinned a little. "Women love guys who raise orphan kittens."

"I think I can get a woman without a kitten."

"Kitten couldn't hurt."

"Are you really in a position to be giving love advice? What happened with the date Cal set up for you?"

Mike's mouth tightened briefly. "I'm going. It's only polite. It's not her fault that Cal went too far." Finn opened his mouth, but Mike held up a finger. "Don't you dare give me any pointers on modern customs or safe sex."

"Wouldn't think of it."

But he bet that Cal and Karl had.

"Have you talked to her?" he asked his uncle.

"Emailed. She wrote back and… I'm going on a coffee date next weekend."

Finn gave him an innocent look. "If you want to take the kitten, just let me know."

MOLLY WALKED OVER to her printer and took out the stack of practice exercises. She had mixed feelings about talking Finn into staying in her class. On the one hand, she'd been the reason he was going to drop the course, and since she believed she could help him, it was a good thing to do. As far as maintaining peace of mind and enjoying teaching the class… Finn had a certain effect on her. Not the he's-so-dreamy effect he'd had on her during high school—up until the fateful date, that is—but something deeper. Baser. More hormone-driven. He was a hot guy, and he unsettled her in a way that Blake never had. She couldn't get a handle on how it was different, and that made her uneasy. She liked to understand these things. Understanding helped one avoid unexpected disaster, and Finn had disaster written all over him, but she persisted in keeping him in her classroom.

Molly set her papers aside, planted her elbows on her desk and pressed her fingertips against her forehead. This wasn't a problem. She was in control of her life and well aware that a guy like Finn—unpredictable and untethered—didn't fit into her master plan. It wasn't as if he could shove his way into her life in the same way that he was shoving himself into her thoughts.

"Excuse me… Molly?"

She looked up to see Jonas—a high school

senior who was taking college courses during his final year of high school—standing in the doorway. She hadn't asked her students to call her Ms. Adamson, but most did. Especially the high school students. "Yes, Jonas?"

"I'd like to discuss this grade." He set the second essay assignment, which she'd returned less than an hour ago, on her desk.

"What can I help you with?" Molly asked, looking at him over her glasses.

"This is only the third week of class, and frankly, I don't believe you've taught us enough to grade so harshly."

Molly almost laughed. She'd given him a B-minus, and if he thought the three or four comments she'd written on his paper were bad, he should have seen Finn's paper. "I'm setting the bar high," she said gently. She'd taught community college classes long enough to know that many students graduating from high school were not fully prepared for college-level courses, and some were stunned to find out what was expected of them.

"I don't understand how setting the bar high is helpful."

"It gives you something to shoot for."

"At the expense of my GPA?" His eyebrows rose in an imperious way.

"Apparently so. And Jonas, this is a very good paper. But there's room for improvement, which is why it's a B and not an A."

He frowned at her and waited, as if expecting her to suddenly say, "Just kidding. You can have your A." When she didn't, he raised his chin and said, "You should know that my parents donated land to this college."

"That is very generous of them." Molly spoke matter-of-factly. "And I'm certain that your parents want you to leave this place with an actual education."

"They want me to be successful."

"So do I."

Jonas opened his mouth, then closed it again. His lips flattened and then he picked the essay up off her desk.

"I'd be happy to go over that with you."

He pulled in a long breath, as if barely containing his impatience at her obvious stupidity, then abruptly turned and stalked out of the office just as Georgina was coming in.

"Who was that?" Georgina asked as she craned her neck to watch Jonas walk down the hall.

"That is trouble with a three-hundred-dollar backpack." Molly just hoped her message sank in. She didn't need trouble at this point in her new career.

"Excuse me?"

"Apparently he's not used to constructive criticism."

Georgina made an exaggerated *O* with her mouth. "Guess you'll be more careful in the future."

"Guess so," Molly said. "What's made you so happy?" Her little sister was practically vibrating with excitement.

"I have a date. With Chase."

"Big surprise there," Molly said with a wry smile.

Georgina curled a dark hank of hair around one finger. "I called him." Her eyes danced. "I figured why wait for him to screw up the courage when I could make the first move. He seemed really happy to hear from me, so…we're going to coffee on Wednesday, which is the day he gets off work early."

"Good for you." He'd seemed like a nice kid, and it was only because her own relationship had blown up so spectacularly that Molly always felt a stab of protective worry for her little sister. And in hindsight she wished she hadn't so blithely shrugged off her mother's concerns about Blake.

"I don't know," her mother had said, thus putting a pinprick in her bubble of happiness when she'd told her she was not only moving in with

Blake—she was buying a house with him. "You two are so opposite."

She and Blake had been opposites. He'd been outgoing and energized by being around people, while she'd found social events exhausting. She loved quiet weekend mornings, and unless they involved sex, Blake was bored by them. They'd been good together in other ways, though, each bringing strengths to the relationship that the other drew upon. Blake had helped Molly gain confidence, come out of her shell. Molly had helped Blake organize his life and had enjoyed keeping the home fires burning while he was on the road. But ultimately Blake had been Blake and had followed in his father's footsteps. And as long as he was discreet, he fully assumed that Molly would follow in his mother's.

It'd killed her when she found out that he was cheating. It was only after he was gone from her life that she started seeing cracks in what had appeared to be a solid foundation and was a bit stunned at how completely she'd turned a blind eye to things she should have been paying attention to.

"Are you coming home for dinner before class?" Georgina asked.

Molly looked at the piles of papers covering her desk and gave her head a slow shake. "I don't see that happening."

Georgina knew better than to argue with her. "I'll have the leftovers in the fridge—just in case you forget to grab a sandwich."

"Thanks." Because Molly didn't feel like eating then. She felt edgy and it was all because of the guy she'd talked into not dropping her class.

FINN TOLD HIMSELF that it was no big deal going back after missing two classes, but he felt as if all eyes were on him when he walked into Molly's classroom—maybe because they were. She was at the front talking to a guy whose name might have been Denny. He'd pay closer attention tonight, try to learn his classmates' names, because he told himself that if he walked back into this classroom, it was for the long haul. Come hell or high water, As or Fs, he was going to finish this class. So what if he felt stupid about what he didn't know? That was what this was all about— catching up.

But he still felt self-conscious, as if everyone in the room knew that he hadn't learned squat about English in high school. That there'd been an unspoken—or hell, who knew? Maybe it had been spoken—conspiracy to pass him along so that he could bring athletic glory to the school. What if everyone here knew that he was a walking cliché—the dumb jock?

Debra waved at him and he went to sit in the

chair directly behind her. She turned, hooking her elbow over the back of the seat.

"I didn't think you were coming back," she said in a motherly tone.

"Neither did I." She frowned and he said, "I had some…scheduling difficulties and I was going to drop the class."

She leaned a little closer. "What changed your mind?"

A belly ring?

That wasn't the real answer, but he certainly thought about that belly ring every now and again. "I was able to work things out in a different way."

Debra reached out to pat his arm. "Well, if you need a study buddy, you just give a yell."

Finn smiled in spite of himself. "Thank you." Like he was going to show the depth of his lack of knowledge when everyone else seemed to be miles ahead of him.

"Okay, everyone," Molly said when the guy she'd been talking to took his seat front and center and opened his laptop. "Time to begin."

Debra turned around to face front as Molly started class, squaring her shoulders and lining her pencils up on her desk. Just as she'd done during the first class, Molly's gaze panned over the class, over him, without stopping. But evidently she knew he was there because her lips curved ever so slightly before she started speaking again. That was when it occurred to him that she hadn't known whether or not he was actually going to show up.

"Last week we worked on using appropriate transitions. This week we'll talk about choosing verbs that convey meaning and feeling..."

Feeling. Yeah.

He was *feeling* pretty self-conscious. Maybe a touch stupid. What the hell was a transition? He slid his phone out of his pocket and surreptitiously looked it up. Ah. He raised his head as Molly turned off the lights so that they could see the interactive whiteboard better.

After a quick review of transitions, she conducted a brief refresher on verbs and various tenses. Then Molly handed out a sheet on which they were to pick the better of two verbs to convey a specific meaning. "Remember—you want to paint pictures, evoke feelings, but you don't want to be hokey."

"That can be a thin line," the guy he thought was named Denny said.

"Good point. It's all about context." Molly drifted by his desk then, lingering just long enough to say, "I have some makeup work for you. If you could stay for a few minutes after class, I'll explain it to you."

"Sure."

"It's easy," Debra whispered over her shoulder.

For you, maybe.

Finn started reading the verb practice sheet, tapping his pencil on the desk as he considered what made a good, non-hokey verb. Debra was done by the time he hit number four of ten, but Finn kept his head down and soldiered on. He wasn't quite done when Molly said they'd start discussing choices, but what the heck? And that was when he noticed that his paper was not the same as Debra's—he had about half as many questions to complete as she did.

Hell. He had a remedial verb sheet and he still hadn't gotten done. A flush started working its way up his neck as he felt himself shutting down. He was even worse off than he'd imagined. *Son of a bitch.*

Molly gave the class more work, laying the sheet on his desk as she walked by. He couldn't bring himself to look at her. Not only did she think that he was stupid, she'd proven it.

"Get this one done and let me check it before you leave." Molly continued to pace through the classroom, answering questions and making comments. Finn sat staring at the paper. Finally, he put his head down and went to work, flinching a little when Debra put her pencil down.

"I'm finished," she said. "Do we have homework?"

"Just a reading assignment. More verb work."

She set a paper on Debra's desk. "You can leave early if you need to."

"Thank you." Debra gathered her belongings and made a signal to her friend Susan, who was also finishing up.

If students weren't to leave until they turned in the exercise, then Finn hoped Molly had a cot somewhere, because even though his assignment was once again shorter than Debra's, he didn't see himself getting done any time soon.

The exodus began shortly after Debra had taken her leave and it wasn't long before Finn and Denny were the only people left in the room. Molly sorted papers and clipped them together, and finally Denny rose from his seat and brought her his completed work.

"I went through everything twice."

"Excellent strategy," Molly murmured. Finn got to his feet while Denny grabbed his backpack and brought his paper up.

"I went through everything three times," he said just for the hell of it. Denny shot him an unsmiling look, then lifted a hand in a salute before heading out of class. He hadn't extended his middle finger, but Finn got the feeling he would have liked to.

Once he was gone, Finn nodded at his paper. "I, uh, noticed that my paper was different than Debra's."

Molly blinked at him. She didn't look as if she'd purposely manipulated things to make him feel dumb or inadequate, but that had been what had happened. "I told you I was differentiating."

"Which is another way of saying dumbing down."

Molly leaned back against her desk, gripping it on either side of the skirt that perfectly outlined her thighs. "You'll have to lose that attitude if we're going to make progress. All I'm doing is adjusting the assignment so that you achieve the objectives in the most efficient manner."

He cocked an eyebrow at her. Fancy talk didn't change the truth.

"Trust me, Finn."

"Trust you." He glanced down at the floor for a moment. He'd trusted her when she told him to come back to class. "I don't like feeling stupid, Molly."

"Then don't. Feel like someone who learns differently."

"How do you grade someone who learns differently?"

Molly wet her lips. "Differently."

"That sounds like a replay of high school." And damned if he was going to have that happen twice in his lifetime. Some people may be fine with being passed along, but he had his pride. Maybe too much pride.

"It isn't." Molly moved around the desk to the box she used to carry her paperwork. She dug through a couple folders, then pulled out a card. "I've written down the addresses of websites with special exercises I want you to work on."

Finn took the card and studied it for a moment. "This will help."

"You're going to have to work harder than everyone else, but yes, I think it will help."

"I want to come out of this with pretty much the same result as everyone else."

"You will. It's the workload I'm modifying, not the result. The way this works is that the in-class assignments are shorter, but you have to do this other work outside of class to compensate."

She tilted her head at him. "Are you game?"

His gaze dropped down to her lips and Molly went still. When he met her eyes again, she was wearing a seriously wary expression.

"Are you?" she repeated. "Because I'm not going to do this extra work if you aren't going to take advantage of it."

Finn felt a twinge of shame. Yeah, she was doing extra work for him. "I'm game."

"Good." She cleared her throat and continued more briskly, back to full instructor mode. "Would it be possible for you to print out the results from the first two exercises and drop them by my office tomorrow, so I can assess before the next class?"

"I'll see if I can do it at work."

"Work. Right. Sorry. I wasn't thinking."

"No. That's okay. I'll try to get it done." He had more free time than he should have once Chase showed up for his afternoon shifts. Why not dive into his studies? Well, maybe not dive, but rather wade in slowly and try hard not to get knocked down by waves.

"My office hours are four to five, but if I'm not there or in the classroom, just slide the paper under the door."

"Right." He tucked the card in the folder he carried and started for the door.

"Finn." He looked back. "You do understand that I wasn't trying to make you feel inadequate. That would be…counterproductive."

His mouth tightened. "Counterproductive. No. We wouldn't want that." He turned and walked back toward her, getting a measure of satisfaction out of the way her eyes widened ever so slightly. "Maybe I'm not so much concerned about inadequacy as the power dynamic."

"How so?"

"You have all of it." His idea of distracting himself—and her—with a sexual vibe was now a smoking pile of ashes. How was he supposed to do that when he was fighting to keep up with everyone else, despite having remedial assignments?

"And you don't like that?" Her voice got just the tiniest bit cold, as if he'd touched a nerve.

"Maybe it'll just take me a little time to get used to it." If he didn't academically crash and burn first.

CHAPTER EIGHT

"WHAT DO YOU THINK?" Georgina held up two dresses, but before Molly could answer, she said, "Or should I go with jeans? You can't go wrong with jeans. Unless it's a formal occasion." She laid the dresses on the bed. "With jeans, I have to find a top. With dresses, I don't."

"The red," Molly said, pointing to the dress on the left.

"You think?"

"You wore it last week. You looked great. It's casual and you won't have to find the right top."

"Yeah," Georgina said as she tapped a forefinger on her bottom lip and studied the two knit dresses. "I agree."

And Molly couldn't remember the last time her sister had put this much thought into what she was going to wear. Or the last time that she, herself, had spent so much time brooding over a guy who wasn't Blake. But while Finn wasn't Blake, he was reacting like him. The fact that he wasn't the one in control bothered him—he'd come right out and admitted it, so it wasn't as if Molly was reading things into the situation.

She was so damned tired of macho men.

"I like this guy," Georgina said, somehow guessing the direction of Molly's thoughts. Maybe the bemused frown had tipped her off.

"You don't know this guy."

"Well…sometimes you just feel that something." She hung the dresses back in the tiny closet she'd finally made peace with and closed the door.

"Have you felt that something before?"

"Nope. First time."

Georgina had dated a lot but had never gotten all that serious about any one guy. That was where Molly had made her mistake. She hadn't been with that many guys before getting together with Blake. After they'd hooked up, she'd been overwhelmed by her good fortune in landing him. He was intelligent, charismatic, sexy. Being with him had helped her take charge of other areas of her life, and then finding out she hadn't been enough had broken that confidence into about a zillion little pieces. If she'd made such a mistake with him, then maybe she was making mistakes in other areas? Maybe she had reason to be insecure?

Thank goodness for anger. If Molly hadn't been so angry about being cheated on, she might have messed up. Taken him back. Given him a second chance, a third, a fourth. She had no idea how many second chances Blake's mother had given his father, but she wasn't about to play that game. Blake had shattered her world, so she set about building a new one, drawing on strength she hadn't realized she had.

And she never wanted to do that again, so she'd made a few strict life rules to make certain she never *had* to do that again. Number one rule—stay in control. Number two—don't be taken in by charm, good looks, sex appeal. There would be no more Blakes in her life. The men she dated would have substance…and small egos. They'd be the kind of men who were comfortable owning up to mistakes, who didn't see themselves as near perfect. Men who could compromise without feeling as if they were endangering their manhood.

Molly ended up calling upon both rules when Finn strolled into her office late Monday afternoon, carrying a printout of the writing exercises she'd asked him to complete. He set them on her desk, then stepped back and shoved his hands into his back pockets, as if he had no idea what to do with them. He sucked in his cheeks momentarily, accentuating the amazing hollows there. The guy had bones. Bones and an ego… and from the looks of things, his ego might be the slightest bit bruised from yet another reality check. Molly was not beyond taking advantage, because she knew from her experiences with Blake that bruised egos healed and became stronger.

"Did you have any major issues?" she asked.

"Define *major*."

"Major as in something that would make you react defensively to a simple question."

Surprise flashed in his eyes. "Actually, there was nothing major. It just took a lot of time."

"Did you learn something?"

"I did."

Molly waited, just in case he was going to expand on his answer, and found herself wishing that he hadn't worn a simple gray T-shirt. Would it have killed him to put on a regular shirt over it, so that she didn't have to be distracted by…him?

She raised her eyebrows in a coolly polite expression. "Anything you want to go over?"

"It was pretty straightforward." He shifted his weight, folding his arms over his chest. "Anything you want to tutor me on?"

Had he purposely made the question sound sexual? Or was that simply where her brain was whenever he was around?

"Not if you feel like you understood these exercises."

"Like I said. I did." His lips curved into a

faint smile as if he realized that she might be repeating herself because, regardless of all the pep talks she gave herself, he still rattled her on some level.

"It must be close to closing time. Would you like to get a coffee?"

A jolt went through her at the unexpected offer. She automatically shook her head as she quickly sifted through possible motives. "I think it's best to keep things between us as they are now."

"Which is…?"

"We're friendly acquaintances. Teacher, student."

"It's coffee, Molly. Something that friendly acquaintances or even teachers and students do."

"Thank you, but no."

FINN HAD TO SAY that this was the first time a woman had ever refused a simple coffee with him. He'd been turned down for date-dates. He knew the sting of rejection. But coffee date rejection shouldn't sting. It was coffee, for Pete's sake. The kind of safe, innocuous date that Mike was going on with his mystery woman, and the kind that Chase was going on with Molly's sister. Coffee was safe. The kind of thing you did with a friend or someone you wanted to know better.

Why was she so defensive with him? It wasn't

all because of the past and it wasn't entirely because she still found him attractive on some level. He was certain on those points—something else was causing her knee-jerk, self-protective reactions. And if that was the case, he needed to get a grip and to stop seeing this attitude of hers as a challenge or an insult.

But still, was wanting to sit down to a cup of coffee, to talk about neutral subjects in a neutral locale, so bad?

Apparently so, judging from the way she'd shut him down.

He drove back to the store where Mike was babysitting the kitten. When Finn walked through the door, Lola put a finger to her lips, and the customer she was helping smiled in the direction of the office. Finn crossed to the office door and looked in. Mike was sound asleep in his reclining chair, the tiny kitten nestled in his lap.

"They both conked out about a half hour ago."

"Late-night feedings," Finn said. Mike had insisted on taking the kitten every other night to feed him every two hours, starting last night. Tonight was Finn's night. Lola came to stand beside him, beaming in at the sleeping pair.

"Little Buddy has put on weight already. We weighed him on the nail scale."

Finn smiled, then pulled the office door partway closed. The store closed in an hour, so he'd let the two of them sleep, then feed Buddy and take him home.

"How's school?" Lola asked as she moved back behind the counter. Finn had decided to let the world know he was taking classes once he committed himself to finishing the English course. Mike had been surprised, but also a little pleased when Finn had explained he needed to expand his horizons and try new things.

"Harder than I remembered."

"The brain is like a muscle. You have to keep it exercised."

"Oh, I'm exercising it, all right."

Lola leaned her elbows on the counter. "What is it you want to do? Or are you just taking the classes for fun?"

Fun. Right. She seemed genuinely interested, so Finn confessed, "I want to get some kind of a degree, but I've forgotten a lot of stuff since high school." Along with what he hadn't bothered to learn.

"And it worries you."

"It makes me wonder about my future."

Lola narrowed her dark eyes at him, making him feel a bit like a kid again. "I know about being worried about the future. Before I got this job…everything in my life was a worry. No money means no way of knowing how you'll deal with tomorrow. But *you* have a good job here. A future. So, no matter what, you have a safety net."

"Yes." He wasn't going to tell her that sometimes he felt as if his brain was dying inside his safety net. "I'd better go roust Chase. He's probably sleeping on the grain bags."

"He doesn't do that!" Lola narrowed her eyes. "Does he?"

Finn just smiled and headed for the side exit.

THERE WERE SOUNDS coming from the art room again, wall thumping and chair dragging, so Molly stopped pretending she could concentrate and headed next door.

"Hey," Allie called from the other side of the room where she was hanging posters on the wall. "Would you mind lending a hand? This thing keeps popping the staple and rolling up before I can get the next staple in."

"You bet." Molly grabbed a chair and dragged it over to the wall and then took hold of a corner of the laminated poster. Allie got up on her chair and thwacked the opposite corner with the stapler a couple times, then handed it off to Molly, who did the same.

"Now...if you'd just keep your hand on your corner while I unroll this..." Allie carefully unfurled the laminated poster and fastened the bottom to the corkboard. "So help me, this thing had better not jump off the wall." She slowly removed her hand and Molly did the same. The poster stayed in place.

"You would think a college would have thumbtacks," Allie said. "I'd kind of banked on them. Three staplers. No thumbtacks."

"Maybe so they don't end up on the teacher's chair?"

Allie laughed. "That's probably it."

She stood back, hands on hips, regarding the poster. "It's not quite straight, but I'm going to call it good."

"I would."

Allie glanced over at the clock. "I'm an hour early. Still kind of excited to be teaching something I like."

"What did you teach before?"

"I student-taught high school art, but my first actual job was working in the elementary school library and, well, let's just say I wasn't a natural there. It was kind of a free-for-all a lot of the time." Allie wrinkled her nose. "I'm much better with adults."

"Me, too." Molly hadn't taught elementary, but she was comfortable teaching adults. Most adults. Not Finn. She wanted to teach him but wasn't comfortable doing it.

"I didn't realize that I'd gone to school with your sister the first time we met."

"Which one?"

"Jolie."

"She'll be back in the area pretty soon. She's moving onto the ranch."

"We didn't really know each other that well," Molly was quick to explain. "I spent most of my time at school with my nose in a book."

"Me, too," Allie said wryly.

Somehow Molly didn't think it was in the same way that she'd buried herself in her studies, or for the same reasons. Allie did not appear to be one bit shy or awkward.

"No. Really," Allie said, somehow reading her thoughts. "My sisters were totally outgoing. Well, Mel, the closest one to me in age, was very serious, but she was also afraid of nothing." She smiled self-deprecatingly. "I was a total geek, focused on my studies. Then I married too young, screwed up my life because I didn't know any better."

"I did something very similar without getting married," Molly admitted. "Which is why I'm here in the Eagle Valley. New life." She smiled a little. "I guess I'm better off because of all the things that happened, but it kind of sucked at the time."

Allie considered her for a long moment. "Let's

go have a drink sometime. I think we have a lot in common."

Molly smiled at her. "I'd like that. A lot."

FINN LEANED BACK from his computer and rubbed his eyes. He hadn't spent this much time staring at a monitor in forever. How did kids spend hours on video games? The website Molly had given him had nothing to do with verbs—it was about organizing writing. Truly, Finn hadn't had a clue about organization. He knew what a paragraph was—or rather what one looked like—but hadn't known much about their structure.

A squeak from the box at his feet had him pushing back his chair and scooping up Buddy with one hand. He held the kitten to his chest and reread the paragraph he wrote. Topic sentence. The three sentences that followed all had something to do with the topic, which was the care of orphan kittens.

He kind of wished now that he hadn't thrown away his first Molly paper, because he already had an inkling of what he might have done wrong. He'd written off the top of his head, and his mind did tend to jump around. Who knew about organization?

Buddy started climbing his shirt toward his neck, a sure sign that he was hungry.

"All right, all right."

The little guy's eyes were all the way open now and when Finn detached him, Buddy stared at him with his serious baby cat expression. "What shall we have tonight?" Finn asked. "Does milk sound all right?"

He tucked the kitten onto the shoulder of his hoodie, his fingers wrapped loosely around him, then headed into the kitchen where he made the formula with his free hand and filled the bottle. Then he settled into his chair for a feeding. There was something kind of soothing about feeding the kitten, rubbing his belly afterward to make him go, cleaning him up. He'd never thought much about fatherhood before, but he felt like a dad. Hell, he *was* a dad. A cat dad.

And Mike was a cat dad, too. Only this was Mike's second kid. Marcel, the big orange cat who haunted the warehouse, had also been a foundling—a few weeks older than Buddy when he'd been found hiding under a pallet, so he hadn't required a bottle.

Once Buddy was fed and changed, so to speak, Finn settled him in his warmed box and headed out the side door of his house to the detached garage. The rain had finally stopped and the forecast was bright and clear for the next several days, but the path to the shop was so muddy that he sidestepped it and walked on the grass. He'd left the hood of the truck up in order to discourage mice and other creatures from building nests on the engine block. When Buddy got older, maybe he could take care of the rodent problem. Finn smiled a little. Right now Buddy was barely larger than a rodent.

He walked over to the bench, where he'd started cutting sheet metal to fabricate a gas tank to replace the rusted-out one on the Ford. He liked working by hand, loved the feeling of losing himself in the process as he made a tank or fender or whatever else had caught his fancy. His dad had been something of a legend before the arthritis got so bad that he had to quit. But he could still play golf.

Finn smiled a little as he put on his pop's old leather apron and then cleaned the glass on the welding hood. He fired up the welder and went to work on the tank, then, when he was done, he attached a couple more bolts and a few odd shapes of scrap sheet metal to Frankie. The freeform monster sculpture was coming along nicely. If he didn't weigh a zillion tons, he'd put him on the lawn for Halloween.

As he cleaned up his tools, cleared his bench, he thought again of his dad, who'd put in a lot of long hours with Mike at the feed store and had expected Finn to do the same. He'd probably still be there if he hadn't been forced into retirement and had his mother not insisted that he move south, out of the cold.

He glanced at the old starburst clock his mom had thrown out and his father had rescued. Too late to call now, but he'd call when he got the chance, tell his dad about his latest projects.

GEORGINA'S COFFEE DATE got postponed to Friday, and somehow turned into early dinner. Molly hadn't caught all the particulars, but Georgina seemed pleased by the turn of events. So on Friday evening, while Georgina dressed for her date in the red knit dress and cute low cowboy boots, Molly climbed into her favorite flannel pants and oversize T-shirt and settled onto the sofa with a pile of grading.

Georgina walked through the living room, her head bent to one side as she put on a dangly earring. She fixed the backing, then shook her head when she saw Molly's nesting spot. "Why you love your profession is beyond me."

Molly made a face at her and focused back on the paper she was reading. She really didn't have to grade at home, but she liked catching up at the end of the week, thereby having a clean slate on Monday as well as having Saturday and Sunday free. Every now and then the plan worked and she actually did have those days free, but most of the time she chose to work even when her grading was done. There was always prep and planning to do. Disappearing into her work had helped save her sanity during the weeks and months following her discovery of Blake's infidelity, and working all the time had become a habit. Not necessarily a bad one, either.

She'd just finished reading the last paper and had slipped it into the appropriate folder when her phone rang. She didn't recognize the number, but since Georgina was out and about and may have had phone issues, she answered. At the sound of the deeply masculine hello, she almost hung up again. Except that Blake said quickly, "Don't hang up, Molly."

So she didn't. But she didn't speak, either.

"Look. I…just wanted to touch base." And it sounded as if he'd been drinking. Another of his small problems that had grown into a bigger problem during their time together.

"Have you sold the boat? Because I can give you the address where to send the check." He was never going to sell the boat, even though he pretended he was going to in order to pay her back all of the money he'd borrowed.

"I'm going to another team."

The curse of the minor leagues. Trades and more trades. Which was why Molly had been glad that he'd been able to stay in Arizona for so long.

"Which one?" She had to ask.

"There are a couple of possibilities. I'll know in a matter of days."

"Why are you telling me this, Blake?"

"Because we had the best relationship I ever had."

"I'm hanging up." He wanted money. He wanted something. And yes, his relationship with her probably was the best he'd ever had, because she'd been so freaking *stupid*.

"You're still my insurance beneficiary."

"Make your mom your beneficiary. And tell me what you really want before I hang up."

"Molly… I've changed. And there are some things you should know—"

She hung up the phone. Blake wasn't in love with her. He needed a caretaker. He liked having someone managing his life. They'd broken up over a year ago, and he still couldn't believe that she wasn't going to take him back.

Molly would have turned off the phone, except that she never shut off communications when her sister was out, so instead she blocked Blake's new number and then went into the kitchen for diet cola and whatever else she could find there.

Not a big deal. Not a big deal.

She grabbed a bag of chips she had stashed away for emergency situations and after opening the fridge, nixed the Diet Coke and pulled out the chardonnay. Why not?

Molly was halfway through a movie she couldn't concentrate on when Georgina let herself into the house, humming under her breath as she hung her car keys on the pegboard next to the door. A few seconds later she came into the living room, pulling off her earrings.

"How was your date?" Molly asked just a little too brightly. She'd have to watch her tone or she'd be on the wrong end of an interrogation.

Her sister pretended to consider the question for all of a split second before breaking into a wide smile. "It was great."

She dropped her purse on the easy chair and disappeared into the kitchen, coming back a few minutes later with a glass of water. She sat on the opposite side of the sofa from Molly and eased off her shoes.

"Chips?"

"When one stays home alone on a Friday night, one gets to indulge."

"When one comes home, one gets to indulge also." Georgina held out her hand and Molly passed her the half-empty bag.

"I gotta tell you, it's refreshing to go out with a guy who isn't all into telling you about himself. I think I got equal time." Her eyebrows drew together. "No. I probably got sixty or sixty-five percent of the time."

"Is he shy?"

"That's probably part of it. But I think he was actually interested in hearing what I had to say."

"That is refreshing," Molly said with a half smile, holding her hand out for the chip bag.

"I thought so. We're going hiking on Saturday. Do you still have your hiking boots?"

"Why wouldn't I?"

"You were a bit purge-happy after...you know."

"True. But the hiking boots live on."

"Can I borrow them?"

"You won't sweat in them, will you?"

"Nope. I'll return them in sweat-free condition."

"In that case, sure."

Georgina reached out for the bag and Molly handed it back. "Chase has a big brother."

"Good for Chase," Molly said.

"Just saying...you know...in case you ever wanted to go to coffee with a guy who listens to you."

"Blake listened." He'd had his faults, but not listening wasn't one of them, which had lulled her into a false sense of security. They'd had some great conversations. Then he betrayed her. And now he wanted her to forget all that. As if.

"I'm not talking about a serious relationship. I'm talking about a casual date with a guy who's…nice. Like Chase."

"Let me think on it."

Georgina gave her a yeah-right look, then got to her feet. "I need more than chips." She started for the kitchen.

"Not me," Molly muttered, pulling another handful out of the bag. She and this bag were in it for the long haul.

SINCE MOLLY HAD blocked Blake's new number, she had no idea if he'd called again. She'd found that there was a pattern to his calls—when he hit a rough spot, he called, and since he was an aging athlete in a profession that was prone to upsets, he seemed to be hitting more and more rough patches. At least he hadn't shown up on her doorstep, and hopefully he would end up on the opposite side of the country when he was traded. That happy thought got Molly through her first two classes. She settled at her desk with a cup of coffee during the hour she had off between her two literature classes and typed Blake's name into a search engine.

Florida. Please, Florida…

Not Florida.

Molly read the lead twice. Blake Cook was no longer playing—he had just signed on as a manager/coach for a Montana team. The Butte Tommyknockers.

Damn it all.

Had this been one of the things he'd tried to tell her Friday night? No doubt.

It doesn't matter. It isn't like he's going to stalk you. Much.

Molly jumped to her feet. She needed to move. She really needed to move. So she did—flat into Finn's chest as he walked into her office.

"Oh. Sorry." She felt her cheeks start to flame as she took a stumbling step backward. "I can't even blame this on not wearing my glasses." Which had slid to the end of her nose in the impact. She pushed them back into place with her forefinger.

"Are you okay?"

"Fine."

"You look rattled."

Probably because she was rattled. Rattled by the fact that Blake was once again in her part of the country. Rattled that when Finn had reached out to take her arm to steady her, she'd almost forgotten. Her awareness of this guy was ridiculous and in some ways worse than it'd been back in her teen crush years. It didn't help matters that he actually looked concerned about her.

"What happened, Molly?"

She shrugged and adjusted her glasses one

more time. "You startled me. That's all. How can I help you?"

He gave her a look that clearly said that she wasn't fooling him. Old Molly, awkward Molly, tried to take over and start blushing or something, but new Molly was having none of that. She nodded at the papers in Finn's hand. "English, I assume?"

He gave an unsmiling nod, his gaze still holding hers.

"I tried to work ahead on those sites you gave me. I kind of hit a wall with the online stuff. I'm missing as many as I'm getting right and I need a shove in the right direction. And these are your Monday office hours. Right?"

"Right." She took his papers and started looking them over. "I'm glad you came by."

"That bad?"

She looked over the top of her glasses. "No. I mean the last time you were in my office…" Her voice trailed off and she realized that she didn't want to say anything that would keep him from coming back if he needed help. Personal feelings and prejudices aside, her job was to teach him English.

"When I asked you to coffee and you said no."

"It wasn't personal."

He gave her a *Really?* look and Molly felt her color start to rise. *Go away, old Molly.*

"All right," she conceded. "A little personal." She heard a tiny squeak as she spoke and frowned at Finn, who shifted uncomfortably. He put his hand in his roomy hoodie pouch, but she would have sworn the pocket moved before he'd stuck his hand inside.

"I...uh..." He looked over his shoulder. "Have a friend with me." He pulled a tiny gray kitten out of his pocket.

Molly's eyes went wide. "Where did you get that?"

"Under my porch. Last week. Something happened to the mother, I guess, after she stashed him there. She hasn't been back."

"How do you know?"

"I've left food out. Nothing. Mike and I are sharing custody because it involves feeding him every three hours. It's my turn to take him and I was on my way home."

She looked past him to the door, then moved around him to shut it, watching the kitten the entire time. "Let me take a look..." She took the papers he held in his free hand and spread them out on her desk. "Okay. I see what you're doing here. Or not doing." She raised her eyes and found herself staring into the hazel depths of his. Too much guy, way too close. And he had a kitten.

"Why don't you sit down and we can go over the ones you've gotten wrong."

Finn sat and Molly positioned the paper on her desk so they could both see it. But her eyes kept straying to the little bundle of fur he held in one hand.

"May I?" she asked.

Finn smiled and handed the kitten to her. "His name is Buddy."

"Hello, Buddy." She held him up to look into his adorable face. "My heart is melting. Right here. Right now. And he's so soft." She glanced up to see Finn studying her with an odd look, but ignored it as she focused back on the cuteness incarnate now snuggled into her palm.

Molly settled in her chair, cuddling the kitty against her chest, stroking his tiny back. A moment later he started to vibrate beneath her hand. "He's purring."

"He just started a couple days ago."

"You aren't carrying him around to get women, are you?"

"Mike suggested that I do just that."

"Somehow I don't think you need a kitten to get a woman."

Had she really just said that out loud? Crap.

"I told Mike the same thing."

"This is a small room, Finn. If your ego joins us, one of us might have to wait out in the hall."

"Ha. Ha. Funny."

"Wasn't meant to be," she said with a straight face. Amusement lit his eyes.

The kitten continued to purr as Molly held him with one hand and she explained the sentence structure issues that were tripping him up. When she was done, she felt as if she were once again in control of the situation. That his…hotness…wasn't getting the better of her. Thank goodness for her teacher self—for new Molly. "I know it's not easy to come here and ask questions."

For a moment she thought Finn was going to deny it, but instead he said, "I have to be honest. I don't know how much of my difficulty is because I might have dyslexia, and how much is because I honestly didn't give two hoots about English in high school."

"A little of both, maybe?" Molly stroked the kitten, rubbing behind his small ears and over his back. "Maybe we should set up a tutoring schedule…if you bring the kitten, of course."

She was only half kidding. Holding the little guy was seriously relaxing. "Maybe fifteen or twenty minutes twice a week. Mondays and Wednesdays. I can answer your questions. We can schedule more time if you need it."

"And if I don't bring the kitten?"

"Ten minutes, once a week."

The corners of his mouth lifted. At least he understood that she was joking. She wondered, from the way he was looking at her, if he also understood how deeply aware she was of him. Not that she couldn't handle it. She could.

"You drive a hard bargain, Molly."

His voice seemed to roll over her, making her heart rate quicken. And that was when she remembered their other bargain. The one she hadn't fully agreed to. The one where he made up for their date. Surely he understood if she didn't do coffee, she wasn't going to repeat that date.

Molly stood and carefully handed the kitten back to him over the desk. Finn's hands were warm and sturdy, gentle as she transferred the little cat to him.

"I'm kidding about the kitten," she said, sounding a touch too formal.

"I know. Thanks for the help."

"What about tutoring?"

He smiled a little. "I'll let you know. I appreciate the offer."

"Do more than appreciate it. Take advantage."

He stopped and turned back. "Here's the deal, Molly…" He stopped for a moment. "Have you ever had trouble doing anything?"

"Like meeting people and feeling comfortable? Like coming out of my shell?" Overcoming paralyzing shyness?

"I think you know what I'm getting at."

"I…"

"Have always been an excellent student. And I have always been an excellent athlete. Now I'm trying to be a student and guess what? I have roadblocks I didn't even know existed. Even if you pass me because of guilt or differentiation or whatever, it doesn't mean I can pass the second English class I need. And then what happens to my degree plans?"

"What degree are you pursuing, Finn?"

He just shook his head. "What I'm trying to say, Molly, is that if you hold my hand through this, what have I actually accomplished?"

CHAPTER NINE

THERE WAS NO reason for Molly to feel frustrated with Finn. So he hadn't gladly accepted her tutoring offer. It was his life, after all. His academic career. No skin off her nose...except that she wouldn't get to see the kitten again.

Yes. That was it. That was why she was upset.

Molly unloaded the last dish from the dishwasher and shut the door.

That wasn't it.

She glanced at the clock. Ten minutes and she had to head back out for her evening class—her Finn class—which was why she was stewing on the guy. Why should it bother her that he bordered on defensive and wanted to do things on his own? He'd come in for help. He just didn't want regularly scheduled help. Or to tell her his degree plans. Or anything like that.

It wasn't as if she wanted to spend *time* with him.

Liar.

All right. She got a physical thrill from being

around the guy—that had been established long ago.

Molly let her head fall back and stared up at the ceiling. Things hadn't changed much since high school in that regard, and how sad was that? Pathetic.

She shoved her hair back from her face, then headed into the bedroom to grab a sweater, since the nights were getting cooler.

High school was over and adult Finn was different from adolescent Finn—he was darker somehow. Not *as* cocky—but still cocky. She had the feeling that he did as he pleased, when he pleased. That despite being in the military, he and self-discipline were not best friends.

He came back to class...

She'd give him that.

A knock sounded on the door as she slipped into her favorite red sweater. Frowning, she hurried to the door and opened it to find a flower delivery person standing on her step.

"Molly Adamson?"

"That's me."

The woman smiled, handed Molly the bouquet, and then turned and hurried off to her van without another word. Molly backed into the house, frowning down at the cellophane-wrapped flowers—twelve white tulips. No card.

Blood started pounding at her temples. Blake's

mother was deeply into flowers and had once explained the meanings of the different blossoms to her. Red roses meant love. Pink carnations meant gratitude. Yellow roses, friendship. White tulips, forgiveness—Molly remembered that one, because she'd thought at the time that Blake owed her a lot of white tulips. Had she mentioned that to him? Yes.

Molly's jaw muscles tightened as she headed into the kitchen where she'd left her purse and car keys.

Blake was sending her flowers and more than that, he was sending her a specific message. *Forgive me. Take me back. Care for me. Put me first in your life and I'll pay you back with good company and infidelity.*

Molly dumped the tulips into the trash. Waste of beauty, but the sight of the flowers made her feel sick.

The thought of once again getting involved with Blake made her feel sick. Never again would she be used by some slick operator who, when push came to shove, put his needs above hers.

Done. Finis.

Late for class.

Molly grabbed a handful of saltines for later and raced out the door. Georgina was studying with a friend, so she hadn't bothered with dinner, which was just as well, because her stomach was a tight little ball right now.

You are in control. He cannot force his way into your life.

But just the fact that he was giving it a shot was enough to put her in a bad mood. Having to park in the far reaches of the parking lot when she was already late didn't help matters.

She yanked her purse out of the backseat once she'd found a spot, jumped out of the car and started jogging toward the building, locking the car as she ran. She hated being late and she hated that Blake still had the power to screw up her life.

MOLLY WAS LATE for class.

Finn leaned back in his chair and fiddled with his pencil, thinking of how this would have been his dream situation in high school—the instructor not showing—but right now he was concerned about the instructor. Molly wasn't the type to be late.

Know-it-all Denny began wondering aloud how long they needed to wait before the class could be considered canceled. Debra had just said she thought fifteen minutes seemed reasonable when Molly rushed in through the door. She almost skidded to a stop, then lifted her chin and continued on to the front of the room in a more dignified manner.

"I apologize," she said as she walked briskly to the lectern and set down her purse. When she turned back, she appeared calm and collected, her expression bordering on serene, but Finn saw tension in the way she held her body, the way her smile was just that much too tight. "We can go ten minutes longer tonight if you want."

A general murmur arose from the class, indicating that once it hit eight o'clock most of her adult students wanted to head home.

"I understand. It won't happen again."

Finn wondered what "it" was as Molly started her lesson. Whatever "it" was, it was still on her mind. She was trying too hard to act as if all were well, and Finn was startled by an upwelling of protectiveness.

Really?

Maybe it was because she looked exactly as he felt when he had to pretend everything was fine when it wasn't. Maybe he didn't want her going through that.

Molly circulated around the room and Finn had one hell of a time keeping his mind on the reading instead of on her. He repeated the first paragraph about six times before moving on. When she stopped to point something out to Denny, who was already on the written part of the assignment, the guy started to talk about a little-known rule that made him right and Molly wrong. Denny droned on until Molly said that he could do whatever he wanted, but that he'd be graded by *The Chicago Manual of Style*.

"What about *The Cambridge Handbook*?" Denny challenged in a snotty voice.

Almost everyone in the class had stopped writing by this point, but a few people were polite enough to keep their eyes on their papers and pretend to work. Finn was one of them, until *The Cambridge Handbook* came up, whatever that was. He sat up straight, watching the confrontation through narrowed eyes.

"If we were in Great Britain that would work well." Molly smiled sweetly. "Unfortunately, we are in Montana."

"Humph," Denny said in a tone that indicated he didn't agree. "What I'm doing is correct."

"Noted. I will mark you accordingly."

And then when Denny realized he had nothing else to bitch about, he looked vaguely dissatisfied.

"You got your way. Now can you please be quiet so that the rest of us can work?" Debra asked in a weary voice.

Denny turned to eyeball Debra, but instead met Finn's deadly gaze from where he sat directly behind her. Finn lifted one eyebrow in silent challenge and Denny started to color, then turned back around. Message received.

Finn went back to work, and a few seconds later, pens started moving again all over the classroom.

Pompous nitwit. Finn gritted his teeth.

After reading the paragraphs, he started making an outline of what he'd just read—Molly had shown them today how to work backward, read and then dissect, in order to see how essays were put together. He was trying his damnedest to do just that, even if it took a while to identify and then translate the main idea of each paragraph into words.

Molly continued to circulate, pausing briefly at Finn's desk to see what he was doing, then moving on. It was as if she didn't know him. And that was probably best. Denny was still red around the edge of his collar, but he let Molly pass by unmolested and Molly did herself a favor by barely glancing at the guy's work. Denny gave a loud sniff as she headed on to the next student.

Twit.

Finn gathered up his materials as soon as class was over and headed for the door. Whatever was eating at Molly was none of his business...even though she'd met his eyes once, about midway through class, and somehow forgot to put her guard up. It was almost as if she had been seeking a connection with a kindred soul, and then as soon as it had happened, her expression had gone blank.

None of your business.

He was halfway across the parking lot when he changed his mind. Molly's car was on the far end of the lot, mostly in the shadows, and even though it was Eagle Valley, Montana, he reversed course and headed back to the building.

Molly came out the main entrance, zipping her purse closed as she walked. She looked up, saw him coming toward her and stopped. "Is something wrong?"

"I thought I'd walk you to your car."

"Because…?"

"It's dark over there," he said patiently.

Molly adjusted the strap of her bag on her shoulder, then started down the concrete steps toward him. "Thank you." The words were clipped. Polite. And the message was clear—*back off.*

Sure. No problem.

They'd made it about three yards before Finn asked, "What's wrong?"

"I was just running late this evening."

"Ah." He focused on the ground a few feet in front of them as they walked. "Being late really puts you in a mood."

"Denny puts me in a mood."

"Denny puts everyone in a mood, but you weren't upset about Denny when you arrived."

They rounded the end of an oversize Ford truck and started crossing the last several yards to Molly's car. "No," she finally said. "I was upset at life." She shot him a look. "You know—the annoying things that happen to all of us."

"What annoying thing happened to you?"

Molly didn't answer until they got to her car. She pulled her keys out of her pocket and beeped the locks open, then turned back to him, folding her arms. "You showed up at my office, all dark and defensive. You wouldn't tell me your major. Wouldn't accept the offer of weekly help, yet you feel as if you can dig into what's now bothering me?"

Finn considered for a moment, then nodded. "Pretty much."

Molly blew out a breath and turned toward her car. Finn put his hand on her shoulder almost before being aware of moving. She automatically stiffened and he instantly dropped his hand.

"I want to major in teaching."

The amazed expression that chased across Molly's face made Finn really and truly wish he'd kept his mouth shut.

"Not normal teaching," he quickly amended.

"What kind of teaching?"

"Automotives. Shop."

"Ah. CTE."

"Uh…yeah. That."

Molly hugged her arms around herself a little tighter, but she didn't turn away from him. Didn't get into her car and drive off. "Yet you bailed from my class at the first sign of trouble—a class you need. I had to talk you into coming back."

"I was going to take the class again," he replied. "From someone who…"

"Wasn't me?"

"Maybe someone who didn't have an ax with my name on it to grind."

She looked as if she wanted to argue, but instead she asked, "What made you decide to teach automotives?"

The Ford truck they'd skirted a few minutes before roared to life and Finn stepped even closer to Molly's car to let the guy by. "I helped some of the new recruits learn the ropes when I was overseas. I was actually good at it."

"I'm not surprised."

"You seem surprised."

"Well, I apologize. Preconceived notions and all that."

"I'm not still the guy who brought you home from a date and then got laid elsewhere."

"That guy's still in there," she said.

"So's the girl who refused to talk to me all evening long." He leaned a little closer. "Molly—that date was painful."

Her pretty mouth tightened and then she briefly rolled her eyes up toward the sky in a gesture of defeat. "Not what I wanted to hear."

"Sorry." Yeah, he'd been bad that night, but Molly had been another part of the reason why they hadn't had a good time. "Maybe you owe me a new date to make up for it."

"Then I can drop you off and get laid afterward?"

Finn laughed. Molly could play. He liked that. Maybe more than he should. "That would be a first," he deadpanned.

Molly's eyes narrowed in thoughtful consideration. "Are you sure about that?"

Finn's smile grew. A small car whipped past them, going too fast for the lot, and Finn stepped closer to Molly, recognizing Denny behind the wheel.

"What an a-hole."

"If you teach, you have to deal with them," Molly said, reaching for her door handle. "Part of the game."

Finn hadn't considered that part of the game.

"I need to go," Molly said. "I hate getting home too late."

"Understood."

Yet she hesitated, bouncing a look down at the ground and then back up at him. "If you need more help…please stop by during office hours."

Back to the neutral corners now, which felt odd after joking about getting laid.

"You bet." He gave her a nod as she opened the door, then turned and started toward his truck a few rows away.

"And Finn?"

He looked back.

"Bring the kitten."

"THIS IS A very bad idea." Mike adjusted his collar in the mirror, then smoothed his hand over his silvery hair. Finn stood a couple yards behind his grandfather and, because his reflection showed in the mirror at which Mike was primping, he kept his expression carefully solemn—no easy task when Buddy kept tumbling out from under the chair to attack Mike's shoelaces before awkwardly retreating back into his makeshift lair.

"This is coffee."

"Easy enough for you to say. You aren't going on a date with a stranger."

"You're going to coffee," he reiterated. Not an orgy. "Maybe you should take Buddy."

"No way." Mike turned away from the mirror. "What if we don't hit it off? I don't want any of that cute kitten charm happening if I want to escape."

"You're right. Kitten effect is better on the second date."

Mike gave a derisive snort, lifted his foot about an inch and waited for Buddy to tumble off and disappear again under the recliner before shrugging into his corduroy sports jacket. Finn had suggested that shirtsleeves were fine for coffee, especially since the day had turned unseasonably warm, but Mike seemed to think that a sports jacket showed more respect. Finn had simply nodded in agreement.

"Cal's going to pay for this," Mike muttered as he thumbed through the bills in his wallet.

"Literally or—" Finn stopped abruptly when Mike raised his eyes to glare at him before settling the wallet into his inner jacket pocket. Letting out a breath, Finn walked up to his grandfather, put a firm hand on each of his shoulders and said, "Relax."

Mike's mouth tightened briefly, then he did seem to relax as he exhaled. "You're right. I'm being stupid. It's just that…"

"You haven't dated since Grandma?"

"Exactly."

"Pretend she's a guy."

"Why would I be dressed up like this to have coffee with a guy?" Mike growled.

Finn spun his grandfather around toward the door. "Go. And I expect a full report when you get back."

"A gentleman—"

"Yeah, yeah, yeah. Don't stay out too late."

Finn settled his hands on his hips and let out a breath after Mike closed the door behind him. Buddy scooted out from under the chair looking for his prey and Finn scooped him up.

"Just the two of us, kiddo."

The kitten's eyes went a little wild and Finn set him back down, smiling as the little cat flattened his ears and humped up, crossing the floor in a series of threatening hops. In a matter of minutes, he'd tire himself out and then the two of them would hit the road, head for the shop where Finn planned to work on his '72 Ford and be on call in case Mike had some kind of dating disaster. It was crazy after the sleepless nights he'd given his own folks, but he felt like a parent and he wanted things to go well for Mike and his mystery date.

"AH, THE NOTEBOOK," Georgina said as she came into the kitchen to pull a box of ginger snap cookies out of the cupboard.

"Yes, indeed," Molly replied, closing the worn cover and smoothing her hand over it. The notebook had helped her keep firmly on track with her life since breaking up with Blake. On the advice of a fellow teacher in Arizona, she'd documented her fears and concerns about the future in the spiral bound book—listed them, then addressed them in writing, one by one. The simple exercise had helped her gain a sense of control over the seeming chaos of her life, spurred her on to write concrete life goals. Helped her define exactly what she needed in life to feel happy, successful and secure.

"Writing in it or revisiting?" Georgina asked as she sat on the opposite side of the kitchen table and dug into the box of cookies.

"A little of both. Just reminding myself of what I'm looking for and what I hope to achieve." *As well as what she was going to avoid.*

The notebook had been buried in a box she'd yet to unpack after the move, but recent events had made her decide to dig it out. Get back on track.

Blake was coming to Montana and there wasn't one thing she could do about it She'd made a note of that in the book a few minutes before and then reminded herself in writing that good things had come out of her relationship with Blake. She didn't need to be tied up with resentment, but rather grateful for the experience. She now understood exactly what she did and did not want in a relationship. The bad thing was over and because of what she learned, she never had to go through it again.

So what if he sent flowers and attempted to call her? Eventually he'd find someone to take care of him—although none of his post-breakup girlfriends had lasted. They'd seen the light a lot faster than she had.

"Do you want to watch *CSI* with me?" Georgina asked as she got back up from her seat. "I'm done studying for the night."

Molly shook her head. "I have grading."

"Suit yourself." Georgina poured a glass of water, tucked the box of cookies under her arm and headed into the living room. A few seconds later the television came on and Molly pulled the stack of papers she'd pushed aside while writing in her notebook closer. But she didn't pick up her pen.

Another reason she had the notebook out was to reinforce the fact that Finn didn't fit into her plans—not even for a little while. She was so damned tempted by the man. Their discussion in the parking lot after class had left her feeling ridiculously on edge. She liked bantering with him and that was not a good sign.

Finally she shoved her grading aside and headed out the back door to get some air. The sun had set and it was getting dark outside, but she crossed the backyard to inspect the flower beds that Georgina had prepared with Mike's help a few days ago. According to the diagram her sister had attached to the refrigerator, there would be daffodils, narcissus, crocus, tulips... hopefully not white ones. Molly pretty much hated white tulips now.

She wandered closer to the boundary fence, where Mike had suggested they plant pansies and violets next spring. She was looking forward to spring and getting this first semester of school under her belt—hopefully with no professional mishaps. She wanted this job nailed down tight. After that she could work on developing a personal life—with the right kind of guy, of course.

Mike's house was dark except for one light in the living room. And Finn's truck was parked in the driveway. Molly instantly headed back into the house.

She had grading to do, and worrying about men had taken up too much of her time tonight.

She'd have to make a note of that in her book.

FINN COULD HAVE taken Buddy and spent the evening in the comfort of his own home. Instead he chose to hang out at Mike's place and wait for his grandfather to return from his date.

Curious?

Totally. And he knew that the window to hear about the date was small. Mike wasn't a big sharer, but if he caught him right after he got home…well, maybe he'd find out how things went. All things considered, he was glad that Cal and Karl had set Mike up. His grandfather lived a rather lonely existence when he wasn't at the shop, and dating would be good for him.

Unless the woman broke his heart. That wouldn't be good. And that was another reason he stayed at Mike's house. What if things went wrong?

"We'll hang here, just in case," Finn told the kitten after he'd fed him. He checked out his grandfather's DVD collection and then he and Buddy settled in for yet another viewing of *Bullitt*, one of his favorite old movies.

"Watch this," Finn murmured as Steve Mc-Queen's car bottomed out on a San Francisco hill, then realized he was talking to a sleeping cat.

Maybe Mike wasn't the only one spending too much time alone.

His life had changed so radically since returning stateside. He'd barely contacted his old friends, and didn't feel his former need to socialize most nights of the week.

Was he getting boring?

Did it matter?

The soft sound of whistling brought his head up after he'd ejected the DVD. Mike rattled his keys, then unlocked the door. The whistling stopped abruptly when he saw Finn still there and the kitten sound asleep on one of the sofa cushions.

"You didn't go home?"

Finn gave a casual shrug and stuck his hands in his back pockets, like he used to do when he and Mike had serious conversations—conversations that often involved Finn learning some important lesson in life, such as "don't break windows in vacant houses" and things like that.

"I watched *Bullitt*."

"I see." Mike dropped his keys in the bowl near the door and shrugged out of his jacket.

"So…how was it?"

The look Mike gave him was not what he'd expected. Instead of withdrawing, as Finn had expected, so that he had to dig details out of him, Mike looked as if he was about to go on the offensive.

"Elaine is an interesting woman."

"Good to hear."

"She taught for a long time. Twenty-five years."

"Cool."

Mike's mouth shifted a little bit sideways. "She was your science teacher in high school."

"What?" Finn pulled his hands out of his pockets. "Really? Huh. Small world."

"It is the Eagle Valley," Mike said drily. He walked into the kitchen and started the faucet.

Finn followed, waiting until Mike had finished with his drink before asking, "What's her last name?" He'd had several female science teachers over the years, but one…

"Fitch."

Ms. Fitch? The meanest freshman teacher in the high school? Couldn't be.

One look at Mike told him that it be.

"Seems you weren't the best student."

"I got okay grades." Probably fake grades, but okay on paper.

"And your deportment?"

Heat started to work its way up his neck. He and his friends had been typical asshole jocks.

"She was our *freshman* science teacher," he said as if that explained everything, and, actually, it did. Fourteen-year-olds were brutal creatures. "I thought she moved away."

"Nope. Just stopped teaching. She said that there gets to be a point where a person gets tired, and that's the time to quit. I experienced the same thing at the feed store."

So had he—just a whole lot sooner than Mike had.

"I, uh—" Finn rubbed a hand over the back of his neck "—feel like the roosters have come home to roost." Sixteen years later. Was high school never going to stop haunting him?

"She didn't say anything bad about you."

"Did she say anything good?"

"Nope." Mike opened the fridge door and then backed out of the fridge carrying the remainders of a ham.

"I thought you went to dinner." And he wasn't yet certain how the coffee date had turned into dinner, but it had.

"She wanted to go to this new rabbit food place."

"Veganomics?" The bar patrons were taking bets at McElroy's as to whether a strict vegan restaurant would survive in the Eagle Valley.

"That's the place. We had salads. Raw stuff." Mike wrinkled his nose. "Didn't mind the tofu as much as I thought I would, though." He looked back at Finn before pulling a knife out of the block. "It takes on the flavor of whatever it's in."

"Good to know. So are you going out with her again?"

"Probably. I told her she needed a steak. We're thinking about next weekend." When he caught the bemused expression on Finn's face, he said, "Nothing wrong with liking salads better than meat and vice versa. There are more important things to consider."

Finn didn't bother telling his grandfather that

it wasn't the carnivore vs. herbivore thing that surprised him—it was the second date. With Ms. Fitch.

Mike carved several pieces of ham off the bone and set them on a plate, glancing up to silently ask Finn if he wanted to partake. Finn shook his head.

"I'm thinking of having her over here. You should come. Say hello."

"Yeah," Finn said on a breath. "Maybe." He glanced at the clock. "I'm going to run. Glad your date went well."

"Leave Buddy." Mike pulled out a chair and sat at the table, raising a hand in farewell.

"I will. See you tomorrow." He stopped to stroke the sleeping kitten's striped belly, then stepped out into the crisp night air.

Ms. Fitch. Wow.

Karma, it seemed, was really intent on chewing his ass.

CHAPTER TEN

THE NEXT DAY, Finn was still getting his ass chewed, but it wasn't by karma. It was by Basic English Comp. It wasn't that he was incapable of understanding *what* he had to do—he'd come to terms with the fear—it was that he didn't know *how* to do it. And that in turn made him doubt his goals. Was he going to be able to power through a degree with minimal writing skills?

After spending the better part of two hours in the warehouse tackling essay organization exercises and then trying to apply them to his own assignment, he decided that he needed to see the master. He told himself it was solely because he needed help with his English—not because he was recalling little things about Molly that kind of turned him on. *She'd drop him off and then go get laid. Right.*

She seemed surprised to see him when he knocked on her door, and even though it wasn't her office hours, she waved him in.

"Sorry I'm not here during the official time. I

have to close the store tonight, so I took a chance that you could squeeze me in."

And was it his imagination, or had her expression shifted when he said "squeeze me in"? He needed to get a grip here. He was going all schoolboy lustful. It didn't help that Molly's cheeks seemed pinker than usual. Was it possible that her thoughts were mirroring his?

"I don't see a kitten…"

Finn smiled in spite of himself. "Buddy is with his other dad."

"Ah. What's going on?" she asked, motioning for him to sit across from her. The desk served as a nice big barrier and Molly was staying on her side of it.

"Take a guess."

"Organization."

"Got it in one. I was wondering if you have any…I don't know…tricks or anything to help me wrangle this beast? My thoughts don't come out in neat categories."

"You're not alone there."

"Good to know."

"Have you tried the note card approach?"

She seemed to think that he knew what she was referring to. He did not. "What is that?" She pressed her lips together and he said, "Let me guess…this is a technique I should have learned in high school…or earlier."

"Good possibility."

"I kind of marched to my own drummer back then. You know…when I passed my classes because I was breathing."

"I would hope you had to do more than breathe," Molly said.

"I handed in all my work."

"There you go."

He leaned back in the chair, enjoying the way rising color was brightening her cheeks, even as she kept her gaze direct and no-nonsense. "Tell me about this method that I blew off years ago."

"You write down one idea at a time on note cards, then arrange them according to categories. You can use something as simple as Who, What, Why, Where, When. Get some three-by-five note cards and write down one sentence on each one. Then organize and write an outline."

"Huh." He gave her a look. "I kind of remember something like this from junior high. I believe I instantly disregarded and fired off a paper from the hip."

"I imagine it was a good one, too."

He smiled at her wry retort. "I'll give this method a go—for real, this time. Thanks."

He got to his feet, but before he could head to the door, Molly said, "You know, if your brain isn't wired to learn in the way you're being taught, there's a good chance you're going to tune out."

Finn gave a slow nod. "That could explain a lot." As could total lack of interest in anything that wasn't sports.

Molly's mouth quirked up at one corner as she idly tapped her pencil on her desk. "That's why dyslexic kids sometimes become discipline problems."

"I was an angel."

She smiled at his deadpan reply. "Then someone was spreading a lot of lies about you."

"I was a victim of circumstances."

"You were a hellion."

"Whom you apparently admired."

Her color was rising again, but she didn't back down. "I was young."

"So was I."

There was a knock on the door and they both turned to see a kid with an imperious expression peering at them through the glass as if he expected Molly to instantly let him in and kick Finn out.

Molly's smile became fixed as she stared at the door.

"I'll get out of your hair. Thanks for the strategy."

Before Finn could move, the kid knocked again, loudly enough that the sound echoed through the room. Molly frowned and got to her feet, quickly moving around her desk to open the door. "Jonas, I have another student here."

"And I have a class in ten minutes. I want to discuss my latest grade."

"My office hours are between four and five. You know that. I'm happy to see drop-ins, but you have to understand that when you drop in there's a good chance I have another commitment. Like I have right now."

"I would like an appointment." The kid spoke as if he were royalty, and Finn's neck muscles started to tighten.

"Fine. Tomorrow at four o'clock."

Molly sent Finn a quick look edged with something that looked like murder, then stepped out into the hall and pulled the door shut behind her. As much as he would have loved to listen at the door, Finn kept his seat. He heard the sound of arguing, one raised voice, cold, just a little whiny, and then a few seconds later, Molly came back into the room.

"Settled?"

"For now. He thinks he owns my time." Molly grimaced. "He is entitled, with a capital *E*."

"Huh. I thought *entitled* was spelled with an *I*."

"All right," Molly said, laughter lighting her eyes. "He's entitled with a capital *I*."

MOLLY DID NOT WANT to be charmed by Finn. He reminded her too much of Blake.

No. That wasn't it.

She stopped digging through the box of sweaters and fleeces to consider for a moment.

He did remind her of Blake in some ways, but what bothered her was that she was *reacting* to him the way she'd reacted to Blake before she knew the truth about him. That was where the trouble lay.

Fortunately, the one thing she could control in life was her reactions.

"Did you find it?" Georgina yelled from her bedroom.

Molly pulled a thick red fleece from the bottom of the storage box. "I have a red one. I don't see a navy."

"That will do," Georgina said as she appeared in the doorway. She reached for the fleece and Molly tossed it to her.

"That's all you need? You're set for your hike tomorrow?" Her sister was seeing a lot of Chase, and while Molly had a few reservations, she kept them to herself. Georgina was a smart girl, and her older sister was a walking cautionary tale.

Georgina slung the fleece over her shoulder and pulled the check-marked list Chase had given her out of one pocket and a plastic disposable rain poncho from the other. "What else could I need?"

Molly had to admit that the kid was prepared. Even though it was supposed to be a two- to three-hour hike, he'd made certain that Georgina was dressed for all eventualities, from heat wave to snow.

"If I like hiking, I'll invest in some stuff." Georgina shoved the list and poncho back into her jacket pockets.

"I truly doubt I'll ever use my hiking boots again."

"Then I'll feel free to sweat in them." Georgina grinned at her and disappeared down the hall. "I'm setting my alarm for five o'clock," she called back. "Do you want me to wake you?"

"No! Tiptoe when you get up."

"In hiking boots?"

"Do your best."

Molly put the sweatshirts and jackets back into the storage box and replaced the lid. The red fleece she'd just handed off to her sister had belonged to Blake. She had no idea how it'd escaped the post-breakup purge, but it had and now it would be useful—as long as Georgina didn't discover who it'd belonged to. If she did, she might just light it on fire.

The protective-loyal gene ran strong in their

family. Blake had hurt her sister, therefore Blake was the devil.

But honestly, just as she'd recently noted in her notebook, there'd been some good to their relationship. Blake had taught her that risk-taking had rewards as well as consequences, and sometimes it was better to throw caution to the wind and feel truly alive than to sit at home, where it was safe. All he asked in return was that she manage his life. Handle the day-to-day stuff. Be there when he came home from the road. Be his partner and his problem-solver.

Where she'd messed up was in believing that they had the same ideas on finance and fidelity. They did not.

Not even close.

The result had been humiliating. Apparently everyone in Blake's sphere had known about the other women. Everyone. And when she'd found out, she'd felt so duped. So stupid.

So very angry.

But thanks to the anger, she'd grown a backbone.

The bottom line was that she didn't mind being charmed, but she wanted to feel…safe… in the process. In control. She was looking for the antithesis of Blake—someone sedate and trustworthy and predictable. She was definitely not getting deeply involved with someone she didn't know inside and out, someone she wasn't positively certain she could trust.

But would she get minorly involved?

That was the question niggling at her. The question she shoved aside as she brewed tea and dived into her grading. Sometimes it was simply better not to think too much.

GEORGINA WAS LONG GONE by the time Molly got out of bed the next morning. Chase had brought a map of the area where they planned to hike, and Georgina had left it on the kitchen table with a note telling her to expect them back in mid- to late afternoon.

And she'd made coffee. Molly gratefully poured a cup from the carafe and hugged it with both hands as she sat at the table. She'd stayed up late finishing her grading, so the day stretched ahead of her. There was so much she could be doing around the house that she really wasn't certain where to start.

Laundry. Always laundry.

So the morning went. Molly caught up on the laundry, hanging out sheets and towels on the backyard clothesline, washing her delicates in the kitchen sink and drying them on a rack in the utility room.

She swept, mopped, polished and then just after lunch, figuring it was five o'clock somewhere, poured herself a glass of wine. She'd no sooner put the cork in the bottle than there was a knock on the door.

Mike stood on the porch and Molly opened the door wider when she saw that it was him. "I'm having a little barbecue this afternoon with a friend of mine. Would you and Georgina like to join us?"

"Georgina is hiking with Chase today. She won't be back until late afternoon."

"How about you, then? You don't want to spend your day all alone, do you?"

Well...honestly...yes...

But something in the old man's expression made her say, "I'd love to come over. What should I bring?"

"Just yourself. I have the steaks and my lady friend is bringing the side dishes. Finn covered dessert."

Molly had half expected that Finn would be there and now she had confirmation.

"What time?"

"We're thinking three o'clock."

"I'll be there." It gave her time to change her clothes, put on some makeup. Pretend she wasn't secretly looking forward to seeing Finn. She was honest enough to admit that she enjoyed the physical rush of being around him. Nothing wrong with that—as long as she remembered her life parameters and goals and acted accordingly.

Right?

Besides, it was damned hard to fight biological responses.

"Sorry about the late notice. Elaine and I were supposed to go to lunch today, but she got waylaid, so I suggested a barbecue this afternoon and she agreed."

"A pop-up barbecue." Mike frowned at her and Molly laughed. "Never mind. Kid talk. I'll be over shortly."

Less than an hour later Molly knocked on Mike's open door, and he motioned her to come inside and then escorted her through the kitchen, where Finn stood at the sink, popping ice cubes out of a tray, to the charming backyard. Finn glanced at her as she walked by, smiled, made her heart go thump.

A plumpish woman with salt-and-pepper hair got up from her chair under the apple tree as Molly and Mike stepped out onto the patio.

Mike motioned at the woman. "Do you know—"

Molly's mouth popped open. "Ms. Fitch!"

"Molly Adamson!"

Molly wasn't much of a hugger, but Ms. Fitch

headed toward her, arms open, so she met her halfway. "Call me Elaine. It's good to see you, Molly."

"It's good to be remembered. Are you still teaching?" Molly asked as she stepped back out of the woman's embrace.

"No," Finn said as he emerged from the house carrying a tray of drinks. "My friends and I wore her out."

Elaine laughed. "You and about two thousand other freshmen. Note to self—do not teach freshman anything."

"I had you my junior year," Molly said, talking a seat on the opposite side of the picnic table.

"Which is why I remember you fondly." She smiled up at Finn as she took the drink he offered her. "This one…" She laughed and Finn's eyes crinkled at the corners.

"Guilty."

"Of what?" Molly asked.

"Probably everything."

"Well, you were a charming hell-raiser. I'll give you that." Elaine lifted her glass in a toast, then smiled up at Mike as he came to take his seat.

"Steaks will be ready to go on the grill in about twenty minutes."

"I wish you would have let me bring something," Molly said.

"Next time." Mike smiled and turned his attention to Elaine, leaving Molly and Finn facing each other with not a whole lot to say. Molly caught the amusement in his eyes and took charge of the conversation.

"I told you that you were a hellion. Now I have confirmation."

"I never denied." He lifted his drink, took a sip, and there was something innately sensual in the action.

"No," Molly said softly. "You didn't." She took a sip of her own drink. Next to her Elaine and Mike began discussing the trials and tribulations of raising headstrong children. Molly could only imagine. No one in her family was headstrong. They'd listened to their parents, did the right thing when they could. None of them were big risk-takers.

Had they lost out?

Listening to the stories Mike told as they waited for the grill to heat and the steaks to come to room temperature, Molly half wondered, then told herself, no. A person needed to be wired a certain way to enjoy risky behavior. Blake had been wired that way. He'd enjoyed his double life. He hadn't come out and admitted it, but it had been pretty obvious as they'd duked it out at the end of their doomed relationship.

He had no regrets about the taking risks

part—only the screwing up the other side of his life part. Thus twelve white tulips. At least there'd been no more flowers, but Molly knew the flowers weren't for forgiveness alone. Blake would follow up; and she'd have to get tough with him…unless she took the offensive.

It was then that she noticed that she was grasping her glass so tightly that her fingers had started to go white at the knuckles, and that Finn was studying her with a faint frown. She relaxed her grip on the glass and smiled at him.

"Taken back by the family tales?" he asked mildly.

"Actually, I was thinking of a few incidents in my own life."

"Care to share?"

"Some things are best forgotten," she said lightly and focused on Elaine and Mike. If only those things would stop trying to get in contact with her.

Mike had just started the steaks when Molly's phone rang in her pocket. Georgina.

"We got back early. Where are you?"

"Mike's backyard."

"Tell her to come over," Mike called. "I have extra steaks."

Molly relayed the message and a few minutes later Georgina showed up, looking windswept and happy.

"How could I have never hiked before?" she demanded.

"Uh…you said you'd hate it when I tried to take you with me?"

Georgina waved her hand dismissively, then turned toward Elaine, who asked where she'd hiked. As Georgina explained where they'd gone and what they'd seen, Molly slipped over to help Mike with the steaks.

"These are gorgeous," she murmured.

"From the Lightning Creek Ranch. Grass-fed." He glanced her way. "It pays to marry into a ranching family."

"When do Dylan and Jolie get married?"

"Next month. On the ranch."

"Sounds lovely."

"I'm just glad to get Dylan married off to a decent woman. His first wife…" Mike's mouth hardened as he poked at a steak.

So Dylan had been married before to a woman Mike didn't approve of. Or maybe it was her actions after they'd married he didn't approve of. The important thing was that he seemed to approve of Jolie.

"They'll be back pretty soon, then."

"Two weeks."

"I bet you can't wait."

Mike gave a satisfied nod. "It's good having both of my boys back."

Dinner stretched on until the early hours of the evening. Molly hung back and watched as Georgina and Elaine entertained. Both were natural extroverts and she was always glad to hand the spotlight over to anyone who wanted it. After dinner, Elaine announced that she was doing the dishes and Molly volunteered to help, since she hadn't brought anything. Georgina continued to share stories with Finn and Mike, and his two friends, Cal and Karl, who'd shown up around dessert after a day of fishing. It was a full house, or rather yard, with a lot of positive, happy energy.

Molly was more than glad to escape for fifteen minutes or so. It was hell being a natural introvert.

"None of my business," Elaine said after loading the dishwasher and filling a sink with soapy water to wash the excess dishes, "but I have to ask…are you and Finn…?"

Molly gave her a startled look. "No." The word came out automatically, adamantly.

Dear heavens…had they come off as a couple? Molly quickly replayed the events of the afternoon and could come up with nothing, other than the vibe between her and Finn. The same vibe that had been growing since he first reported to her class.

"Oh. My mistake." Elaine smiled a little and reached for a serving plate, which she submerged in the soapy water. "I misread things."

"He's a student in my English Basic Comp

class at the community college," Molly murmured, as if that explained the time she'd spent studying Finn from behind her sunglasses, feeling totally safe because, hey—dark glasses. "We know each other that way. Teacher. Student."

Elaine's eyebrows lifted as she washed the plate, but she did not look at Molly. The shift in her expression was enough to tell Molly that the dark glasses hadn't been enough.

"Finn's attractive," she allowed in a carefully casual voice. "But I'm looking for more than a pretty face."

"And he is good-looking. Finn looks a lot like Mike did when he was young."

"You knew Mike when he was young?"

"I knew who he was. He didn't know me." She handed Molly a dish to rinse. "Well, if you're not just looking for a pretty face, then what are you looking for in a partner?"

Molly frowned at her. "If someone had told me thirteen years ago that I'd be trading man-talk with my science teacher…"

Elaine smiled back. "Life is funny." Then she raised her eyebrows in a clear invitation to continue.

"I'm looking for someone who probably doesn't exist," Molly said on a laugh. She'd made a list of qualities in her notebook and rattled off the top few. "He'll be steady and predictable. Definitely professional—someone settled in their career. Maybe another college teacher."

"Kind of a male version of yourself?" Elaine asked shrewdly.

"I don't think that's such a bad thing. Compatibility and all that."

"Not going for the excitement of opposites attract?"

"Been there. Done that." Molly let out a long breath. "I won't do it again." She shot her former teacher a look. "Give me boring and sedate any day." She gave a soft snort. "Wild attraction is fun, but it can also—" she looked for the right words and finally settled on "—lack substance." Molly placed a plate in the drain rack. "Guess that's why I need more than a pretty face."

WHAT WAS THAT thing his mother used to say about eavesdroppers never hearing anything good about themselves?

Finn knew for a fact that wasn't true, having secretly listened in on the occasional girl conversation back in the day, but it sure as hell was true in this case.

He finished scraping the barbecue grill into the trashcan, which just happened to be next to the open kitchen window. Molly and Ms. Fitch were still discussing the best qualities in a man. Qualities he apparently didn't have, according to Molly.

He could deal with not being her dream guy, but lacking substance and being just a pretty face?

That pissed him off.

"Looks good," Mike said.

Finn glanced down at the grill that he'd been scrubbing with dry steel wool and saw that, yes, it was probably cleaner than it had been in years. Maybe since it was new.

"Yeah. I like a shiny grill."

"Since when?" Mike asked.

Finn hefted the grill without answering and carried it back to the barbecue, where he set it in place.

Let it go.

And he did…right up until Molly went into the house for bowls so that he could dish out the ice cream he'd brought. He followed her into the kitchen and she smiled at him from cupboard.

"I got this. Seven of us, right?"

"Yeah." Molly stopped counting bowls and glanced back at him with a slight frown. Part of him said to walk away. Another part, one that he couldn't quite rein in, refused to back away, as he well should, in the name of peace and harmony.

"Is something wrong?"

"Not unless you count lack of substance and just being a pretty face."

Molly's cheeks went bright red. She opened

her mouth. Closed it again. Finally she managed to get out a single word. "How?"

"I was cleaning the grill on the deck, next to the kitchen window. I hadn't intended to listen, but when you hear your name…" He gave a shrug.

Molly lifted her chin. "I didn't say *you* lacked substance."

"Yeah. I'm pretty sure you did."

"What I meant was…" Her voice trailed as she gave him a look that bordered on pleading. Finn wasn't going to give her any help. Or a break. But he didn't mind turning up the heat.

"What *did* you mean, Molly?"

"That you aren't right for me."

"Ah." He briefly sucked his cheeks in and sauntered just a little closer, frowning as he asked, "Since when then was that an issue, me being right for you?"

If her cheeks were red before, now they were on fire. "It's not an issue. Elaine—" She stopped abruptly and shook her head. "Nothing I can say here will help."

"No. I don't think it will."

"Maybe I'd better go."

Now he shook his head. "No. I think you should have ice cream so that Mike doesn't get worried about you…then you should go."

CHAPTER ELEVEN

THE WEEK STARTED in a rush, with Molly meeting with her supervisor to discuss the first steps in the instructor evaluation process at the college, and then covering classes for a fellow English teacher, Luis Cortez, who had a family emergency. She'd had to cancel her office hours, leaving a note on her door explaining the circumstances, as well as sending a group email to her students. She didn't go home for dinner as usual after her afternoon class, but instead ate a sandwich at her desk as she prepped for her evening class. The class where she'd see Finn for the first time since the barbecue. She couldn't say she was looking forward to that. What really stung was that she was in the wrong. She'd said things she shouldn't have instead of steering the conversation with Elaine Fitch to a safer place.

None of her students had emailed questions or concerns, so Molly assumed all was well when she walked into the room—with the students who weren't Finn, anyway.

"Did any of you try to see me during office hours today?"

She scanned the class, taking care to let her gaze pass over Finn as if he were any other student.

Finn returned the favor, meeting her eyes in a detached way before opening the spiral notebook on his desk.

"Great," Molly said. "Glad no one needed assistance while I was away. Okay, tonight you'll finish your project outlines, if you haven't already done so, and then start hammering away on the rough draft. Questions?"

"Is everything all right?"

Molly turned her attention to Regina, a grandmotherly type who, like Mr. Reed, was finally reaching for a lifelong dream and attending college.

"In what way?" Surely she hadn't been able to read the dread Molly had felt walking into the room and facing Finn for the first time after insulting him.

"I heard rumor of an emergency, and if you needed to end class early for any reason, I'm certain we, as a class, would be fine with that."

"Thank you," Molly said, "but that won't be necessary. The emergency was that of another faculty member. I just had to cover classes."

Regina gave a silent "ah" then started to work.

Denny opened his expensive leather briefcase and took out his laptop along with a sheath of papers. With a sigh, he put his laptop back. Molly had made it clear that she wanted the class to do the preliminary steps of the first project on paper, and Denny wasn't happy about it. Tough. Molly continued to circulate through the room, passing by Finn's desk as he pulled out the note cards he'd made as per her suggestion.

"What are those?" Debra asked as Molly walked by toward a student with his hand in the air.

"Note cards," Finn said.

"How clever." The older woman cocked her head. "I wish some of these methods had been invented when I was in school. How does this one work?"

"What you do is to write one thought on each one, then arrange them—"

"Why don't you just write your outline on paper? You know. Like a grown-up."

Denny's loud voice brought Molly's head around. The man belonged in a kindergarten class. She was about to intervene when Finn growled, "Because I'm special."

"How so?"

"I have a learning disability."

The class went still. Molly went still. Denny went red.

"Then you're going to have a hell of a time in this class," he finally said in an obvious effort to save face.

"That's *so* rude." Everyone turned toward the quiet woman who'd just spoken. Since Martha Simmons never, ever said a word in class unless directly addressed, her statement was all the more powerful.

"It's also true," Finn said quietly. "I am having a hell of a time. But I made a deal with myself to get through and I'm going to use whatever tools it takes…whether you approve or not."

Debra glared in Denny's direction before Molly stepped in. "Learning is different for everyone. The important thing is that we all get tools we can use to help us tackle life." She shifted her attention to Denny, gave him the teacher look, which felt odd with an adult, but seemed to work. "The note card method is tried and true. There are even computer programs for it. You might want to check those out."

She gave him an unsmiling nod and then walked on, feeling a dozen sets of eyes on her back before she stopped to help Mr. Reed, who thankfully had a question about the opening of his essay and not about note cards. By the time she finished, the rest of the class was focused on their work—or at least pretending to focus—

despite the aura of tension that still hung between the two men.

Finn continued to work on arranging cards on his too-small desk while Denny kept his head down. He was blessedly quiet for the remainder of the class and for the first time ever he left without sharing some bit of obscure knowledge meant to make him look smarter than everyone else in attendance.

After the chime ending the hour sounded, Finn quickly gathered his stuff. He was heading for the door when Martha caught up with him.

"Mr.… Finn… My son has a learning disability," she said in a rush. "And…well, thank you for being so open about it. I wish my boy could have seen what you did today." She patted Finn's arm and then disappeared out the door and down the hall.

Finn glanced over at Molly, his expression cold, bordering on icy, as if he blamed her for the Denny attack. Not knowing what else to do, she turned to Mr. Reed, who had a question. When she glanced back, Finn was gone.

Ass. Hole.

And what was wrong with him that he couldn't just shrug off the petty attack of a bullying jerk? Easy answer there. Denny the Douche had hit a nerve—the same one Molly had hit a few days ago.

Mike had custody of Buddy for the night, so instead of heading home, Finn gave in to temptation for the first time in weeks and pulled into McElroy's on his way by. Maybe Denny was there. Yeah. That would be fun. He didn't know the guy, but he had seen him at the bar now and again. Unfortunately, Denny was not there, but the crowd was larger than it had been the last time he stopped on a weeknight, and wonder of wonders, Wyatt was not among the patrons.

"The usual," he said to Jim, who frowned deeply.

"What would that be? I haven't seen you in weeks."

"I'm a student now." *Kind of.* Jim cocked an eyebrow and turned around to pour a draft. "Takes a lot of time," Finn continued. And when he wasn't at the feed store or being a student, he was forging ahead on his '72 Ford, hammering a little metal. He'd built a sweet gas tank for the big truck.

"That doesn't help my bottom line," Jim said, setting the beer in front of Finn.

"I'll send a monthly check to make up for it." Finn jerked his head toward the group of young guys gathered around the pool table. "How old are these guys?"

"They're legal and *they* help the bottom line.

Come here most nights. Unlike you old guys, who stop by every couple of weeks and have to be home by nine." He smirked a little.

The door swung open and Finn heard his name. He turned to see a familiar group, led by Terry Tyrone. The door no sooner closed than it opened again and a group of college-age girls came in behind them. The place was going to be packed soon, and it was a little strange to feel like one of the older people there on a week night.

"Looks like some old guys," he said to Jim.

Jim snorted and wiped the bar. "You'll all be gone by nine."

Finn hated to tell Jim that he was right, but the last time he'd been with his old wild friends, they honestly had gone home early. To wives. Kids. They'd probably do the same tonight and then they would get up in the morning and go to jobs they liked. Terry was a lineman for the local electrical utility. Lowell worked as an assessor for the county. The other guys they hung with led similar lives.

It seemed as if everyone had settled into regular adult existences while he was overseas, and now he was the only one who was still at loose ends. It made him feel oddly inadequate…like he lacked substance.

His mouth tightened and he picked up his beer.

"Finn!" Lowell raised a hand and motioned

to the tables they'd pushed together in the back of the room.

"Guess I'd better get my partying in fast, before we all fall asleep."

"Good one," Jim muttered as Finn picked up his beer and went to join his old crew who were enthusiastically signaling the server.

Jim was exaggerating, but the fact of the matter was that they were all older now. More responsible—but he had to admit that the guys weren't look all that responsibly minded tonight, even though it was Monday.

Maybe tonight was the night to let loose.

THERE WERE A lot of cars in McElroy's parking lot for a Monday night. Molly gave a bemused snort as she stopped at the light next to the popular bar. How did people party on Monday night, then go about regular life on Tuesday?

Maybe they held their liquor better than she did.

Good possibility.

The light changed and she was about to pull forward when a truck caught her attention. Finn's truck. The car behind her blasted its horn and Molly jumped before accelerating. So Finn was one of those Monday-night drinkers. He went to class and then hit the bars, just like a regular college kid. No reason that should bother her.

Nope. None.

She turned onto a side street and headed back to the bar. After parking a few spaces away from Finn's truck she got out of her car, took a deep breath and headed for the door.

This is dumb. You know it is.

She told herself that she wanted to discuss the Denny matter, but what she really wanted to address was the situation between herself and Finn. Old Molly would have let sleeping dogs lie. New Molly was going to confront, apologize, make peace.

Old Molly wondered if this was really the time and place. New Molly conceded the point, but by that time the door was open and she'd stepped into the bar. All eyes did not swing toward her, but it felt as if they had. Pulling in a breath, Molly lifted her chin and started toward the table at the other side of the room where Finn sat with his back to her.

Someone at his table, a guy who looked vaguely familiar and whom she might have recognized if it hadn't been for the thick black beard, zeroed in on her, and Finn turned in his chair before she followed her last-minute survival instinct and veered off for the ladies' room.

A look crossed his face that could only be described as stunned. "I saw your truck," she said before he could say anything. "I wondered if we could talk for a moment."

That raised a few eyebrows. All eyes at the table may not have been on her when she walked into the bar, but they were on her now. Her and Finn.

"About class?" he said.

"Yes."

"Everything's fine."

Was that it? Was she dismissed?

It appeared so. She'd known it was a dumb move before she made it. What had she expected? That he'd invite her to sit down with his friends? No. She'd kind of hoped he'd be alone. Probably a bit stupid.

"Glad to hear all is well." Careless comment. *Check*. Forced smile. *Check*.

Molly headed for the bar, where she pulled up a stool as if she drank there regularly. The man next to her smiled and nodded. She smiled back and hung her purse from the hook below the counter. When the bartender approached, she ordered a beer, figuring she didn't have to finish it, and then toyed with the napkin he placed in front of her before he turned toward the taps. A moment later she felt someone at her shoulder and knew without looking that it was Finn.

"Come here often?" he murmured.

"First time," she replied. "I wasn't of drinking age when I left the Eagle Valley."

"Just thought you'd visit the bar for the first time tonight?"

"I think it's pretty obvious that I stopped because I saw your truck and I was concerned about you," she said, still not looking at him.

There was a person on either side of her, so Finn couldn't move in beside her, and she kept her gaze stubbornly focused straight ahead, on the bartender's back. He turned and placed a mug of beer in front of her and Molly immediately lifted it to take a big drink. Foam tickled her top lip and she dabbed at it with the back of her hand.

"Why the concern? Because of that douche in class?"

Now swiveled on her stool toward Finn, meeting his unreadable hazel gaze dead-on. "That and what happened at Mike's." She thought she was going to apologize again, but she wasn't. Once was enough.

His eyes narrowed slightly. "I thought we'd already dealt with that."

"So did I." Molly took another drink. The beer tasted good, and it gave her something to focus on, which made it taste even better. "But class was pretty damned awkward and I wanted to see if I could do something about that."

"I was just putting our relationship back where it should be. Teacher-student."

"Ah." She turned back to the bar and held her

beer between both hands. He waited behind her for her to say more, but she really didn't have a lot to say. Maybe this was the way their relationship was supposed to be. It wasn't as if she were losing anything...

He touched her, laid his hand lightly on her arm and made her nerves jump. She turned back, taking her beer with her this time to stop all the swiveling.

"You should get home," he said softly. "School night."

There was something in the quiet words that made her heart rate speed up even more than it had when he touched her, but she'd rather chug her beer than let him know that. "I'll be fine. Go back to your friends."

"As you wish." He took a step, then stopped and looked back at her. "Are we good now?"

Molly frowned at his coolly asked question. *Good now?* What the hell did that mean? When had things ever been good between them? Maybe for a few moments while they'd bantered in the parking lot or when he'd brought the kitten to her office. Other than that...not good.

"I...don't know what you're asking," she muttered.

Finn have her a long, silent look. "Neither do I." He reached past her to set his empty mug on the bar beside her almost-full one. "But I am going home. If you want, I'll walk you to your car."

Molly realized that she wanted. She wasn't comfortable here, knowing that Finn's friends— people she probably knew if he mentioned names—were looking at her. Knowing she shouldn't have stopped here in the first place. She could be home right now. Safe and comfortable, except for the nagging thoughts about Finn. But no. She was in a bar, with Finn at her elbow, offering to walk her out.

An odd situation for someone who wasn't all that impulsive.

Molly reached down for her purse, opened it and pulled out a ten and laid it on the bar before sliding off the stool.

"Generous tip," Finn said as she started for the door.

"That's me. Generous." The truth was she wanted to get out of there rather than wait for change. Once she stepped out into the chilly night air she headed straight for her car.

"We seem to talk a lot at your car," Finn said as she beeped the lock while still several yards away. She wanted that door unlocked and ready to go when she got there.

"We'll break tradition tonight." Molly could only think of one other time they'd spoken at her car, and she recalled it being unsettling because she'd enjoyed it so much. And she'd talked of getting laid.

Dear heavens. Sometimes she was her own worst enemy.

Finn waited until they'd reached her parking spot before saying, "So you came here tonight because of me."

Molly gave him a tight-lipped look. "I think we both know that it wasn't because I'm a regular."

"And you came because you were concerned about me." He was frowning now, as if he didn't quite buy her story. Fine. He could think what he liked.

"I wanted to apologize one more time, and I felt guilty, okay? But I've since changed my mind about the guilt. Now we can segue into that strict teacher-student thing you were speaking of—and Denny the Douche can give you all the crap he wants."

He smiled a little. Like he knew something that she didn't.

Before she could ask what was so funny, he moved another step closer even though her brain whispered something about danger, but she didn't move. Didn't try to head him off when he slid a hand around the back of her neck, even though a jolt went through her as his calloused fingers brushed over her sensitive skin. His palm was warm against her neck as he held her and his lips came down to touch hers. And even though pulling back was the right thing to do, Molly didn't. She wanted to see how this played out, because she'd probably never be in this position again.

She sucked a breath in over her teeth as his mouth moved away, then she leaned toward him, pulled his head back down, made contact again. His fingers tightened on the back of her neck and Molly opened to him, answered his kiss, allowed herself the freedom to seize the moment. Revel in it.

His free hand came up to the side of her face as the kiss deepened, his tongue introducing all kinds of knee-weakening responses as it stroked and teased.

He backed her up a step or two, but when her back came up against her car door, he pulled back, leaving her blinking as his hand dropped away.

It took him a few seconds to say, "Let's not do anything you'll regret in the morning."

Molly drew in a breath as she held his gaze, not really caring that it shook a little. His breathing wasn't exactly even. "You make it very easy not to." With a poor attempt at a smirk, she jerked open the car door and got inside. Finn stood where he was until the lock went down on her door, then raised his hand in the barest of salutes and walked away toward his truck.

She'd expected him to go back into the bar, had assumed that "going home" was a ruse to get the better of her, but his door opened and closed as she backed out of the parking spot and the headlights came on. He followed her out of the lot, but whereas she turned right at the stop sign, he turned left.

She hit the heel of her hand on the steering wheel as she stopped at the light. A quick glance at the clock told her that less than thirty minutes had passed, but a whole lot had changed in that time.

She knew that Finn could kiss like no one's business. She knew that she reacted to him in a crazy way.

She knew that she was never kissing him again.

And since Georgina was home, she knew she'd better act normal when she got there.

AFTER THE KISS in McElroy's parking lot, Finn decided to give both himself and Molly a break and keep his distance. Maybe it was because kissing Molly had been nothing like he'd thought it would be. He'd acted on impulse, expecting something pleasant, but not the instant heat that had flared between them. It was all he could do not to back her up against her car, fist his hands into her hair and find out what else the two of them could do together. In the parking lot.

Bad idea. Not only for the sake of decorum, but because he wasn't messing with a woman who'd made it so clear that, while she found him attractive, she also found him lacking. She'd come after him in the bar out of guilt, but he'd be a fool to twist that into caring for him more than she did. When people did things out of guilt, they did them for themselves. He knew. He'd done things out of guilt a time or two.

For the next three weeks, he went to class, arriving just before the bell rang, so that he didn't risk being alone with Molly before the rest of the students—some of whom were chronically late—arrived. He did his best to be pleasant, yet distant. A student to Molly's teacher. He didn't ask for help, didn't go to her office with questions. He haunted the internet and also started doing something he should have done from the beginning—he started FaceTiming with Dylan. And the fact that it'd taken him so long to think of that showed that he might be a little slower on the uptake than he'd first thought.

Dylan was busy with his own studies, so it was often Jolie—who'd sucked at chemistry, but excelled in English—who helped him. When he didn't ask for help, he faltered, which made him wonder if it was actually possible for him to get an honest degree and, more than that, to use it. Even teaching a hands-on course, there was a lot of paperwork and grading.

He hadn't been aware of that until he'd spent time in the college automotives lab, saw what the classes looked like today. They were different from the classes he'd taken in high school, both in form and content. More computer usage. More writing, because apparently *literacy* was the new buzzword in education.

Was he wasting his time trying to get an education degree? Setting himself up for failure?

A bigger question was did he want to sell feed and Western-themed doodads for the rest of his working days?

Meanwhile, as Finn questioned his life, Mike seemed to be taking great satisfaction with his since taking up with Ms. Fitch. No matter how many times she asked him to call her Elaine, it just seemed strange, so she remained Ms. Fitch in his head.

She and Mike ate dinner out several nights a week, cooked together on the weekends, went for long walks and drives. When Finn mentioned that they seemed to be moving mighty fast—not that he was getting parental or anything—Mike had laughed and said at his age, he couldn't afford to waste time.

The best part was that Cal and Karl were both now trolling dating sites for real, trying to find their own Elaines. Wise man that he was, Cal had changed his profile photo to one where his eyes weren't rolled back in his head, and Karl had taken about fifty headshots before he found one that he could live with.

"What do you think of her?" they'd ask Finn at least once a day, and he would give his honest opinion of a woman's profile, pointing out any red flags he might see. The boys were getting as addicted to their online dating sites as Chase was to social media—most of which Finn was totally unfamiliar with.

He was getting old and he needed to figure out a career before he simply settled for the status quo.

His math class continued to go well, but his last English assignment hadn't done his confidence any good. Molly now wrote neat comments in the margins in pencil instead of screaming red pen, and she tried to include examples and places where he could find helpful information. Of course they both pretended that that kiss had never happened, because what else could they do? He wasn't about to put the moves on a woman who didn't want him, even if she did haunt his thoughts at times. She'd surprised him by kissing him back in the parking lot—he had a strong feeling she'd also surprised herself.

Molly was distantly friendly during class, treating him no differently than any of the other students—other than modifying his assignments.

At the bottom of each graded paper she wrote a short note encouraging him to see her during office hours if he had questions, but she never voiced the invitation aloud. He did have questions, but the thing was, he had to do this on his own as much as possible. He'd never expected to need help every single step of the way.

Again, not a confidence-builder. At night, after finishing his assignments and exercises, he'd head to his shop and lose himself in his work. If he had the kitten for the night, Buddy would come with him and practice his mouse skills. So far, the little guy was batting zero, but he continued the enthusiastic search for rodents. Finn thought it might be for the best that he hadn't yet encountered a mouse, because he was still very small and a mouse could probably take him in a fair fight.

Frankie the Monster was almost finished. His idea of putting the sculpture on the lawn for Halloween in a few weeks was squelched the first time he'd rocked the creation with one hand. He could probably move it on a handcart, but if the thing fell over, it could do some serious harm.

His newest project, a hobbit-like creature, would be squat and have a more solid base. It'd be ready next Halloween. One scary sculpture a year was a good production schedule.

In the meantime, he was hammering out new fenders for an old motorcycle that Terry Tyrone had sold him for a few hundred bucks and rebuilding the Ford engine as he could afford the parts. Not a bad life...but missing something, and that something was causing a gnawing inside him. He needed purpose and he needed an outlet. A guy simply couldn't pound metal all day to take out frustrations—he needed...substance.

CHASE WAS BECOMING a fixture in Georgina's life and Molly told herself she was okay with that. Her sister was an adult. She had a good head on her shoulders. And Chase was a nice kid—who worked in a feed store. He'd been out of high school for three years and had bounced from job to job, a victim of the recent recession, until finally landing a part-time gig at the store and another part-time job at a local grocer, stocking on the midnight shift three nights a week.

When Molly commented on his jobs, Georgina had been quick to defend. Jobs weren't easy to find in the Eagle Valley. Molly concurred... but she thought that some post-high school education would have helped his chances.

Molly was also smart enough to keep her mouth shut. She liked Chase. Twice now he'd cooked dinner for her and Georgina when they'd had overloaded schedules, and he was always willing to pitch in with dishes or whatever else needed to be done around the house.

And he hiked. Georgina had fallen in love with Montana on their day trips. "You can't believe all the cool stuff outside the city limits," she told Molly after her most recent excursion with Chase. Molly was aware of all the cool stuff, but didn't mention how often she'd tried to get her little sister to leave the city limits. Nope. Nothing to be gained by that conversation except for sisterly discord.

Every now and then Chase mentioned Finn in an offhand way while telling a story or explaining something that had happened at the store. Hearing Finn's name always made Molly's pulse bump a little, almost guiltily, and she hated that.

So the guy was hot. So he could kiss. So she called him a pretty face who lacked substance— that hadn't been meant for his ears, it didn't truly describe her feelings for him, and she had apologized. She certainly wasn't going to explain any of that stuff to him. That would be courting disaster, pure and simple. Finn was not predictable. Finn kissed her in parking lots.

And you kissed him back.

True. But since then, she'd come to her senses. Now if she could just shake this edgy, unsettled feeling she got before, during and after her night class. This feeling that things weren't right and she needed to make them right.

No. Simply, no.

The only problem was that Finn was still having difficulty with his classwork—more and more as time passed. Despite his talents on the sporting field and in automotives, his brain was wired for scattergun when it came to English, and English was a skill he would need as an instructor—especially a high school instructor, as they were now directed to include writing in every aspect of education.

"So do you want to go hiking with us next time?" Georgina asked Molly as they tidied up the kitchen after both had survived a long day of classes. "Chase says it'll take four hours and we'll see two alpine lakes."

"I'd go, but I have no boots," Molly said.

"I think we can work around that," Georgina replied. "They're having a sale at the Recreational Outlet. Chase and I are going tomorrow morning before he goes to work."

"Sounds fun, but I think I'll stay at home and grade."

"You are *so* much fun," Georgina said with mock enthusiasm.

"I'll do my best to tone it down."

"*Mike* dates more than you do."

It was true. He could have dated once and dated more than she had since arriving in Montana. As it was, Elaine Fitch was spending as much time at Mike's house as Chase was spending at theirs. She always waved cheerily when she caught sight of Molly, and Molly found herself hoping she'd be that happy when she reached Elaine's age.

Maybe it was surviving teaching that had put her in such a good mood.

Molly was once again in drowning mode, feeling as if she were never going to catch up, but doing her best to look as if she had everything totally under control—a normal state for any teacher.

The thing was that she wasn't certain she had everything under control. The first round of student evaluations—part of her overall professional assessment—had been given the week before, and to her surprise, she'd received one abysmal review. She had a strong feeling that Denny had penned the assessment, and even though she told herself she couldn't control what people thought of her, that she'd been professional and fair with him, the fact remained that she had an unsatisfactory student review.

Even worse, she didn't see Denny changing

his opinion of her before the semester was up, so she was simply going to have to excel in all other areas.

She had a formal in-class observation coming up in a matter of weeks and the second set of student surveys would be given during the first week in December. Until that time she had to focus on being the best instructor she could because she wanted to keep this job and eventually work her way into tenure—one of her life goals.

And, even with Finn issues, she loved the Eagle Valley and wanted to make it her permanent home. If she lost this job, she'd have to embark on another nationwide search, a move…

Molly went to the cupboard and took out the chips for a quick pick-me-up.

A couple handfuls in, she decided that she was overthinking things, making bonfires out of tiny sparks, but the worst-case scenario here was one she didn't want to face.

She simply couldn't afford to lose this job.

CHAPTER TWELVE

MIKE DIDN'T SHOW up for work Wednesday morning. Cal and Karl arrived around nine, emptying the coffeepot and then settling in for news and the occasional check of their computer dating profiles. Finn figured that Mike was simply late, until Cal asked if Finn had heard from Mike that morning.

"He was here yesterday, but left early."

"I tried to call a few times, but it went to voice mail," Karl said.

"Huh." Finn pushed a hand over his head. Since Mike had come out of retirement, he rarely missed a day at the shop. "I'll drive over and check on him."

The boys nodded and went back to the news. Finn started for the side door. "I'm heading over to Mike's."

Lola lifted a hand without looking away from her computer screen and Finn headed out the door. He dialed Mike as he walked, and as the boys had said, it went straight to voice mail. There was always a chance that he was entertaining his lady friend in an intimate way and had shut his phone off, but Finn couldn't see his grandfather playing romantic games early in the day.

There was always a chance, though, so he checked for Elaine's car when he pulled up at Mike's house. Her usual parking spot was empty and the curtains were drawn on Mike's windows. Maybe Mike was at Elaine's house…

Finn took the steps two at a time and after a brief hesitation, knocked on the door. He heard shuffling inside and tried the doorknob. It was unlocked so he pushed the door open. Mike stopped halfway across the room, Buddy held against his chest. The kitten peeked out over Mike's big hand, but for once, Finn was immune to that crazy cuteness. His grandfather's usually neat hair was practically standing up and his eyes were red-rimmed, as if he hadn't slept. If Finn needed any other indicator that something was wrong, there was a Jameson bottle next to his grandfather's favorite chair. Mike never drank alone, but it appeared that had been exactly what he'd been doing last night.

"What the hell?" he asked as he closed the door behind him. "Why isn't your phone on?"

"I needed some time."

Mike turned and slowly moved back to his chair. Once he was seated, Buddy scrambled up the back cushion to the top, behind Mike's head. Finn knelt next to the chair. "What happened, Grandpa?"

Mike moistened his dry lips, then said simply, "Elaine."

"Did you guys break up?"

Mike met his eyes and Finn was rocked by the depth of pain he saw there. "Cancer. She has cancer."

"Damn." The word came out softly. "I'm so sorry."

Mike just shook his head and then settled it back against the cushions, staring at the opposite wall.

"Do you have any details?"

"Not a lot."

His grandmother, Mike's wife, had died of breast cancer. Losing his beloved Annie had ruined Mike, and then he'd lost his nephew, Dylan's father, not long after. A double whammy it had taken Mike years to recover from.

Finn put a hand on his grandfather's knee. "What kind of cancer? Do you know?"

"Esophageal."

"How's Elaine taking it?"

"Better than I am," Mike said. "I need… time…to get used to this."

"I'd tell you that you need to be strong to help her through this, but you know that."

"That's exactly why I did my drinking last night. I got it over with and now I can focus on the inevitable."

"Are you sure it's inevitable?"

"I haven't had a good batting record so far when it comes to dread diseases."

Finn got to his feet, clearing the thickness from his throat before saying, "Do you want me to hang with you here for a while?"

"Somebody needs to run the store."

"Lola's there. Cal and Karl—not that they're employees, but they've been there for so long, I think they could run the place without either one of us."

Mike smiled weakly. "I'm not one for feeling sorry for myself," he said gruffly.

"No shit. Or for letting me or Dylan feel sorry for ourselves." Finn took a seat in the recliner. "But sometimes it's okay to grieve."

Buddy caught sight of Finn in the adjoining recliner and poised himself at the edge of his chair, wiggling his rear end as he prepared to leap up onto Finn's lap. Mike reached behind him to scoop the kitten into one palm and stop the disaster before it happened. "Not yet, little guy."

The kitten walked up Mike's shirt and settled on his shoulder, tucking his little head against Mike's neck. The old man's expression relaxed an iota.

Finn leaned forward, loosely clasping his hands between his thighs. "I...uh...was thinking. I'm not home as much as I used to be, what with night classes and stuff. Maybe Buddy should just, you know, move in here."

Mike gave Finn a sharp look. "Then your house will be as lonely as this one is."

"I have my shop. The metalwork." He shrugged one shoulder. "Maybe Buddy could get a little brother or sister."

"Have to be mighty damned little, considering Bud's size." But Mike didn't seem displeased by the suggestion.

"He needs to settle in one place or the other," Finn said. "Cats are territorial. He'll be happier if he has one home."

"Are you sure about this?" Mike asked gruffly, stroking the kitten with the tips of his fingers.

"I'll still have visitation rights. And if you need me to take him because...you know...then Buddy has a place he knows. But we'll go into this assuming that is not going to happen."

Mike gave a silent nod and Finn leaned back against the cushions again. It wasn't like he was losing Buddy, but he was going to miss the little guy while he was in the shop. And regardless of what he'd just told Mike, he didn't think another kitten was in his immediate future.

MOLLY PUSHED DOWN hard on her briefcase, trying to contain the overload of papers she planned to take home that evening to grade while Georgina was out with Chase. She might honestly have to think about accepting papers over email and marking with track changes…at some point in the distant future. She still liked paper. She'd just gotten the case locked when someone knocked on her door, then pushed it open before she could answer.

Finn. Tall, dark, truant.

Molly straightened and pushed her glasses a little higher on her nose, telling her heart to slow down. Just the guy you've been having hot, impossible dreams about. "You missed class yesterday."

"Mike needed me."

She put both hands on the handle of her briefcase. "You're supposed to let me know when those things happen."

"Yeah." He hooked his thumbs in his front pockets. "I didn't think about it at the time."

"Did…something happen to Mike?" she asked, alarmed by his grim expression.

"Elaine." Molly frowned as she tilted her head and he added, "Cancer," making her heart slam against her ribs.

"I'm so sorry."

"It's scaring the hell out of Mike and I didn't want to leave him. Elaine came over and we discussed her prognosis and I did my best to calm Mike down. He…uh…my grandmother died of cancer."

"I see." Molly glanced down at the floor, her gaze running smack into Finn's boots. She looked up again. "I'm truly sorry about this. Your work will be excused, of course, and I'll give you the assignment." She started to open her briefcase, but Finn stepped forward, shaking his head.

"Do you really think you should?"

Molly shook back the hair that had fallen over her shoulder. "I don't understand."

"I guess my question is…is my being in this class a waste of time for both of us? Honestly, do you think I can achieve my goal?"

Molly's chin sank to her chest. "You've already paid for the course and you're halfway through. Why not finish?"

"Because I'm really wondering if I'm actually the one doing the work. It seems as if my hand is being held every step of the way."

She took a couple of steps toward him, stopping at the edge of her desk. It was the closest she'd been to him since they'd kissed in McElroy's parking lot. Her body mentioned this to her in a couple of different ways, both of which she ignored. "Have you learned anything?"

Finn considered for a moment. "I...guess I can identify some of my issues, even if I need help fixing them."

Molly made an open-palmed gesture. "So you're leaving better than you came in."

"Yeah, am I wasting our time?"

He wanted a definitive answer, so she gave him one. "No."

"You're sure."

This Finn was so very different from the Finn of her teen years. Of course everyone had insecurities, but back then she'd never once considered the possibility that amazing Finn Culver would struggle at things she did easily. Yet she had no difficulty in believing the opposite—she had trouble with things Finn did not. Socializing, for one. Basketball, for another. But being bad at social activities and intramural sports wasn't going to affect her chosen career. Difficulty with English could hurt Finn's.

Molly glanced up at the clock, then back at Finn, who was studying her bulging briefcase with a faint frown. "Let me buy you a cup of coffee."

He brought his gaze up to hers. "You're being ironic, right?"

Molly smiled a little. "No. Just less standoffish. We can go to the student union."

Finn gave a small nod. "Sounds good. I'll buy."

"I think you missed the first part of the invitation, as in, 'Let *me* buy *you* a cup of coffee.'"

"Fine. You buy."

They crossed the common and Finn snagged a table in the nearly empty cafeteria while Molly got two black coffees. She set the mugs down and took her seat. "I like that they give a choice of paper or ceramic. Paper is… I don't know… temporary, I guess."

"Not a big fan of temporary?"

"When you move as many times as I did as a kid, one of two things happens—either you get really good at being temporary or you really resent it. My brother and sister were good at it."

"You resented it."

"When you're shy, being uprooted every one to two years is not much fun."

"You stayed here three."

"We moved here so that my dad could put the big grocery store back on track. It took a year and a half and I begged him not to make me go with them on the next move. Offered to live with my best friend, Julie Faraday."

"Didn't she—"

"Move. Why yes, she did. Shooting that plan

all to pieces. Anyway, Mom and Dad decided that Dad could commute to Spokane for the last year and a half while he worked on a department store there. So I got to go to most of high school in one place."

"What exactly did your dad do?"

"He saves stores." Molly set down her cup and did her best to explain her father's occupation, which still had him on the road. "They're in Alabama now. I think this might be one of his last consulting jobs, but he's said that before."

"Do you like what *you* do, Molly? With the Dennys and the grading and all that?"

Finn had obviously been spending some serious time thinking about his future and Molly considered her words carefully before she said, "I do. There are days, sometimes weeks, when I wish I'd become anything except a teacher, but… all in all, I like it. I feel good when most days are done. The Dennys…that part can be challenging. Staying tactful can be challenging." And apparently she'd failed at the tactful part with Denny.

"I worry about that," Finn said matter-of-factly. "I might keep my patience for a while, but the Dennys of the world would wear me down." He gave her a look. "I would break."

"It gets better with practice," she said. "In the beginning…it can be rough. I won't lie. You have to grow a thick skin."

"You have to learn to take crap from nitwits as near as I can tell."

Molly fought a smile, but it faded as she said, "Thinking of changing your career goal?"

"Wondering about my aptitudes." He gave her a humorless smile. "I hate wasting time."

"Education is never a waste of time."

He gave her a surprised look. "I…guess not."

"Tell me about Elaine and Mike."

Finn swirled his last bit of coffee but didn't drink. "She has esophageal cancer. Mike has already lost my grandmother and my uncle, and he's not ready to lose someone else."

"They haven't been together for that long."

Finn considered for a moment. "Yeah. I know. If they were younger, I'd be concerned. But they know what they want." He drained the last of his coffee. "Lucky."

Molly gave him her empty cup when he held out his hand and he took them both to the counter where the used cups were collected. "I need to get back to the store," he said when he came back to the table. "Lola's there, but Chase had to take the afternoon off. I don't want Cal and Karl loading grain."

They started back to her office and after he'd opened the door to her building, Molly said as casually as possible, "About Chase…?" Finn gave her a curious look and she continued, "He and Georgina are getting kind of serious."

"I gathered."

"He's a good kid, right?"

"What do you think, Molly?"

"You know him better than I do."

"He's overcome some decent odds to get where he is today. I don't see him going anywhere but up."

Not what she'd hoped to hear. Not even close. She wanted someone who was already "up" for Georgina. They rounded the corner leading to her office and before she could say anything else, Finn said, "You have a customer. A surly one from the looks of things."

Sure enough, Jonas was leaning against the display case opposite Molly's office. And even though he was looking at her as if she was a lower life form, she knew for a fact that Jonas hadn't given her a poor review because his class had been chosen for the second round of student evaluations.

"Hi, Jonas. What can I do for you?" Molly asked, doing her best to sound positive.

"Well," he said in his overly precise voice. "You could be on time for your office hours."

Molly's smile froze. So much for positive, but she told herself not to react, because that was what people like Jonas fed on, although it was a

bit of a challenge to keep her composure when
Jonas held up his phone, which read 16:05, and
snapped, "Some of us have schedules to keep."

"And some of us need to learn to treat people
with respect," Finn growled. "She is your instructor."

Jonas's gaze jerked toward Finn. "Who are
you to give lessons in deportment?"

"Your elder," Finn said calmly, but when he
turned to Molly to say goodbye, she could see
the tension in his face. He was doing his best
not to pop the kid and she appreciated his effort.

"Do you want me to stay?" he asked. "I could
hang here in the hall."

It took Molly a surprised second to say, "No.
I'm fine. I'll see you later."

"You're sure?"

"You're wasting time," Jonas muttered.

"And you're a little…" Finn closed his mouth
and after a quick look at Molly, headed down
the hall.

Jonas watched Finn go down the hall through
narrowed eyes, then turned back to Molly, waiting with barely contained patience for her to
open her door.

She walked inside and took her time putting
her purse away. Two could play the discomfort
game. "What do you plan to major in when you
go to college, Jonas?"

He seemed surprised at the question. "I plan to be an electrical engineer." He pulled yet another assignment out of his bag. "I have an issue with your marks on this essay."

"Have a seat, Jonas."

"I also have an issue with your condescending tone."

Molly's eyebrows rose. "I have an issue with your rudeness and I suggest that until you can conduct yourself politely, you leave my office." She might want to keep this job, and student evaluations might play a part in that, but there was also the small matter of self-respect.

Jonas blinked at her. "You work for me."

"I work for the state of Montana, which pays me to give you an education. It doesn't pay me to sit in my office while you take potshots at me."

"This is why I'm getting Bs, isn't it? You don't care for me."

"You're getting Bs because you're doing B work."

"I'm a high school student taking a college class."

"The grade of which will go on your college transcript. College. There will be no notation that you were a high school student at the time and got a break because of it."

"I bet *he* gets breaks."

Molly's blood went cold. "Excuse me?"

"I think you understand my meaning." Jonas snatched the paper up from her desk and strode out of the room without a backward glance. Molly stared at the empty doorway, and then pressed her palm against her forehead. Finn wasn't the only one who sometimes had difficulty keeping his cool. But this was her job and she wouldn't let the Jonases of the world ruin it.

AFTER LEAVING MOLLY to deal with Jonas the mini asshole, Finn helped Lola close down the store, then picked up barbecue tri-tip, coleslaw and rolls at the local market and drove over to Mike's place with his dinner. His grandfather was doing better. The shock had worn off and he was putting on a braver face. Buddy trotted along behind him, attacking his pant leg and his shoes, making Mike smile at a time when he probably didn't feel like smiling, and Finn knew in his heart that giving Mike full custody was the best move. Even though he was going to miss his little feline friend.

"Are you coming to the store tomorrow?"

"Probably. Elaine and I are going to lunch." Mike met Finn's gaze, his expression solemn, still a little bemused. "I kind of thought losing two people close to me was enough for one lifetime."

"I know." Finn knew his grandfather meant

two untimely losses and he didn't bother with platitudes. "Just know that I'm here with you. And Dylan and Jolie will be back shortly. We'll tackle this together."

"Thanks." Mike bent down to scoop up Buddy and headed for his chair.

"Are you staying for dinner?"

"I ate a sandwich a little bit ago, but I'll sit with you while you eat?"

"To tell you the truth, I'm not that hungry right now."

"But you will eat."

Mike gave him a weary nod. "Yes."

"You want me to stay and watch television with you?"

"I want you to go home and work on your Ford."

Finn gave his grandfather a long look. "Go," Mike repeated. "I'll see you tomorrow."

Finn headed out the door, doing his best to tamp down his frustration at the new difficulties his grandfather faced, at least until he was outside the house. As he walked down the steps, Molly approached the fence separating her property from Mike's. She looked tired yet friendly. Amazing what a shared coffee could do.

"Hey," he said. "Did you beat that kid to a pulp?"

"Did my best. He's pretty bulletproof." Molly

gave him a dark smile but her face was still set in tense lines as she added, "His parents donated land to the school, you know."

"Very important people."

"Important people annoy me." She dropped her hand from the top of the fence. How's Mike?"

"Doing okay." Finn shifted his weight and glanced over Molly's head at her house as he debated, then back at her. "You want to go beat some metal?"

The look on her face made him feel like laughing. He managed not to.

"That isn't a euphemism for…anything? I mean…you're not getting parking lot ideas again?"

Now he did laugh. "I'm talking actual metal hammering."

"For what purpose?"

He sauntered forward a step, closer to the fence, closer to Molly. Yes. He could smell what he now thought of as Molly scent. Sweet. A little floral. A little citrus. It made him want to bury his nose in her hair and breathe deeply. He'd probably get smacked in the process…

"The purpose is to take out frustrations in a productive way." He smiled a little at her wary expression. "You won't know what I'm talking about until you've hammered out a dent."

"It's therapeutic?"

"Very." He could think of only one thing that was more therapeutic and Molly wasn't on board for that as near as he could tell—more's the pity. He cocked his head. "Come on, Molly. Take a chance with a guy who lacks substance."

"You aren't going to let that die."

"You struck a nerve." Which was true. No one wanted to hear that they were just a pretty face.

"I only meant that you weren't right for my life plan."

"Maybe I'm not interested in being part of your life plan, so it's a moot point."

"Ouch."

"But you're relieved, aren't you?"

Molly cocked her head. "This is one strange conversation."

Finn jerked his head in the direction of his truck. "Coming?" She hesitated, so he added, "No kissing." Her eyebrows went up at the candid promise. "Scout's honor."

"Were you a Scout?"

"Honor is honor. Come on."

WHAT ARE YOU DOING?

Molly clutched the steering wheel a little tighter as she followed Finn's truck into his driveway, then forced her fingers to relax.

Living life on my own terms. Which was legit and part of her overall life plan.

Don't get burned. Also part of her life plan.

Hammering metal shouldn't get her burned. She and Finn could be friends, and she was certain that was now the direction they were heading in. They'd kissed and it had almost gotten away from them—a warning sign to both of them to not go there, to the point that Finn had made no kissing a condition of her visit. Or had he simply been trying to put her at ease?

Whatever. She was here now and there would be no kissing...which kind of freed her up to enjoy the view as he led the way to his workshop.

This tug between what was possible and what was logical was killing her.

Finn opened the door and stood back as Molly stepped inside the shop, pausing to take in the brightly lit space. A pickup truck with its hood up dominated the center of the shop. Long workbenches and tool chests lined two of the walls, while machinery and racks of wood and metal took up the other two.

"Oh my gosh." Molly made her way past the big Ford truck to what could only be described as a monster standing next to the rear exit.

"Frankie."

"Original name." Molly grinned as she reached out to touch the intricate pattern of bolts that formed his hair. "You made this?"

"I hated throwing away all the scrap. I could

have sold it by the pound, but it was more fun turning it into Frank."

"And you have another one." A smaller frame of a squat little creature stood a few feet away, on the opposite side of the welder.

"As yet nameless. He will be shorter and lighter. I want to put him on the lawn for Halloween. I had similar plans for Frankie, but he wouldn't be that stable on uneven ground. I don't want to squish a passerby or anything."

"Never a good thing."

She looked around the shop, then back at Finn. "I like the way this place smells."

"It smells of grease, oil and fuel."

Molly shrugged. "Guess I'm a grease, oil and fuel kind of girl." She was also still a touch nervous being there. No, not nervous. Self-conscious. Finn in his own environment was a bit overwhelming. Being in the shop seemed to double his Finn-ness, his basic masculinity, and parts of her were starting to pay close attention. Was it possible that she would never move past this physical connection? What had attracted her to him in high school before she'd known one thing about him, still attracted her, would possibly always attract her, despite logic and reason to the contrary. And there were viable reasons to the contrary.

While she didn't really think Finn lacked substance, she knew he'd never fit into the world she was building. The nice quiet world where everyone knew where their next paycheck was coming from, nobody spent too much time hanging in bars. Where careers were settled. Life was settled. Boring. Sedate. Wonderfully comfortable.

Finn didn't make her feel comfortable. He made her feel the way she'd felt when she first met Blake, and that was a red flag of ample proportions.

"About that metalworking?"

Finn jerked his head toward a bench with pieces of sheet metal on a rack nearby. "We'll just do some practice hammering today."

"And if I'm good at it?"

"I'll put you to work. Double my production."

"Tempting, but I have enough on my plate. More now that my observation is coming up."

"Observation?" Finn took a smallish piece of sheet metal off the rack and took it to a disk-shaped piece of equipment sitting on a sturdy bench.

"Part of my professional evaluation. I get observed once formally, several times informally. Two student evaluations. If I pass the first evaluation, then I get evaluated once every six semesters."

Finn placed the metal next to the disk. "What happens if you don't pass?"

"That won't happen." Molly spoke automatically, because it wouldn't happen. Even with a tiny ripple in the student evaluation area, she knew she was good at what she did. There was always room for improvement, but as far as the basics went, she had them down. "If it did happen—to someone else—they're put on probation and have opportunities to remediate. Or they get fired."

"That would sting."

"Yes." For a brief moment she teetered on the brink of telling him about the horrendous student review that was now in her file. She hadn't told anyone, not even her sister, but to let it out...to have someone say, "One review? How could that possibly matter?" would make her feel better.

She couldn't do it.

Finn picked up a pair of safety glasses large enough to cover her own glasses and instead of handing them to her, carefully slid them onto her face, then stood back to judge the effect. "You appear suitably bug-eyed."

"Always a goal of mine." Not. It had been hell being the girl who wore glasses, but contact lenses bothered her. Finn grinned and then bent over to dig around in a bin beneath the bench, coming up with a thick pair of gloves.

"Keep you from getting metal cuts."

Molly put on the gloves and held up her hands. "Awkward."

"You'll be glad of them later. You come more often and I'll see if I can dig up a pair that fits you."

"You think I'll need to take out my frustrations often?"

"Is Jonas your student?"

"Point taken." But she couldn't see herself coming to Finn's private lair all that much, not when she kept breathing just a little more deeply to draw in his scent. *Bad Molly.*

Finn gestured toward an array of hammers, ball peens and some with odd flat heads. "This is a chasing hammer. Metal moves away from the area you pound, thinning." He put the sheet of metal over the disk and started tapping away at the center and moving out. "As you hammer, you pretty much chase the metal as it thins and it shapes to the dolly, the form, that is." He handed Molly the hammer.

"Have at it."

"Okay." Molly started tapping away, felt the metal give beneath the hammer.

"Move it in this direction…"

Molly followed Finn's instructions, hammering from the center out until her flat circle was now a lovely, relatively smooth dome.

"I made a hubcap." She laid down the hammer and picked up her handiwork.

"Kind of." Finn smiled at her. "I'll show you how to do some different textures…"

Half an hour later, Molly had used a variety of hammers for a variety of different techniques. Finn was a patient teacher and she could see now why he wanted to make it his career. He made her feel confident, even though she'd been patently uncertain when she'd walked into his shop.

"You're different here," she said without really thinking.

"You are, too."

Molly wanted to ask, "How so?" but didn't. This was not a real place for her. She was visiting Finn's world, which was far different from her own.

"Have you made any other artwork?" she asked.

"Artwork?"

"Frankie?"

Finn gave a scoffing laugh. "That's not art. That's recycling."

Molly disagreed, but wasn't there to argue. "Do you have any other recycling?"

"A few pieces in my backyard. Smaller."

"Can I see them before I go?"

"You're leaving?"

Molly bit her lip. So very tempting to say,

No. I'm not leaving, and then see what unfolded. "I think I'd better."

He didn't argue. Molly took off her glasses
and her gloves, set them side by side on the
bench. "This has been fun."

"You'll have to come back." He said it in a way
that told Molly that he didn't believe she would.
He was right. Being here...she saw too much potential for trouble. For getting in over her head.
as she'd gotten in over her head with Blake.

They left the shop and walked by the light of
the full moon up the short path to his house. He
veered to the right and opened the gate of the
chain-link fence. His back porch light was on,
illuminating the metal pieces in his backyard.
Molly went from piece to piece. A funky glass
table supported by what looked like a twisted
tree, a chair made entirely of old rusty bolts,
a swan with raised wings supporting a rustic
wooden planter.

"That's it. These three pieces."

"You're talented. Ever thought of making this
your career?"

"I was thinking that I wanted something more
stable." He shot her a sideways look. "Surely you
understand that."

"I do." She smiled a little. "You are a good
teacher."

"I know."

"Can you handle the Jonases of the world?"

"Do those guys take automotives?"

"The Dennys do."

Finn let out a breath. "You had to say that."

"Reality bites." She reached out to touch him, to lay her hand on his upper arm. His gaze jerked toward her as his muscles tensed beneath her fingers. "I don't want you to give up the idea of teaching. Not for a second. But it's important to go into it with eyes wide open. It's not what it looks like from the outside. Many students are not empty vessels waiting to be filled. They're there for a credit and to cause trouble."

"Rosy picture." He started back out the gate and Molly followed as they headed down the driveway toward her small car. "Sometimes I envy Dylan. He may have taken some side trips, but he always knew what he wanted. And now he's accomplished it." He stopped next to her car. "I imagine you always knew what you wanted to do, too."

"Guilty."

Finn lifted his chin, looked over the top of the car off into the distance, then back at her, making an obvious effort to push unsettling thoughts aside. "Did hammering help with your frustrations?"

"Yeah. It did." The mental ones, anyway. The

physical ones…not so much. "Thanks for inviting me."

Molly opened her car door and Finn stepped back. "Hey," she said softly. "Since I'm here—" and since they were not at odds with each other "—tell me about Chase. What did you mean about him going nowhere but up?"

One corner of Finn's mouth tightened briefly. "His dad died in prison."

Molly's mouth fell open. "I…uh—"

"Chase is not his dad. He's a good kid."

"But still."

"We can't all come from Ozzie and Harriet backgrounds."

"I realize that. I just feel protective of my sister. I don't want her involved with anyone who would—" she made a helpless gesture "—I don't know, screw up her life?"

"I get that. I'm sure Chase doesn't want to be involved with anyone who would screw up his life, either. He's working hard, Molly."

"What's his mother like?"

"Not dangerous, if that's what you're asking. She's a sweet woman who got hooked up with the wrong guy."

And that was exactly what Molly was hoping her sister wouldn't do. She suddenly had more questions. Lots of them.

"He's never been in trouble."

"Not like I was."

She gave him a dark look over the top of her glasses. "That's not reassuring."

"He thinks Georgina is perfect."

"Well, I'll give him a couple points for that." She let out a sigh. "I don't want to come off as a snob." A lift of his eyebrows told her that was exactly what she was coming off as, which ticked her off. "I'm just being protective, okay? There's a difference. If I was a snob, I would look down on Chase because of his background. I don't. I think he's a nice kid."

"But not nice enough for your sister?"

Molly crossed her arms. "Positions reversed… how would you feel?"

Finn considered. "I'd be okay with it. His dad is dead."

Molly pressed her lips together, then unfolded her arms. "I don't want to ruin what's been a nice evening."

"Then trust me when I say that Chase is a nice kid who won't do your sister wrong."

Molly bit her lip, and then opened her car door. "I wish I could, Finn…but I just don't know."

"Here's the thing, Molly…"

His tone stopped her as much as his words. She glanced over at him and he said, "Like it or not, you judge people. Chase is not good enough for your sister, and I'm not good enough for you."

"I never said you weren't good enough."

"It was heavily implied."

"What I said has nothing to do with your worth as a person. It has to do with what I can and cannot deal with in my life."

"How am I so lacking?" He reached out to put his hand on the top of her open car door, essentially caging her in.

She dropped her chin, tried to find words before looking back up at him. He was watching her closely, as if her answer honestly mattered—whether he wanted it to, or not. "It's not a lack. It's incompatibility."

"So you say without really knowing me." She didn't answer, even though she thought he was wrong. She did know a lot about him. She knew he was compassionate and took care of small orphan animals. He was there for his grandfather. But he was also a guy meandering through life. He had a goal, but he may not be able to achieve it. What then?

Finn shifted his weight and then said with a touch of impatience, "Not every guy you go out with has to be husband material, Molly— for you or your sister. Have you ever thought about just having fun and not worrying about compatibility?"

"I don't think I'm wired that way."

His hand dropped away from the top of the

car door. "Your life, Molly. You've got to live it the way you see fit."

"Thank you. I will," Molly said, not missing the censure in his words. *Who was judging whom now?* "And for your information, it isn't about me not *wanting* to have fun…it's about me trying to make the best choices possible. There's nothing wrong with having a plan and sticking to it."

Especially when the objective of that plan was peace of mind and security.

"Tell me about this damned plan of yours."

"What?"

"I'm also trying to make a plan. Maybe I can use yours as a prototype."

She gave a short laugh. "I don't think so."

"Guys like me can't use a plan like yours?"

"You have different objectives."

"Tell me about your objectives."

For a moment, they faced off, then Molly slowly stepped out from behind the safety of the car door and swung it shut. Now there was nothing between them except for a couple feet of gravel and a healthy dose of animosity. She walked around him to the front of her car, put a foot on the bumper and hoisted herself up to sit on the hood. If she was going to have an uncomfortable discussion, she was damned well going to be physically comfortable while she did it—or pretend to be comfortable.

"You'll scratch your paint doing that."

"So?"

He folded his arms over his chest again and waited while Molly massaged the tense muscles at the back of her neck with one hand. So much for feeling better after metal hammering.

"I hooked up with a guy who looked really good on paper," she finally said. "A semi-professional athlete." Finn's eyebrows lifted and she glared at him. "Don't be so surprised."

He took a couple steps closer. "I didn't think you were into athletics."

"I can watch quite nicely." And she had once enjoyed hiking and skiing. "Anyway, eventually it became…very clear…that we had different expectations in life and that being together wasn't going to work. For me, anyway." She ran her fingertips over the smooth, cool metal of the hood. "I wasted a few years of my life on a guy who blindsided me. I'd been… I don't know… amazed that he and I had hit it off so well. I totally bought into the opposites-attract thing."

"How'd he blindside you, Molly?"

She shook her head. He didn't need to know all of her humiliations. "Let's just say he did. And to keep it from happening again, I did a lot of soul searching. I wrote down what made me feel most comfortable and secure in life. Made a long list. Then I pared it down to a short list of nonnegotiables."

"What's your number one objective, Molly?"

"Security." She wanted to feel as if her world was safe and predictable. And she wanted the people in her world to play by her rules.

"Not love?"

"Not if it interferes with security."

Finn gave a slow nod. "This guy must have taken you for quite a ride."

"Yes. And I'm not about to get on board again.

He considered her words for a moment, then said, "What if a guy didn't want anything from you that would interfere with your security?"

"What are you getting at, Finn?"

"What if a guy just wanted to have some fun? Would you be on board for fun?"

Her stomach did a small freefall. Fun with Finn conjured up all kinds of unsettling images.

"I…uh…would have to believe that I wasn't heading toward another big mistake." She stretched her legs out then dropped them again, the heels of her shoes bouncing on the bumper. "This guy you're talking about wouldn't happen to be you, would it?"

"Well, you could see where I would be a lot of fun."

The wry note in his voice helped ease some of the tension in her neck and shoulders.

"That's what Sheena said."

"Shayna. And that doesn't have to be the kind of fun I'm talking about."

She cocked an eyebrow. "Doesn't have to be?"

"Well… I'm open to a lot of stuff."

"I bet you are." Banter she could handle. Serious Finn telling her she was judgmental, not so much. "But as you know, I have strict rules and parameters." She made it sound as if she were exaggerating, but the sad truth was that she really wasn't. She did have strict rules and parameters, that helped keep her safe from nasty surprises in life—as safe as one could be anyway.

So why did safe suddenly seem…lame?

Finn.

His lips tilted into a careless half smile, but his gaze was serious as he said, "Afraid you'd fall for me?"

"Well…you are Finn Culver."

He laughed, genuine amusement lighting his eyes.

"You'd better go home, Molly Adamson, before I provide you with too much temptation."

"Yeah. Right." She spoke lightly, but the truth was that he *was* tempting. There was never a time she didn't find him tempting—even in the heat of an argument.

He was right—it was time to go home.

Molly slid off the hood of the car, ignoring his pained expression as her jeans made a light scratching noise. She dusted off her behind, then once again met Finn's dark gaze. "Thanks for an interesting evening."

"Anytime." One corner of his mouth tightened as his gaze slid down to her lips and Molly felt a tingle go through her. In another time and place he might have kissed her...but not after this conversation. Besides, he'd promised no kissing.

You could change that...

She wasn't going to. She opened the car door and slid into her seat. "I'll think about what you said, Finn." Because she wanted to be open-minded, and open to change. She just didn't want to get hurt again.

"Do that, Molly. I'll talk to you later."

MOLLY UNLOCKED THE front door and walked into her silent house. Georgina's books were stacked on the coffee table and her laptop was open, but her purse was not hanging on coat hooks as usual. Molly wandered into the kitchen where she found a note propped against the sugar bowl. *Out with Chase.* Big surprise.

Finn approved of Chase.

She still wasn't convinced that a guy who came from a wildly dysfunctional background was the guy for her sister, but she'd hold off saying anything for a while. It was totally possible that nature would run its course and that her sister and Chase would break up. No sense creating a sisterly rift when it wasn't necessary.

Besides, Finn had given her other things to think about.

She almost went to the cupboard for chips, then decided she was woman enough to tackle this business without a crutch. Her notebook was now neatly filed with the cookbooks and she pulled it out, laid it on the table and flipped the cover open.

When her life had been in shambles, not all that long ago, this book had helped her put things back together. It contained goals, insights and, most importantly, promises she'd made to herself. The act of writing those promises down in the form of a life plan was the closest she could get to carving them in stone. She'd stepped outside of her comfort zone with Blake, reaped some benefits, but, in the end, had lost more than she'd gained. Confidence was good, but losing trust was brutal.

But…she rifled through the pages, recalling how lost she'd been when she first started the life plan book…maybe trust didn't only involve another person. Maybe she needed to trust herself—trust that she could have fun, as Finn had suggested, and not lose herself, or her heart, in the process. It didn't need to be an all-or-nothing deal. She could cut loose. Date a little.

Trust herself not to slip into a Blake situation.

Her strict parameters had been utterly necessary when she'd first started healing her life, but now that she'd moved forward and gained her confidence back, maybe they *were* a little too strict.

Surely there had to be a way to address her very natural needs without losing herself in the process.

Molly reached for the pen lying next to the grocery list and turned to the page where she'd listed her goals. She hesitated, then put the pen to the paper and wrote *Have a little fun*.

MOLLY SEEMED PREOCCUPIED during class, teaching with a brisker style than usual, but a couple of times she caught Finn's eye and it seemed as if she relaxed a little. Then Denny or Mr. Reed would ask a question and she fell back into all-business mode. The result was that Finn had no idea what the aftermath of their last conversation was. Whether she was going to give him a wide berth, and whether she was going to loosen up a little. He was shoving his notebook and folders into his old backpack after class had ended when Molly approached his desk.

"Can I speak to you before you go?" she asked in her cool teacher voice.

"Sure." He had to admit that he loved her cool teacher voice.

She glanced around to see if anyone was close enough to hear, but the class was emptying rapidly, with the exception of Denny, Mr. Reed and Martha, who always took their time. "I've given your suggestion some serious thought—the one about having some fun."

"And…?"

Her mouth tightened again and she shot a glance over at Denny who was eyeing them as if he was looking for some kind of infraction to report. "Maybe I should talk to you later."

She was worried about Denny? Really?

An idea hit him. "Hey… Dylan and Jolie are coming back earlier than expected and we're going out on Thursday night. Why don't you join us?"

This time Finn glanced at Denny, who seemed to be taking a longer time than usual to pack up. In fact, the guy was barely moving.

"Are you waiting to talk to Molly?" Finn asked.

Denny gave him a dark look. "No. *I* understand the assignment."

"Well, I don't," Finn said easily, before turning back to Molly. Actually it was a lie, because for once the stuff she presented made perfect sense. "Thursday at McElroy's."

"Just a casual thing, right?"

"No. An orgy." Her lips twitched at the corners, as if she were fighting a smile. "Yes, casual. All you have to do is relax and enjoy my pretty face."

Molly leaned closer to him "You're a jerk," she whispered pleasantly.

"I try."

It was then that he noticed that Denny really was watching them closely while pretending to pack his stuff. He worked up a frown. "Okay. I'll look up subordinate clauses when I get home, but I don't think I ever learned about those."

He looked over at Denny as he spoke just a little too loudly. Molly rolled her eyes.

"Do that. I promise they exist."

He knew they existed because he'd learned about them the week before. He shouldered his backpack and headed for the door, then waited for Molly outside the main entrance.

"Six-thirty?" he said when she pushed through the glass doors.

"I'll be there."

"What's the deal with jerk face?"

"Denny?" Her eyes cut sideways toward the

hallway, when it remained clear, she said, "I think he gave me a really bad review. I don't want to give him any more ammo."

"He what?" Finn was surprised at the surge of protectiveness that welled up inside him.

"No big deal, Finn. I want to keep it that way."

"Are you sure?"

She actually laughed a little. "Positive. I'll see you at McElroy's. Six-thirty."

He gave her a nod, glad that she'd agreed, and headed for his truck while she jiggled her keys and waited for Denny and Mr. Reed to finish their slow journey out of the classroom.

If teaching meant patiently dealing with the Dennys of the world, then there really was a good chance that it wasn't the profession for him.

FINN WAS WAITING near the entrance of McElroy's when Molly pulled her car into the lot and parked a few spaces away from his truck. She'd stopped wasting time worrying about where she should be edging ever closer to the slippery slope that was Finn—whether she was really in control of the situation. She was doing it. She was going to have some fun. Instinct was pushing her forward and she simply had to stop letting knee-jerk fears keep her from living her life. Finn wasn't looking for anything heavy and deep, and since she wasn't, either, this made sense.

Finn met her halfway across the parking lot and, as he closed the distance between them, he smiled that crooked smile, which made her stomach tumble a little. "Glad you could come. Dylan and Jolie are looking forward to meeting you."

And she was nervous about meeting them. This seemed a lot like a real date.

A thought struck her. "They know we're just friends, right?"

Finn opened the door and Molly walked inside. "They know you're here with me. They have no more information than that…but they'll be curious."

"Then let's put an official title on our relationship. We're friends."

He frowned at her. "How close of friends?"

"Not screw buddies. And if you get laid after you drop me off, I have no right to complain."

He took her hand and squeezed her fingers. "I don't see myself getting laid after dropping you off. If I was dropping you off. You drove. Remember?"

"By the way, Jolie ordered beer. Are you okay with that or do you want to order something else at the bar?"

"I like beer."

"Good to know." Finn kept hold of her hand as he led her through the fairly crowded bar toward the table where Dylan and Jolie sat and

Molly told herself it was because he didn't want to lose her in the crowd. Dylan stood as they approached, looking very much as Molly remembered him—tall, dark-haired, handsome. He extended his hand as Jolie got to her feet and offered a quick hug of greeting.

"Hi, I'm Jolie. I don't know if you remember me."

"Of course I remember you." Molly spoke easily, drawing on her teacher self to overcome her suddenly shy self. Jolie had been one of the movers and shakers during high school—confident and bubbly and fun. A cheerleader, while Molly had been a geek. "I was kinda invisible."

"You were one of the brainiacs."

"Uh...thank you?"

Jolie laughed. "It's a compliment." She glanced over at Dylan. "I have a thing for brainiacs."

Dylan smiled in a way that reminded Molly of both Finn and Mike. "Good to see you again, Molly. Table C, right?"

Molly laughed. "I'd forgotten, but yes."

Table C had been her favorite table in the library, where she'd spent most of her free time hiding out and studying.

"Uh... Table B?"

Dylan shook his head. "I haunted Table D. Close to the biology reference section."

"Yes. I remember now." Dylan had kept his

nose buried in books almost as much as she had
and she remembered how she'd always thought
he seemed like a nice guy. Handsome, like his
cousin, but lacking the devil-may-care aura that
had so entranced her.

"You know," Jolie said with mock serious-
ness, "I kind of feel like a loser because I never
had a table."

"You kind of had to study to have a table,"
Dylan pointed out as he slipped a hand around
the back of Jolie's chair.

"Studying…" Jolie made a dismissive gesture.
"I did okay with gut instincts and a little luck.
Is beer all right, Molly? We ordered a couple of
pitchers."

"Beer is great. Thank you."

The words were barely out of her mouth when
two pitchers clunked down on the table. Finn
did the honors, pouring perfect, almost foam-
less glasses for everyone.

"Haven't lost your touch, I see." Dylan raised
his glass in a mini salute.

"Some people study. Some people pour beer,"
Finn replied. "I didn't have a table either, because I was busy learning other skills."

Molly raised her glass. "Here's to other skills."

Jolie smiled and drank, then leaned against
Dylan's arm, which rested along the back of her
chair. The two radiated contentment, which was

so odd after their epic high school feud. If Mike had succeeded in bringing the two of them together, as he'd intimated to Georgina, then he truly had skills in the matchmaking department. What would it be like to be so content?

Molly took a healthy drink. Actually, she *had* been that content at one time, but it had all been an illusion.

No more illusions for her. She went into things with her eyes wide open, not expecting more than she could be absolutely sure of.

"How long have you guys been seeing each other?" Jolie asked.

"We're a casual couple," Finn said solemnly. Molly almost choked before he added, "Which means we're friends."

"Testing the waters, so to speak?" Jolie asked. It was not an intrusive question.

"No, we're just friends," Molly said. The kind that held hands and made each other's hearts beat just a little faster. She'd felt Finn's heart rate ramp up when they'd kissed. "Better make sure Mike understands that," Dylan said.

"At least if he were matchmaking, it would give him something other than Ms. Fitch to think about," Jolie said softly. Molly's eyes went wide at the mention of matchmaking, but the conversation immediately moved on to other Culver family matters—how to be there for Mike while he dealt with Elaine's illness without being so obvious about it that he grew impatient with them; Jolie going back to work managing the store and how that would affect Lola; Dylan's and Jolie's roles in rebuilding the Lightning Creek Ranch after the fire. Molly sipped her beer and listened until Finn said that they hadn't come to discuss family matters. They'd come to enjoy themselves *before* family matters took over their lives.

"Hey, sorry for being boring," Dylan said. "Finn didn't ask you out to listen to us bitch, plot and plan."

"I don't mind," she said honestly. It was nice seeing a family that was concerned about one another. And the beer was somehow acting as a filter, making everything clearer. Better.

She wasn't drunk. Maybe slightly buzzed. Whatever her condition, it was pleasant to be out. Even more pleasant to put her hand in Finn's without hesitation when the music started and Dylan and Jolie automatically headed for the dance floor.

"How do friends dance?" Finn asked as he settled his hands on her waist, keeping a good six inches of air between them.

Molly made a face at him. "Let's go with the usual way. You know…actually touching? So we don't look dumb?"

He pulled her closer, the length of their bodies now lightly pressed together. "Like this?"

"Uh…yes. This works." At the very least, it felt good. Maybe too good as her legs pressed up against his muscular thighs and her breasts came up against his solid chest. "I'm glad we agreed to be friends." The beer might have loosened her tongue a bit, but it was the truth.

"Why wouldn't we be friends?" he asked, his voice rumbling seductively close to her ear.

"Uh…all the stuff that's gone down between us?"

He leaned back to look into her face. "I guess there has been some…stuff." He pulled her against him again, resting his cheek lightly on top of her head, and she felt him smile against her hair. "I like you anyway. And you kiss well."

"Gee. Thanks." The words came out drily and hopefully kept him from realizing that heat was now flooding her midsection. It was more than remembering the kiss; it was him. Having him hold her close, his hand moving over her back in a distinctly possessive way, making her want…more.

Was he doing this on purpose?

She tilted her head back to look up into his surprisingly dark eyes. "Are you doing this on purpose?

"Doing what?" he asked in a way that told her that he knew exactly what she was talking about.

"Trying to get me all hot and bothered."

He laughed. "Maybe."

"Won't work," she said against his chest.

"Maybe."

"We're friends," she murmured against his chest as the music ended. And she was here to have fun. Hot and bothered could work into that.

Molly danced four—or was it five?—dances with Finn before the band took a break and they settled back at the table. Not long after that, Finn told Dylan and Jolie that he had to open the store and that Molly had an eight o'clock class.

"Fine," Dylan said, slipping an arm around his fiancée. "Be responsible. We'll close the place down without you."

"I didn't realize they closed at eleven-thirty," Finn remarked straight-faced.

He and Molly left the bar the way they'd come in—hand in hand—only this time it had a different feel to it. Maybe it was the beer. Maybe it was the dancing, but Molly felt freer than she'd felt in years. She squeezed Finn's fingers as they crossed the parking lot to where she was parked but didn't look at him when he shot her a glance.

"Are you okay to drive?" Finn asked as she pulled out her keys.

"I had a beer and a half over a long period of

time." She leaned back against her car instead of opening the door. The air was crisp, so she folded her arms over her chest. "I'm not much of a drinker."

"I noticed."

"Well, I *did* have a table in the library."

"While I developed other skills."

Molly smiled at him, liked the way his eyes crinkled sexily at the corners as he smiled back. "I enjoyed being out with Dylan and Jolie."

"And me."

"And you."

"We can do it again."

"Yeah." She glanced down at the pavement with a slight frown, her gaze coming up again as Finn reached out to touch her chin.

"No pressure, Molly."

She smiled tightly, then made an effort to make it feel more real. "I've worked hard to get control of my life. To overcome shyness and make a career and get…secure… I guess. I like being your friend, Finn." Even though she hadn't thought of him as a real friend until tonight. She'd thought of him more as a crazy-sexy distraction.

"I sense a 'but' coming on."

"No 'but.'" Molly pushed her hands through her hair, smoothing it back away from her face.

"I had that…guy problem…not that long ago, and as I said, I'm still dealing with it."

"You made strides forward tonight."

"That I did." She bit her lip and then smiled up at him. "Thanks to you. But I have to be honest… In ways I'm still dealing with all that."

Finn reached out to touch the edge of her face. "I hate to think of you hurting."

The touch, the stroke of his fingers down her cheek, about did her in. Her voice was husky as she asked, "So you understand?"

"That you're cautious? Yes. I'm not sure what to do about it, but I understand." He stepped back then, putting his hands in his pockets, giving her space.

Suddenly she didn't want space. She wanted human contact. "Will you kiss me?"

"Like a friend?" His voice was low, the question legit.

"I don't…know." And that killed her because she was supposed to be in control of her life. "What else you got?"

He reached out to take her face between his palms, gently drawing her near. Molly stepped forward as their lips met in a slow, deep, soul-searing kiss. Not casual.

He raised his head, his lips gently pulling away from hers. "Better?" he asked, somehow

understanding what it was she had asked for.
Had understood that it was more than a kiss.

She briefly rested her head against his chest before looking up at him and saying, "Yes. Better."

CHAPTER THIRTEEN

MOLLY WOKE UP with a start, stretched out her hand and realized the bed was empty. She sat up, clutching the sheets to her for a moment, then collapsed back into the pillows, wishing her bed was not empty. She rolled over, dragging the sheet with her. The clock read 4:30. Too early to get up—especially since she'd gone to bed around 1:00 a.m.

She shouldn't have kissed Finn.

Molly squeezed her eyes shut. Maybe not, but she'd *needed* to kiss him. To be kissed. To feel somewhat alive again. She'd walled herself off for protection after Blake, but the wall was cracking and she was afraid.

Finn understood, though. He'd said that he knew she was wary. He knew she wanted to be friends, not lovers. She grimaced against the pillow. She shifted, still feeling the throb of sexual desire even though she couldn't remember the dream that had woken her.

It must have been a good one and it had to have involved Finn, because he'd been her first thought upon waking. She rolled over, resigned herself to staring at the dark wall until it was no longer dark, then fell sound asleep.

Georgina was making tea, when Molly rushed into the kitchen at 7:30 a.m. By pulling her hair up into a knot while it was damp and pulling the first outfit her hand touched out of her closet, she would make it to her eight o'clock class with a few minutes to spare.

"You're still here? I thought you were gone."

"Overslept."

"Obviously." Georgina popped up her toast and put it on a plate. "Here."

Molly took the plate. "Thanks. I have an eight o'clock, covering for Mr. Cortez again."

"I know."

She poured hot water from the kettle into her travel mug, popped in a tea bag, closed the lid, grabbed the toast and headed for the door.

"You were out late last night," Georgina called.

"And paying for it now."

Molly arrived at Mr. Cortez's classroom with almost two minutes to spare and after she caught her breath, class went well. The toast, which she'd eaten while driving, and the tea had perked her up and she'd prepared everything she needed the day before. All she had to do was to skid into class and start the lesson.

During her first class after lunch, she had to stifle the occasional yawn as the effects of the long night set in, but all in all it was a good day…right up until the dean stuck his head in her office just as her office hours were ending.

"Do you have a few minutes to meet? Or would it be handier to set up an appointment for Monday?"

"I have time now." The last thing Molly wanted was to go the weekend wondering what the dean wanted to meet about.

"Five minutes? My office?"

"I'll be there."

When Molly showed up at the dean's office a few minutes later, his secretary, Penny, told her to go straight in. Molly knocked lightly on his door, opened it and then closed it behind her as he waved her to the seat on the opposite side of his desk.

He set down his pen and lightly clasped his hands. "How are things going? In general, I mean. Any challenges or situations of note?"

Molly folded her hands in her lap. Preliminary stuff before he got down to the business at hand. She'd searched her brain but couldn't imagine what the business at hand might be, unless Denny had struck again. "Things are good. I am finding the workload challenging, but I've been able to stay on top of it."

The dean nodded, then said, "I had a talk with a concerned parent this morning."

"A parent?" That seemed…odd, since she taught at a college.

"Mr. Simon. Jonas Simon's father. As you know, Jonas is still in high school so…I guess that's why we got the parent call."

"What's the problem?" Molly asked, thinking it was better to know exactly what she was dealing with rather than to confess to something that might not even be an issue. Maybe the parent was on her side. It could happen.

The dean frowned down at the floor as if looking for words. Never a good sign. When he looked up, he said, "Succinctly, you are grading harshly, you are rude to students and you're apparently overly friendly with another of your students. To the point of making Jonas uncomfortable."

Molly's mouth dropped open. "Excuse me?" She didn't know even where to begin refuting and her stomach was in the process of curling into a tight little ball. This was no way to start a new job in a place where she hoped to stay.

"That's the story. And Mr. Simon is close to Dr. Womack." Dr. Womack, as in the president of the school. This just kept getting better.

"I understand that the Simons donated some land to the school."

"They did."

Molly blew out a breath. "I stand behind my marks. If anything they are on the generous side."

"That's the easiest of the claims to refute. Jonas has agreed to bring his papers in for examination."

"I keep copies of everything, so he needn't bother."

"Good. Now…the alleged rudeness."

"Have you ever spoken to Jonas?"

"Do you mean have I been spoken to by Jonas?"

Molly felt a twinge of relief. The dean understood. That didn't mean Dr. Womack would.

"No matter how our students speak to us, professionalism dictates a tactful reply."

"I don't think I strayed far from tactful, given the circumstances," Molly said, trying to recreate the conversation in her head.

"In the future try to stray less far. At least until Jonas is gone."

"I'll do that."

The dean uncrossed his legs, looking uncomfortable. "Now…are you having some kind of an amorous relationship with a student?"

"Amorous?" she asked incredulously, half wondering if Jonas had been spying on her last night, because other than going to coffee… and Finn not giving up his tutoring time upon Jonas's demand…

That little fink.

"Not my word."

Molly cleared her throat. "I went to high school with one of my students. We're…friends. We've known each other for a long time." She hoped that the words sounded more convincing to him than they did to her. They were friends. For the most part. Friends who had shared one hot kiss last night.

"You were seen in a bar together a few weeks back and the parent specifically mentioned that fact."

A few weeks back—as in no one had seen them kissing in the parking lot last night. Relief slammed into her, even if she hadn't done anything wrong.

"Is there a rule against that?"

"No. But there are perceptions and rumors and the snowball effect."

"You can't have a student dictating what goes on," Molly felt compelled to point out.

"You are correct, but we have a unique situation. A high school-aged student in a position to raise you-know-what. The family is wealthy and they've donated."

Fine. She'd just been given a directive to kiss ass.

"Jonas's parents back him to a fault. I would be careful not to give him any ammunition in any way, other than giving him an honest grade—one you can defend without difficulty. I don't want the academic standards of EVCC to be compromised."

But Molly bet that if she fudged *A*s for the kid, the powers that be would be fine with it. He was undoubtedly going to attend a larger, more prestigious college once he graduated from high school. Why not give him what he wanted to keep him quiet?

The dean let out a breath. "This conversation is the extent of my 'investigation' into allegations, but in the future…watch out for that kid. You will, of course, be involved in the review of the grades."

"For the record, are you telling me not to be seen with my friend? Or to not go to bars?"

"I'm telling you that you are a probationary instructor in her first year, and even if it's not fair, you should be careful of anything that can be used against you by a disgruntled student and his influential family." His mouth tightened. "If we have another complaint that is at all viable, there could well be some kind of documented investigation. Letter in the file, that kind of thing."

Which was a lot more serious than a single outlier student evaluation. She'd been worrying about the wrong thing.

"Thank you for the warning," Molly said

faintly. She swallowed drily after the dean had given her a tight smile, then disappeared into the hallway. A seventeen-year-old kid was trying to ruin her life.

FINN STOPPED BY Molly's office on Friday afternoon to discuss the paper her was working on, but he was honest enough to admit to himself that he would have stopped by even if he hadn't needed clarification on some grammar issues. He wanted to see her.

Just…see her.

He wasn't certain if that was good or bad, and he didn't have an opportunity to find out because her office was locked up tight. It was barely five minutes after five and Molly always worked late, but apparently not tonight.

Damn. He shouldered his backpack and headed to his truck.

Even though it was Dylan's night to sit with Mike, Finn could legitimately stop by his grandfather's house, see if Molly was around, but instead he headed home. He wasn't about to pressure her. She wanted to be friends. Fine. They'd be friends.

So what if she made him horny as hell? They'd figure that side of things out as they went.

If they went. She may never see him again.

Finn didn't like that idea. There was something about Molly that made him want to find out more about her—to do what his teenaged-self had been too stupid to do and discover the things that Molly was too shy to share.

But he'd been too much of an arrogant jock back then, and she'd been too closed off. A geek, like Dylan. She still had a touch of geekiness, but it didn't define her as it had in high school. Molly was not the same girl who had blushed whenever their arms accidentally touched on their date.

Damn but that had been painful, but now he wished he had a do-over.

So how did he handle this situation? He'd promised friendship. He wanted more.

The sensible thing to do was to bide his time, let her make the next move or two. He didn't want to put himself out there to get slapped down...although that was a novel feeling. Since when had he ever worried about getting shot down in the romance department?

About the same time that he started to find glasses sexy.

How MANY HOT DREAMS could one woman have before she did something about it? Molly had lain awake long after going to bed on Friday and Saturday nights, worrying about Jonas Simon, only to fall asleep and dream about Finn. It was getting to the point that sleeping was as exhausting as staying awake and worrying.

Molly pushed the sheets aside and swung her feet onto the cool wood floor, gripping the mattress on either side of her legs. Her subconscious was sending her a message and it was coming through loud and clear. *You've been neglecting yourself and you should stop doing that.*

Yeah? Well, what's the next step?

Her subconscious didn't have an answer for that.

Since it was Sunday and she'd actually gotten her grading done early, she went to the kitchen, poured a cup of coffee from the carafe Georgina had made for her before heading out close to dawn. Molly wasn't certain what today's activity was, but Georgina always left a note on the fridge and sure enough, there it was.

Molly took a bracing sip of coffee and then slipped the note out from under the magnet. Georgina and Chase were going otter watching at the river. Molly gave an appraising nod as she attached the note to the fridge again. Sounded like fun.

She, in the meantime, was going to sit at her kitchen table, prep for next week's classes and try to convince herself that Georgina and Chase would break up soon, so she wouldn't have to go into protective sister mode. Because damned if Georgina was going to make the same mistakes she had. It had nothing to do with liking or disliking Chase and everything to do with common sense.

Meanwhile, she was debating about the Finn situation—whether to address their obviously mutual attraction. Hypocritical?

She thought not. She was twenty-nine. She'd learned a few lessons the hard way and was trying to keep her sister from doing the same.

Damn, but she hoped they broke up first.

Molly took another big drink of coffee and set the cup aside.

Ten-to-one that, when push came to shove with Finn, she'd play things safe. Finn would get bored being just a friend and she'd be left with hot sexy dreams.

Molly wrinkled her nose and got back to her feet. Why did a perfectly sane solution to the Finn situation seem so…unsatisfying?

But at least it gave her something to think about other than entitled Jonas Simon and the ways in which he could impact her job.

FINN WAS GETTING seriously concerned about Mike. He was a rock when Elaine was around, but when she wasn't there, he sank into silence, staring off into space as if he'd already lost her.

Even Buddy couldn't snap him out of it—but he came closer than Finn.

"You need to come to work," Finn told him. "Or come to the shop with me. Help me with the truck."

"I'm fine."

And surly. Very unlike himself. Even though the outlook for Elaine was cautiously optimistic, Mike couldn't bring himself to believe the worst was not going to happen again. Even Jolie, who'd once had a similar experience with loss, couldn't get through to him.

"We should let him be," she said when she and Dylan met Finn at McElroy's late Thursday afternoon. She took a sip of her iced tea. Dylan studied the table and Finn debated going to math that evening. He was ahead in that class and could probably get away with skipping and staying with Mike. Unlike Jolie, he didn't think his grandfather should be alone.

Dylan caught his eye. "I'll hang with Mike tonight."

"I think we should let him be," Jolie repeated as she set her glass down.

"He shouldn't be alone."

"Why not?" Jolie asked.

"He gets morose," Dylan said.

"Maybe we should ask him if he wants company," Finn suggested.

"I'll do that," Dylan said. "When I hang with him tonight."

Finn pushed his chair back. "I've got to run home and get my stuff for math class."

His English classes that week had been…awkward. He could think of no other word. He'd stopped by Molly's office after class on Monday and she'd been friendly yet somehow distant. Not in the same self-protective way she'd been before, but…distant. Thoughtful. And he didn't think it concerned him, so as Jolie had suggested with Mike, he let her be. Wednesday, she'd left the building almost as soon as class was over, leaving him to wonder what the hell was going on. And if he should ask or back off.

He wasn't going to back off—not until she gave him a direct order.

He was falling for a woman who didn't want to be fallen for. A woman he could have had if he hadn't been such a dickhead back in the day. Now some guy had hurt her, screwed with her life—and he'd like to meet the guy, whoever he was. All he needed was a few minutes… He could do some damage in that amount of time. Not that it would do Molly any good, but it might cheer her up a little.

The math class released early, so Finn headed by Mike's house on his way home. Dylan's truck was no longer there, so Finn gave a quick knock and let himself in. Mike looked up with a deep frown.

"This has got to stop."

"Yeah. I agree."

"No. You guys have got to stop. Give me space. Give me my time."

Finn blinked at him. "We're worried about you."

"You are suffocating me. Let me work through this. Yeah. I'm sad. I'm going to stay sad until I get some time to process, and I'm not getting that with you guys smothering me."

Finn held up a hand and took a backward step. "We thought…"

Mike's expression shifted from angry to weary in a heartbeat. "I know what you think. And I understand why. I love you guys. I want your company, but Finn, I've lived alone for a while now. I'll be okay. Just…give me some privacy."

Finn moistened his lips. "How much?"

"Can you call before you come by? Not forever…but for a while."

He gave a nod. "We can do that." Buddy lifted his head from Mike's lap and Finn had a feeling that the little cat was one reason that Mike probably didn't need human company as much as he and Dylan had thought he did.

"Did you give Dylan this talk?"

"I did," Mike said on a sigh. "Cal, Karl and Lola, too. Between all of you it's been like Grand Central Station over here. I need some time alone. Some time to deal." Finn opened his mouth and Mike said, "Yes. I know the prognosis is good. Thank you. But it's still cancer. Elaine is a dear friend. Allow me my worry."

So Finn left his grandfather to his worries and went home to a few of his own. Was he supposed to just stand back and do nothing while his grandfather refused to sleep or eat? To watch grief turn the guy inside out?

How was that helping anything? He paced through the house, his stomach getting tighter with every step.

He'll be fine. Mike will be fine.

But he didn't know that for sure.

MOLLY HAD A FEELING that the Jonas situation was far from over, since the dean had popped in at least once a day every day this week, staying for fifteen minutes each time. Informal observations were part of the evaluation process, but not on a daily basis. This was not a good sign. If she lost this job…

She wasn't going to think that way, because she'd done nothing wrong. Let the dean come and watch. She was an excellent instructor. Jonas had an ax to grind because he couldn't handle the real world and he was the one who needed to change. Not her. This wasn't a case of trying to be nicer to Denny. If she let Jonas get away with this, she was setting the stage for him to do it again, to someone else.

She had copies of all of his work, as well as that of the other two high school students enrolled in her English Basic Comp class, as well as a sampling of other students. She'd been generous with him. He was smart enough to perform better, but he was also entitled and, even though she hated to say it, lazy. Things had come easily to him up to this point and he'd gotten used to phoning things in.

But even though she talked her way through the situation on a daily basis, it still ate at her. She was, after all, human.

She'd just gotten to her car when she got a call on her cell.

"Hey. It's Finn."

She gripped the phone a little tighter. It'd been a week since they'd gone to McElroy's—a week during which they'd had little contact with the exception of class. But, despite the Jonas fiasco, he'd never been far from her thoughts.

"Hi. What's up?"

"I was wondering…can I see you tonight?"

There was something in his voice that told her not to say no, even though common sense decreed that no was the only logical answer. She didn't need to give Jonas any more ammunition.

"I can't meet you at McElroy's." Despite all of her "it's a free country" speeches to herself, she honestly didn't want to court trouble with the school.

He sounded perplexed as he said, "Maybe your place?"

"Or maybe I could come by your shop. I feel a distinct need to hammer metal."

THE LIGHTS WERE ON in Finn's shop when Molly pulled into the driveway, so she parked at the edge of the drive, close to the shop. The muffled sounds of AC/DC's "Highway to Hell" filtered through the metal walls as she got out of the car, and she hoped that it wasn't an indication of something bad. Finn had not sounded like himself when he called. She hesitated, then gave a quick knock and pushed open the door. The music got louder, swelling around her. Finn was at the metalworking station, hammer in hand, but he turned almost as soon as she stepped inside the brightly lit building. He set his hammer aside and wiped his hands on his jeans.

Molly hesitated just inside the door, teetering on the brink of…something. Unsettled business would be settled tonight, at least temporarily. Maybe by talking. Maybe by other means.

She was ready for other means. She'd had a week to think, a week to come to terms with the fact that yes, she was human. She made mistakes and she had needs. But indulging her needs was not synonymous with making a mistake. That had happened once. That didn't mean it was the only possible outcome.

And something was up with Finn. She'd sensed that during their short conversation and now, as he met her gaze over the hood of the old Ford, she knew that all was not well.

He smiled, a guarded tilt of his lips, making her feel as if their positions were now reversed—he was the wary one and she was the one who had a pretty decent idea of what she wanted.

And looking at him now, all long legs, broad shoulders and lean muscle, she definitely wanted.

"Hey," she said, her voice barely audible over the loud music. Finn reached out to turn off the radio and the ensuing silence was almost as jarring as the music had been.

"Thanks for coming." His voice was low, still a touch guarded.

"Not a problem. I wanted to see you anyway."

"You did?" The statement sounded like a question.

She gave a solemn nod, and then, since he didn't move, she did, her shoes echoing on the concrete floor as she walked. She needed to do something with all the nervous energy balled up inside her. Crossing the shop would burn a little of it. The rest…?

As she got closer, his smile faded and his gaze remained watchful, as if he wasn't as certain of himself as usual. He had no reason not to feel certain. Teen Finn had been hot, but adult Finn was blazing. Tonight she felt like getting burned.

Just a little. Just enough to feel.

She stopped a good three feet away from him, next to the big truck. Something rustled in the engine block and she jumped.

"Damned mice." Finn came closer, peered down into the engine.

"Maybe Buddy needs to take up residence."

"I left him with Mike full-time. While he… deals."

Again that note in his voice. Worry.

"How's he doing? Mike, I mean."

"He's…not himself."

A silence fell between them and Molly finally asked, "Is that why you called?"

Finn nodded. "I stopped by his place tonight and he essentially kicked me out. Kicked all of us out. He wants to be alone. I thought…maybe you and Georgina could keep an eye on him from a distance. Make sure lights come on when they should and stuff."

"You know we will."

Finn needed someone close by to keep an eye on his grandfather, but Molly knew for a fact that wasn't the only reason he'd called. Intuition, maybe…or perhaps the way he was looking at her.

"Jolie thinks it's the best thing, and she's been through this stuff before, but Mike's been through it twice. He's afraid it's number three."

"You can't grieve for him, Finn. He has to do it himself."

Finn blinked at her. "We're fine letting him grieve, but he needs to eat."

"And maybe for a day or two he needs time alone to come to grips with this situation. He won't die of starvation and I bet that he does eat."

"Maybe…"

"We all want to ease the pain of those we love. When Georgina had her first big breakup, I wanted her to stop hurting now, because seeing her hurt, hurt me."

"So you're siding with Mike. Telling us to back off."

"For now. You can change tactics after a day or two if necessary."

Finn picked up his hammer, weighed it in his hand, then set it back down again. "I guess that makes sense. I'm just so damned worried about the guy."

"I get it, Finn. I totally do."

Silence fell and then he gave her a sideways look. "Want to do some metal work while you're here? Like last time?"

"Last time we had an argument."

He quirked an eyebrow up. "We also figured some stuff out."

"True."

More silence. He shifted his weight, then met her gaze. "So where are we now, Molly? What happens next?" His mouth tightened briefly, before he asked, "Do we talk some more?"

The way he was looking at her made his meaning crystal clear.

D-day.

"I…"

She could tell him, yes, she wanted to talk. Or she could turn and walk out the door. Run to safety.

Instead she reached out to lightly touch the front of his shirt, stroke her fingers over the soft gray cotton. His hard muscles tensed beneath her touch. She lifted her chin, met his eyes. "What if I don't want to talk just yet?"

"What would you like to do?"

And suddenly she felt very calm. In control. "I would like to find out if you're as good in person as you are in my dreams."

She felt his heart do a double beat beneath her

palm. His voice was rough when he said, "I'm fairly positive that I'm better."

"Yeah?" she asked softly. "Prove it."

She felt his heart do an odd double beat and then his mouth came down on hers, the first touch exploding into something hot and demanding.

Molly wrapped her arms around his neck and pulled herself closer, molding her body against his long frame. The kiss pulled her in, obliterated her sense of up and down, right and wrong. All that mattered in her world for this one moment was the man whose mouth was ravaging hers, demanding a reaction that she was more than willing to give.

She pushed her hands up along his face, over the light scruff on his cheeks, answering his demands, pressing her body against his.

Molly, who overthought everything, did herself a favor and stopped thinking. She reached for the bottom of his T-shirt, dragged it up over his head and tossed it on the bench behind her. He returned the favor, his gaze pausing on the swell of her breasts, then moving on down to the jeweled bar in her navel.

"This," he said in low voice, "surprises me."

"Wait until you see my other one."

His eyes went wide and she laughed, pulling his mouth back to hers for a long kiss. "Kidding," she said softly. "This is my sole sign of rebellion."

"I approve," he murmured before undoing her jeans and pushing them down her thighs. Her panties followed, and she kicked out of them as he reached behind her to clear the bench with his arm, then took hold of her waist and lifted her butt onto the cool metal. Molly didn't think it would be cool for long.

Finn leaned back, took a long look at her, his heated gaze traveling over her. "You're ridiculous," he muttered. "Perfect."

Molly liked being perfect, and she liked seeing his erection straining against his jeans. She nodded toward it.

Finn gave a short laugh at her silent directive, then followed orders, the hard length of him springing free as he shoved his jeans down. He was gorgeous, and Molly was glad she was sitting because her legs were getting wobbly.

He leaned in as he smoothly undid her bra, their last remaining barrier, then gave her breasts the attention they deserved, first with his hands and then with his mouth. Molly gasped. Arched. His tongue trailed lower and he played with the jewelry that so fascinated him—her freedom-from-Blake jewelry—and then continued lower as she opened her thighs for him.

Molly arched again, against his mouth, gasping as he hit the spot. She almost came but instead scooted backward.

"First time you're in me."

He gave her a look, then went to his pants, dug around in his wallet and came back with a condom. Once sheathed, he took hold of her hips and pulled her forward until he was pressed firmly against her. Molly wrapped her legs around him and slowly slid herself forward on the smooth metal bench until they were fully joined.

Perfection.

Her mouth opened in a silent "oh" as he started to move. Slowly, oh so slowly, rocking against her, filling her. It felt so ridiculously good that Molly almost couldn't breathe…and then she could as he changed things up, started moving faster. Her breath came in short gasps as his rhythm increased, and all she could do was hang on until her body exploded against him. She saw the gleam of pure male satisfaction before he finished, plunging deeply, holding her body tightly against his until he relaxed and his head came to rest against her shoulder.

She closed her eyes, stroked her hands over his damp skin, his hair, then hugged him to her.

Finally he lifted his head and smiled at her.

"Better than dream guy?"

She laughed and took his chin in her hand. "Much."

He helped her off the bench and to her amusement handed her a couple of shop towels. "Always prepared," he murmured.

They got dressed without speaking, but it was not an uncomfortable silence. Molly picked up the hammer that Finn had set aside before they made love and gave the sheet metal sitting there a tap. "There. My mission is accomplished." She smiled at him. "I did come to beat metal."

"Right."

He took her by the hand and led her over to a vinyl sofa beneath the midcentury starburst wall clock that Molly estimated was worth a lot more money than Finn probably realized.

"Want a beer?"

There was a small fridge next to the sofa. "No thanks. For now." That was when Molly noticed the television mounted on the far wall, up high, above the door. "This truly is a man cave of extraordinary proportions."

"I prefer to call it a man arena."

Molly smiled, leaned her head back and closed her eyes. Maybe she could just sit here with Finn, shut out the world. Breathe in the scents of grease, oil… Finn. Yes. That would be nice.

Warm fingers started moving up her thigh.

"I have a hammer," she said without bothering to open her eyes.

"So do I."

Her eyes came open at that and he laughed,

the sound low and sensual. "Thought that might get your attention."

"It certainly did before."

He took hold of her hand then. "What's going on, Molly? Why couldn't you meet me at McElroy's?"

"I'm…under scrutiny."

He shifted so that he could look at her while still holding her hand. "What does that mean?"

"Jonas has brought in the big guns."

Finn blinked at her. "You don't mean…"

"Yep. His parents. They filed a complaint against me. I have to defend my grading, which I'm fully prepared to do."

She gave him another sideways look as his fingers tightened on hers. He knew there was more, so she didn't hedge. What was the point? She'd come to talk to him and she'd talk. Even if it wasn't the most comfortable topic ever. "I've been rude to him—"

"Holy—"

"And I'm in an amorous relationship with a student, which makes Jonas uncomfortable."

Finn let go of her hand and shifted in his seat so that he could see her face. "Me?"

"Well, it's not Denny." She bit her lip. "We were seen in McElroy's—and even though there's no law about me going to bars, there is public perception and you are my student."

Finn stared at her. "What now?"

"Now I walk the straight and narrow and wait for this to die down."

"Should I drop your class?"

"No." She gave a small sniff. "Besides losing your money and your credit, it makes us look guilty."

Finn settled back in his seat. "We are guilty." He took her hand again, laced his fingers through hers.

"I feel better because of it," she admitted.

"For how long?"

"Meaning do I have regrets?" She smiled a little. "More like concern for the future."

"I won't screw with your future, Molly."

"If I thought you would, I wouldn't be here."

"So...you're saying you trust me?"

She turned her head to look at him, her cheek pressed against the vinyl of the sofa. How did she tell him that she trusted him to a point, just as she trusted herself to a point? As long as they had clear sight of the boundaries of their relationship, she could let herself go. Trust him within that parameter.

Because the truth was, she fully expected to get burned again. Guys like Finn, guys like Blake, guys who didn't know what they wanted in life, or couldn't pin down what they needed... they'd move on as they searched. Molly was staying put. But the difference between this relationship and the last was that she knew what to expect. Forewarned was forearmed.

She reached out to touch Finn's face, to trail her fingers down the scruff on his cheeks, loving the feel. Not yet ready to give it up. "I'll be here for you, and you can be here for me…but I'm not putting any kind of label on what we have."

She hadn't answered his question and she could see that he was fully aware of that fact.

"I won't hurt you, Molly."

Not on purpose, anyway.

"Can we leave things status quo, while I figure a few things out?"

She felt him withdraw, but made herself stay strong. She *would* be there for him. At this point she might fight tigers for him. But she wouldn't put herself into a position where her world crumbled when he moved on.

CHAPTER FOURTEEN

GEORGINA SPENT THE weekend hiking and camping with Chase, leaving Molly home alone, catching up on her grading and avoiding any hint of public scandal that Jonas's parents might pick up on and use to put the screws to her. It was nice to be alone when she had so much to do, but she was becoming concerned about the amount of time Georgina was spending with her beau, not that she had any reason to address the issue other than the fact that Chase came from a questionable background. Honestly, though, she would have been concerned regardless. Her sister was an adult, but she was also only nineteen—not that much younger than Molly had been when she'd begun to embark on the biggest mistake of her life.

Molly had told Finn that Mike needed to deal with his own issues in his own way, and now she needed to listen to her own advice—but how did one stop feeling protective of their little sister?

One did not.

So one attempted to focus on other matters.

Making love to Finn sprang to mind a number of times. He'd called on Friday to touch base and ask her if everything looked normal at Mike's house and on Saturday he'd been at Mike's, but he didn't make his way over to her house. She didn't know if he was giving her space, or if he was being careful of not giving the appearance that she was involved with him.

She would have liked to see him. Touch him. Wrap herself around him.

This was new territory for Molly. When she'd hooked up with Blake, she'd practically been a pseudo-wife from day one. She'd loved being needed. Loved the perks of a close relationship, disregarded the part about seeing to her own needs. Caring for Blake was her need. If she did that, she felt great.

And he felt up someone else.

Jerk.

Molly forced herself to focus on her prep work. On Monday she had *the* meeting—the one where she defended her grades—and she wanted everything to go smoothly that morning so that she could focus on exonerating herself.

Jonas had bullied his way through the system for too long, and he needed some comeuppance. For his own good and the good of those he'd have to deal with in the future. Molly was all about giving it to him.

Her fingers stilled on the keyboard. How would she have reacted to this situation two or three years ago—while she'd been Blake's caretaker?

Would she have rolled over? Fought?

She hadn't been a fighter then. Hadn't really taken control of her own existence. She coexisted, until Blake had forced her to become a solo act with his egregious behavior. She was stronger now. In control.

Except when she wasn't—like while making love to Finn.

But what a great way to lose control.

As Sunday passed, Molly thought less about Finn and more about her future. Yes, she was alone and probably overthinking, but she had a difficult time living with unfinished business and she wanted the meeting over, conclusions drawn. She wanted to get on with her professional life, which was essentially her anchor.

Molly needed that anchor.

On Monday morning she dressed carefully in a navy suit with a pin-striped blouse. An outfit that screamed "I'm a professional, good at what I do. Don't question me."

It also shouted "boring" with its at-the-knee skirt and matched jacket.

Good. Boring was dependable. Boring was trustworthy.

Trust me...your son is behaving like an entitled egomaniac.

Words she could not say.

IT WAS THE DAY of Molly's big meeting and Finn hoped that she'd get hold of him afterward, tell him how it went. They had class that night, but for the rest of the semester, he was going to be just another student. He probably wouldn't stop by office hours, either. Molly's job was important to her and more than that, it was what kept her in the Eagle Valley, and Finn wanted her in the valley. He wanted a shot at helping her move past guy-mess.

She hadn't been able to tell him that she trusted him, but she had to trust him to a point or she wouldn't have made love to him. Molly wasn't a one-night-stand kind of person, and, funny thing, neither was he anymore.

It felt good to admit that.

Now if he could just figure out what to do with his life. Try to muscle through the teaching degree? Try something else? Now that Jolie was back at the store part-time, they needed him even less. Chase was beginning to fill his hours and Finn knew he needed to find a job that made him feel that he was actually doing something.

He'd thought about Molly's suggestion to try the metal-art thing, wondered if she'd suggested it because she knew that he'd never succeed in his current goal. That would bite. It wasn't possible to make a steady living doing artsy shit, but maybe he could fabricate.

Again, he wanted more.

But what?

At the moment, he needed a beer because he was getting tired of being uncertain about every damned thing in his life except for the fact that he could stay at the feed store forever.

At least if he fabricated metal, he'd have a specialization.

THE DEAN'S SMALL OFFICE was packed to capacity by the time Molly arrived for her meeting. The dean stood and introduced an unsmiling couple as Mr. and Mrs. Simon. They were in their midforties, Molly estimated as she extended her hand to both and received cool handshakes in return, both blond with angular Scandinavian features that, combined with their elevated noses, gave them a distinctly snooty look—exactly what she expected after dealing with their offspring. Mr. Simon was dressed more formally than the dean, with slacks and a jacket. Mrs. Simon wore a suit that looked very much like Molly's.

"We're here today because Mr. and Mrs. Simon have issue with Jonas's grades."

"And his treatment." Mrs. Simon's mouth closed tight once the few words had escaped.

"As far as treatment goes, we have a his-word-against-hers situation."

"He has a log."

Somehow Molly kept her mouth from falling open. Jonas had kept a log? "Amazing." The word slipped out, bringing the attention of everyone in the room squarely onto her, as if it hadn't been there before. The dean caught her eye then and Molly got the message loud and clear. He didn't want to get into the log, and she didn't blame him. That could be a messy affair, especially since she wasn't going to allow herself to be steamrollered—unless she had to in order to keep her job. She had her pride, but she also had bills.

"I'll be happy to go over the grades with you," Molly said pleasantly. "I have copies of his work here." She indicated the folder she held in her lap.

"We have copies," Mrs. Simon said in a clipped voice. She turned to the dean. "What we would like is for these papers to be graded, blind, by another instructor. Then we can compare those marks to the marks of Ms. Adamson."

Molly gave a nod. It seemed fair to her. A burden on whomever had to grade, but her marks were reasonable. The Simons were not.

"We would also like to have other papers included. A general sampling."

The dean looked as if he was about to draw the line at that request, when Mr. Simon added, "We have it on good authority that one of Ms. Adamson's students is passing her class despite a distinct lack of ability."

"How do you know he's passing?" Before Mr. Simon could answer, the dean turned to Molly. "Do you have any failing students?"

"Not at the moment."

Mr. Simon smiled with a touch of cold smugness. "We want his papers graded blindly, too."

"We can't do that. Privacy laws—" The dean sucked in a breath and pressed his lips together. "May I have a moment alone with Ms. Adamson?"

The Simons exchanged looks, then rose to their feet. Molly didn't look at them as they left. Instead she focused on prying her fingers loose from the arm of the chair. After the door closed behind them, the dean's shoulders literally slumped. He was a nice guy, but by no means a tower of strength.

"Well?" he asked.

"I have a student that I'm differentiating for. He has a disability."

"Diagnosed?"

She shook her head. "But it's pretty obvious that he's dyslexic."

"Yet no diagnosis, so no Americans with Disabilities provisions. Are you grading him more easily than Jonas?"

"He's working to the best of his ability. Jonas is skating."

"That wasn't the question."

Now Molly's shoulders slumped. "I've been helping him. A lot."

"Are his grades reflective of his abilities?"

"Not at the moment, but he's improving." She raised a hand. "I know. Not the answer to the question. No. They are not reflective."

"You've put me in a bind here." An odd expression crossed his face. "Please tell me this isn't the student that Jonas accused you of being amorous with?"

Molly opened her mouth. Closed it again. She couldn't truthfully say they weren't amorous.

The dean put his elbows on his desk and pressed his fingertips against his bowed head. "I want to keep you."

Molly's stomach tightened. "I want to stay."

He raised his head, his expression grim. "Two choices. You give all of your students a writing assessment to be completed by Wednesday. Or you get permission to share this student's work. Either way, another instructor grades. I can tell you which one would be less work for said instructor."

"I'm sorry about this," Molly said. "I honestly was trying to get him up to the point where he could pass the class without discouraging him. He had years of work to catch up on."

"I understand the motivation. However…it's now a problem."

Molly let out a sigh. "I have copies of his work. I can obliterate the name so as not to violate privacy laws."

"Please have those to me at the end of the day."

"Do you want me to continue this meeting with the Simons?"

The dean's eyebrows lifted. "And risk getting into the log?" He shook his head. "You have class and I have waters to smooth."

As did she. Waters to smooth. Confessions to make.

MOLLY SMILED AT FINN as he walked into her classroom, and he smiled back. That was the last contact they had for the next hour, but Finn sat in his truck and waited for Molly to leave the building. As she walked by his vehicle he rolled down the window and she said simply, "Your place. We need to talk."

He nodded and drove away. Fifteen minutes later, Molly pulled up at his house.

He opened the door and she slipped inside under his arm, glancing behind her as if checking to see if she'd been followed.

"This isn't good," he guessed, reaching out to pull her against him.

She breathed deeply, as if drawing strength from him, then eased back. "Not good." She took a backward step, hugging her arms around herself. "I don't know how to begin to say this."

"Yeah?" he asked softly.

"Things happened that I can't get into, but the bottom line is that your work is going to be graded by an outside instructor."

"Why?"

"To prove that I'm guilty of favoritism."

Finn went still. "Are you?"

"No, but it might look that way."

"I thought this…stuff…you were doing was aboveboard."

"It is," she said fiercely. "By the end of the class you would have earned your grade."

He folded his arms over his chest. "I don't know that I totally buy that."

"What do you think I'm doing, Finn? Stringing you along so that I can nail you at the end? By the end you will have an honest C."

"But right now?"

"High D."

"On a good day."

"It's better than when you walked into my classroom."

"Yes. My F days."

"You've come miles."

He had. But miles still didn't mean average, which were the grades he'd been given—on his remedial papers.

"Can you trust me on this, Finn?"

He let out breath, shifted his gaze to the opposite wall. "Looks like we both need to work on trust."

"I guess." She started to move past him, toward the door. "I'm sorry this happened. It wasn't my intention."

"Where are you going?"

"Home?"

He shook his head, his body stirring as her gaze jerked up to his. "Not unless you really want to."

Her lips parted as she stared up at him, and he reached out to take her glasses by the bows and slowly pull them off.

"Now I'm blind."

"So I can take you where I want you to go." He brought his hands up to push her silky hair back over her shoulders. "Will you come?"

"Loaded question," she said softly.

He took her face in his hands, held it as he kissed her, waited for her to make her decision. It took only a matter of seconds for her to answer his question, pull him closer, deepen the kiss. She wanted him. Didn't trust him, or maybe didn't trust herself, but wanted him all the same.

He swung her up in his arms, and still her lips clung to his. She wrapped her arms around his neck, hanging on as he carried her down the hall to his room.

"A real bed?" she murmured. "Uptown."

"I'll show you uptown." He nudged the door open with his toe and then kicked it shut behind them.

AFTER MOLLY LEFT, Finn pulled a beer out of the fridge and settled on his sofa. He didn't bother with the lights or the television. He needed the quiet and didn't mind the darkness.

He was a D student.

An honest to goodness D student…unless Molly had been amping up his grades even more than she let on.

Why would she do that? To encourage him? Because she liked him? Because she felt sorry for him.

The last thought made his stomach twist a little, but he knew that wasn't the case. Women like Molly didn't sleep with guys they felt sorry for. So was he going to become a teacher with Ds in English? He probably wouldn't be the first.

But what if he couldn't handle the other English classes he needed for his degree? What if, as a teacher, he had to write long reports and evaluate…things? Like student writing? Molly had told him that writing was becoming more and more important in all aspects of education. His weak point was the new buzzword.

Finn took a long pull on the beer. Did he want a career that made him feel inadequate? Wasn't that why he was trying to get out of the feed store? So that his specialty in life wasn't lifting grain?

At least if he fabricated metal, he'd have a specialization, a name for what he did. There was nothing wrong with owning a business. It was damned tough work, but a person was either wired for business or he wasn't. Finn wasn't. He wanted to work with his hands and he wanted to pass those skills along.

It now appeared that he needed to get real and accept that he'd be working with his hands only. He needed to shift his goal and move forward with Plan B. It wasn't as prestigious in his mind as Plan A—Finn Culver, teacher, but it was still a career he could be proud of. He could hone his skills, take a couple fabrication classes or maybe finish an entire course, since his skills were for the most part self-taught. He was good, but there were still things to know.

He brought the beer can up to his forehead, pressing the cold aluminum against his skin. There was no shame in shifting and adjusting goals. His real goal, as he saw it, was to do something he felt good about while at the same time becoming the kind of dependable nine-to-five guy that Molly was looking for. He could fit into her Mr. Right mold…and as crazy as it was after only a matter of months, that was exactly what he wanted to do.

"WHY DO EGGS never peel right when you need them to?" Georgina asked as she picked off tiny bits of shell, trying to make deviled eggs for Mike's barbecue.

"Something to do with a guy named Murphy and his law," Molly murmured. She was half looking forward to the barbecue and half dreading it. Allie would be there, with her husband-to-be, whom Molly knew of but had never met, as would Jolie and Dylan and Elaine. A nice group of people. A nice reason to relax and enjoy one of the last pretty fall weekends before winter set in, but she still felt unsettled about it.

She'd obliterated Finn's name on several examples of his work—the least differentiated. She'd included his final essay, which was short, but not bad. His latest research paper. Again, short but not bad.

But she had been generous on the grades, to make up for the way she'd treated him before. That wasn't what she was supposed to do, but she'd discovered during her first years of teaching that encouragement and praise worked better than punitive measures for students who were willing to work to improve themselves. And damn it, Finn was trying.

He might also have sunk her.

She wasn't going to allow her thoughts to go that way. Not today.

"What time is Chase coming by?"

Georgina looked up from the eggs. "He's not coming. He has some family issues. One of his little brothers got into trouble and he's dealing with it."

"What kind of trouble?"

"Underage drinking."

"Ah." Molly sat down to help peel eggs. "Where's the mother?"

"She's not well." Georgina frowned as she removed the last bit of shell from the egg she held and then placed in the bowl to be rinsed.

"How not well?"

Georgina shrugged. "I'm not sure. Chase has to take care of the kids a lot, though, which is hard when he works two part-time jobs. I think that's one reason he loves hiking so much. He can get away. Really away. Where no one can contact him about the latest emergency."

Molly concentrated on her egg, somehow keeping herself from asking Georgina how deeply she wanted to get involved with a guy who had to spend most of his time putting out fires for his family.

"I heard that Chase's dad died in prison."

Georgina's dark gaze came up. "Yes. Hepatitis. Not a shanking." She held Molly's gaze for a long moment as if challenging her to make something of it. She wasn't going to. Not now, anyway, before they were going to an event. But they were going to talk at some point. Meanwhile, she kept hoping that the new would wear off and that Georgina would find a nice college guy from a similar background as their own.

The street was lined with cars by the time Molly and Georgina left their house with the cake and the eggs, which had come out very well, if Georgina did say so herself. Elaine opened the door and ushered them in.

"Mike's out back, preparing the grill," she said.

"Great. How are you feeling?"

"Good. Good." She smiled, but Molly got the impression that she was tired of people asking about her health even if she was understanding of the fact that they need to.

She went into the kitchen where Finn was digging around in the fridge. He looked over the door as soon as she set foot in the kitchen and she felt an instant tug of attraction. He smiled at her, then went back to his search for whatever.

After setting the cake on the table, she followed her sister out the back door to the yard where the rest of the guests were relaxing in lawn chairs. Allie waved her over and the guy sitting next to her got to his feet. Molly had to tip her head back to see his eyes.

"Molly, this is my fiancé, Jason Hudson."

"Nice to meet you." He smiled congenially as his big hand swallowed hers. She'd known him by reputation only, since the former professional wide receiver had graduated from high school before she and her family moved to town.

"Same here."

Dylan and Jolie were on a blanket in the shade of the big apple tree that dominated the small backyard and Mike was at the grill, just as Elaine said. Cal and Karl were milling around nearby, both holding cans of beer and wearing loud Hawaiian shirts.

"Where's Buddy?" Molly asked Mike after saying hello.

"Safe in the house. I can't keep as close of an eye on him out here and he's still mighty small."

Mike the protector. She could see why he was so upset about Elaine, in addition to having lost two other people in his life. She patted his shoulder and went to join Georgina and the rest of the Brody-Culver-Hudson clan under the tree. When Elaine and Mike approached, Jason and Allie vacated their chairs and stretched out on the grass. Jason settled his big hand on Allie's thigh and she casually settled her own hand on top and leaned back against him. Just as with Jolie and Dylan, she was struck by the level of sheer contentment. She'd been content once, too. Believed in the dream. The dream could happen…but it was a bitch when it didn't work out.

But her dark thoughts didn't keep her from smiling when Finn joined them, sinking down into the grass beside where she was stretched out and propped on her elbows. He waited until the rest of the group was discussing new restaurants that had recently opened to lean closer and ask, "Doing okay?"

"Nervous for this upcoming week."

"Yeah. Me, too."

She dropped her head back to look at him. "This won't affect you."

"It'll force me to face the hard truth."

"The only hard truth is that Jonas is a butt."

Finn laughed. "Maybe he'll grow out of it."

"Not unless he leaves home soon and life gets a couple good swipes at him. As it is, he'll be protected for the next ten years."

He lifted a few hanks of her hair from the ground where it had pooled behind her and let them slide through his fingers and drop to the grass. It was an intimate gesture and one that Georgina caught. She sent Molly an "ah" look and then smiled a little.

Cool.

Elaine got out of her chair and Mike was instantly out of his, too. "I need to start cooking dangerously," he said. Elaine smiled at him and the two of them ambled toward the house.

"They're together because of me, you know." Cal beamed like a proud parent.

"Good job," Georgina said.

"Yeah," Cal agreed. "I wish they didn't have this health challenge ahead of them, but at least Elaine's not facing it alone. She has us."

And that was true.

The dinner was excellent—steaks, side dishes, homemade ice cream and pies. Molly ate until she was full, then ate some more. Elaine started cleaning up and Mike tried to stop her, but she waved him off. He opened his mouth as if to try again, then seemed to change his mind. Molly got to her feet and went into the house under the pretext of using the restroom, but instead intercepted Elaine in the kitchen.

"I'm going to help and you aren't going to stop me." She turned on the water in the sink as if to emphasize the point.

"You can help," Elaine said. "I just don't want Mike to be doing everything for me."

Molly smiled a little. "I can take care of that." She pulled out a phone and sent a text to Georgina that said We're doing dishes. Mike's not invited.

A few minutes later Georgina and Allie showed up at the back door, each carrying two serving dishes in each hand.

"Jolie stayed to manage Mike. She's better at it than the rest of us," Allie said.

"Who would have thought doing dishes could be fun?" Georgina remarked ten minutes later as she finished wiping the counters. She went outside to help Allie clean the picnic table and grill while Elaine stood with her hands on her hips, studying Jolie and the guys parked under the tree.

"I'm impressed she was able to keep Mike in check."

"He's driving you crazy?" Molly asked gently.

Elaine turned her gaze toward her. "He's the best guy, but...now that I'm sick, he treats me as if I'll break. He does everything for me, but he won't touch me."

"Ow."

Elaine's eyebrows went up. "No kidding. I'm doing my best to convince him that I'm not my disease. That I'm still me. We haven't been together for that long, but it feels like forever and I need more...contact than I'm getting." She blinked a couple of times and looked away, but not before Molly saw the moisture clinging to her eyelashes. "Sorry to vent. More than you wanted to hear, no doubt."

"Honestly... I don't blame you for being irked."

"Mike's hardheaded, but if I keep hammering away, maybe I'll get through." She let out a small snort. "Keeps me from thinking about my treatment, so maybe it's all good." She glanced over at Molly, then back out at the men under the tree. "Forgive me for saying that it's interesting to see how things have changed between you and Finn since the last time we spoke in this very kitchen."

Yes...that awesome conversation that Finn had overhead. Today she was going to set the record straight before moving on to safer topics.

"They haven't changed that much," she said. "We're friendlier than before, but still just friends."

"Do you honestly believe that?"

Molly narrowed her eyes at her former science teacher. "What do you mean?"

"I've made a career out of reading people. I had to for survival. Trust me, Finn isn't looking at you like a friend."

Molly's stomach tightened at the woman's adamant tone. She moistened her lips and tried again. "We know each other well…"

Another cocked eyebrow, and Molly gave up. She followed Elaine's gaze out to where Finn was sitting next to his grandfather and pressed her lips together. It wasn't fair of her to string Finn along if he wanted more than she could give.

Did he?

Why wouldn't he be happy with a mutually beneficial relationship that didn't involve the prospect of a broken heart?

She'd so thought they were on the same page. She glanced over at Elaine.

"Are you sure?"

"All I can do is tell you what gut instinct tells me. That boy likes you."

CHAPTER FIFTEEN

Monday came too soon.

Molly woke up with a headache and it only intensified when she discovered that the dean had called in sick that day. She felt like going home sick, but what good would that do?

She muscled through her classes, muscled through her evening class. When she stopped at Finn's desk after her lecture she simply said, "No results yet."

"See you later?" he asked quietly.

Molly shook her head and moved on. Denny was also out sick, so she could have probably spent more class time with Finn without fear of someone reading something into it, such as her giving him the answers or being involved in a relationship with him, but her head still hurt and she just wanted to go home, go to bed and shut out the world for a while.

Every now and again one was entitled to do just that. Tonight was her night and that was what she told Finn when he came into her office after class.

"You're sure you're okay?"

"I'm just tired." Confused. Frustrated on many levels. And uncertain as to her next move in the game of life.

"Maybe we should go hiking with Georgina and Chase this coming weekend. Get away."

"I'll have a lot of work next weekend."

"And maybe we shouldn't be seen together?"

"There's that," she agreed.

"Hell of a way to live, but I understand. I don't want to mess with your job."

"And I don't want to mess with you."

Finn stilled. "Meaning?"

"Meaning it's very important that we are on the same page here…about what we have and what we want."

He reached out to gently brush her hair back over her shoulder, his fingers caressing her neck. "I guess I want you."

Not what she'd hoped to hear. Twelve years ago she would have died of happiness at those words. Today they scared her death. He wanted her and, if she were honest, she wanted him… but wanting was the first step toward heartbreak. The first step toward getting into a situation where control was out the window and another person's actions could destroy you.

"Finn." Her voice grew husky. "That isn't going to happen. Not in the way I think you want."

"What? In like a real relationship way?"

"I don't want a real relationship, Finn. I can't handle one. I don't want to deal with the uncertainty that comes with a relationship."

Finn stepped back and regarded her for a moment, then wiped a hand over his face. "We all have baggage, Molly."

"True."

"We don't have to carry it alone."

"Some of us choose to carry it alone."

"Why?"

"I fought hard for my independence and I don't want to compromise it."

"How will being with me compromise your independence? I'm not pushy."

"I don't know that, Finn. We haven't been together."

"And you won't risk getting to know what I'm like in a relationship?" He moved closer. "You can always leave later."

It was too damned hard to leave *now*, and they'd barely gotten started. "That isn't fair to you."

"It is if I know what I'm getting into."

Molly tipped up her chin. "You knew it a few days ago and you're fighting me now."

"Are you not willing to take a chance because I don't fit your cookie-cutter description of your perfect guy? The one you mentioned to Elaine? Mr. Boring and Dependable?"

"The one you heard about while eavesdropping."

He narrowed his beautiful eyes at her. "Yeah. That one. Would you loosen up and take a chance if I were that guy?"

"But you aren't that guy. You will never be that guy."

"The problem is you, Molly. You let one bad situation color everything in your whole freaking life. We are good together. We are great together. And guess what? I am dependable. You don't need a college degree to be dependable. I can show you plenty of guys who do have the paper who aren't."

"I'm not some kind of a snob. I just know the characteristics that will work best for me."

"Invisible and absent?"

Molly mouth hardened. "Those will do for a start." Her chin dropped for a moment. This wasn't good. It wasn't fair. She looked back up at Finn. "I love your company. I love being with you in bed. But it—"

"Has no substance?"

"Damn it, Finn. I'm trying to save us both some heartache."

He jerked his chin up. "Guess what? It's too late for me." His mouth clamped shut and then he muttered, "I can't believe I just said such a douchey thing."

"Finn…" The look he gave her stopped her from saying more. Froze the words in her throat. A moment later he was gone, the door closing behind him with a cold *click*.

Molly leaned back against her desk, her fingers gripping the edge. What in the hell had she done? Right move? Wrong move?

The only move.

DEAN STEWART WAS back at work on Tuesday and he invited Molly into his office after her last class of the day. She settled in the hot seat once again, folded her hands in her lap. And waited.

The dean made a show of studying the papers in front of him, although Molly was certain he'd already been over them—probably a couple of times.

"Your marks are high," he said.

"I told you. I might have erred on the side of optimism."

"I see from the dates that you've given me a progression over time."

"I wanted you to see that he's improving."

"And he has." The dean leaned back in his chair, tapping a pencil against his lower lip. "But we aren't in the business of remediation during our normal classes, English Basic Comp being one of those."

Molly took a deep breath. "I thought I could help him. And we don't have a remedial English class offered until next semester." The instructor was on paternity leave and everyone else's schedules were overloaded.

"We need to adjust this student's grades."

"It's not fair to fail him when he's come this far." And she'd just emotionally skewered him less than twenty-four hours ago. She had to stop thinking about that. If he wanted more than she could give, then it was the only thing she could do.

The dean set his pencil down. "I didn't say fail. But he's a D student."

"What if he gets a diagnosis?"

"He can retake the class with provisions for his disability. I'm totally on board for differentiated assignments. Given the lack of a remedial class, it makes sense. But he has to have the skills we say he has when he finishes the course."

"Of course he does." Molly leaned forward. "I don't want this guy to feel like a failure. That won't do any of us any good."

"Are you involved with him?"

"I'm not." Her words were instantaneous and adamant. She was no longer involved with him—and the short time she was, she would hold close. "But I want him to succeed. I want all my students to succeed. Even Jonas. I use grades to encourage and inspire. In Finn's case they encourage and in Jonas's they were supposed to inspire him to try harder."

"You did well there, as you will see with our next Simon meeting."

"Another?" Molly asked weakly.

"Tomorrow at five o'clock."

"What happens to Finn?"

"The grades will change, but since the midterm and final projects count for the most, he can rescue himself."

He. As in him alone. That was how it would have to be, if he even continued in the course.

Molly felt like growling as she left the dean's office, but she managed a smile at Penny and a few cordial nods on her way down the hall. Teachers were such great actors. She went into her office, closed the door and leaned back against it.

At least she hadn't heard the words *You're fired.*

Yet. She still had quite of bit of time left in the semester and the remainder of the evaluation process to get through. She gathered her grading into her briefcase, jammed the lid shut and thanked her lucky stars that the hallway was now empty. She started for the entrance, her footsteps echoing on the tile floor—a sound she usually loved because it meant she was where she wanted to be. Now she wasn't.

You wanted to teach. You signed on for this.

She had. Most of the time she loved her job, and she'd known going in there'd be conflicts with students, parents, other instructors, administrators.

She hadn't counted on the Finn part.

MOLLY SEARCHED THE CUPBOARDS, then finally gave up and leaned back against the dishwasher and put her forehead in her hand.

No chips.

How could that have happened?

She paced into the living room, turned around and paced back. She was never one to pour her problems out to others, but now she really and truly wished that Georgina was home so that she could discuss the events of the day—even if it meant coming clean about things that had happened between her and Finn. Her sister was an adult and she'd already clued in to the fact that she and Finn were more than mere acquaintances…or at least had been. Her sister had a good head on her shoulders. She could deal and damn it, Molly needed to talk to someone. And she needed chips.

But Georgina wasn't at home, which meant that Molly had the whole empty house to herself. The place had never seemed so big. Or echo-y. And she hadn't felt so uncomfortable with herself since Blake had first left—before the anger had set in, when she'd been dealing with the bewildering pain of his betrayal. Mourning the loss of an illusion.

But now she was once again dealing with a loss. Things between her and Finn were never going to be the same, and she'd never be in his bed again. She probably shouldn't have been there in the first place, but at that point their perceptions of their situation had been in alignment. They were enjoying each other. A lot.

Now they weren't because their wants, needs...perceptions...were no longer in line with each other's.

Temporary mourning. That's all. She hadn't been with Finn long enough for it to be anything else.

She went into her room and flopped down on her bed, dragging a pillow over her face, shutting out the light. Darkness felt right. She could deal with entitled Jonas and his influential family and whatever they might throw at her. She could even deal with losing her job—even though she hoped it didn't come to that.

She just needed to gather her strength, get it together. She needed to reassess.

FINN COOLED HIS HEELS in the waiting room of the administrative office, feeling very much as if he were waiting to see the principal, which in essence, he was. The only difference between now and high school was that back then, he'd at least had an inkling of the crime he'd committed. Right now, he didn't have a clue as to what was about to happen. He assumed it had something to do with Molly and his grades, but until he saw the dean, he wouldn't know for certain.

At the moment he was more concerned about Molly than his grades. It hadn't taken long after their recent blowup for him to realize that he'd essentially reneged on his promise to her. They'd had the fun times he promised...but he'd also been moving in the direction of a relationship. It was part of a natural progression. They did well together, so why not spend time together? A lot of time.

But Molly wasn't ready and she'd been candid about that. She had strong ideas about what she needed in life to achieve that security that was so important to her and he needed to give her time to understand that he was trustworthy and dependable—that he wasn't like the jerk she'd cut loose after he'd done whatever to her.

"Finn Culver?"

He looked up to see a slightly built man in a neat suit standing in the doorway. "I'm Dean Stewart. Thank you for coming."

"Not a problem."

The dean ushered him into his office and closed the door. He waved him to a chair and then, instead of moving behind his desk, took the chair beside him.

"How has your experience been here at Eagle Valley Community College?"

"A little bumpy in the beginning, but it's gotten better."

"Glad to hear that." The dean hesitated for a moment, then said, "Do you know why you're here?"

He shook his head, having learned a long time ago to give nothing away.

"We've been investigating some grading practices here at the school and your grades were some that we took a closer look at."

"I can understand that."

"You can?"

"Ms. Adamson was trying to teach me four years of English in one semester. I…wasn't all that motivated in high school English. Plus, it appears I'm dyslexic."

"I see."

"So to help me deal with my problem, Ms.

Adamson shortened my assignments, saying it was better to practice something well a few times, rather than to practice it badly a lot of times."

The dean considered for a moment, then nodded. "Good advice."

"My brain is not a big fan of organization—not the kind involved in writing, so she helped me with some techniques to help me sort things out. She's done me a lot of good."

The dean glanced down at the floor, then back up at Finn. "Your grades are too high."

"How much too high?"

"You have Cs. You should have high Ds, according to other instructors who have read your work."

"Yeah. I can see that. But I'm getting better. Before Ms. Adamson knew about my difficulty, she graded my first paper...thoroughly. Once she figured things out about the dyslexia, she came to me, encouraged me not to drop the class and offered extra help." He drummed his fingers on the arm of his chair as he tried to figure his best tactic. He decided to go with honesty. "She's a good teacher. She shouldn't get in trouble because of me. I'm not your usual student. Hell—" he cracked a smile "—I'm barely a student. But I feel more like one now than I did when I first started."

"I see that your math scores are good."

"Never had a problem with math. I still don't."

"What is your career goal?"

"I'd hoped to…" He couldn't say it. How could he tell this guy that he couldn't handle basic English, but he wanted to teach? "Figure that out. Guess I won't be an English major."

The dean allowed himself a weak smile. "I guess not. You understand that the majority of your grade comes from the end-of-term project. You can still earn a C, but the daily grades will be reduced."

"Do what you have to do."

"We value you as a student, but you understand that we have a reputation to uphold."

"And students like me don't help you out much."

"That wasn't what I said."

Finn simply smiled and got to his feet. "I appreciate the heads-up about the grades. Ms. Adamson is a good instructor. You'd be foolish to let her go."

And he'd be foolish to continue as he was, wasting people's time. He was better, but he was never going to be much more than a D student in English. He had other skills and maybe it was time to see about using them rather than trying to teach them.

Rather than go back to the feed store, Finn did

something he probably should have done a while ago. He consulted the campus map and found the ag mechanics building. Since he attended night classes, most buildings were closed by the time he arrived, so he never investigated what ag mechanics had to offer. Perhaps the instructors would have an idea of how he could best use the skills he did have—whether they had career and course options more in the line with his specific talents. Maybe he wouldn't be making a huge difference in society, helping people achieve their goals, but he could fix their cars and bend their metal.

When he pulled open the door, he was hit by smells that made him feel instantly at home— diesel, lubricants, engine sludge. The hall was only half-lit and all the doors were closed with the exception of one at the very end of the hall. A faint metallic banging came from inside, making Finn feel even more at home.

Having perused the college catalog many times while trying to decide what he wanted to do with his life, he knew EVCC offered certification in diesel mechanics, ag mechanics, automotives and metal fabrication. While all those subjects interested him, he didn't need training in them. He'd wanted to *do* the training. Make a difference. Help people. Kind of like Molly had helped him…

Once he reached the open door, he stepped inside a brightly lit shop that put his to shame. The banging came from a corner to his left, where a guy in a blue shop coat was hammering away on a vintage fender. Finn ambled closer and the guy suddenly stopped hammering as he realized he wasn't alone. He straightened up and Finn realized the guy was a woman.

"Hey," she said, setting the neoprene weighted hammer down on the bench. "Can I help you?"

"I hope so." Finn tucked a thumb in his front pocket. "I'm a metal fabricator and a student."

"You're Finn Culver."

He squinted at the woman. "Barney?"

She smiled widely. "Yes!"

Julia Barnes had been a fixture in the ag shop at high school. Some people thought she never took any other classes, although he'd had history with her once, which killed that theory. "Your hair's a lot shorter."

She pushed her fingers through her two-inch-long brown hair. "Made sense to cut it. I got tired of trying to keep it out of machinery."

"That does seem like a good idea."

She moved closer, smiling widely. "Age didn't hurt you none."

"Uh…thanks?"

"You're welcome." She settled a hip on a piece

of I-beam standing on end next to her. "What can I help you with?"

"I… It's kind of a long story."

She motioned to the tractor seat welded to a large stiff spring. "Pull up a seat."

Finn knew looking at it that he wouldn't be pulling that thing anywhere. He sat and found it surprisingly comfortable. "I served overseas with the Guard."

"I heard."

"Came back and wanted to do something other than the feed store." He paused and then said, "I wanted to do what I think you're doing."

"Teaching ag shop?"

"Yeah. Only I wanted to do automotives. I signed up for a math class and an English class here at the college to test the waters. I'm doing great in math and I suck in English. I think it'll take me about ten years or taking English over and over again to get an education degree, because you have to take several classes."

"You want to teach high school."

"I thought that would be better than junior high."

"Why not teach community college? You only need a two-year degree for that."

Finn blinked at her. "That wasn't in the catalog."

Barney leaned forward. "They pretty much

take any two-year degree as long as you have the skills…" She gave an appraising nod. "If I recall, you do."

"I worked in the motor pool in the service. All kinds of vehicles."

"I'll tell you a secret, Finn. We have trouble keeping people because they can make more money elsewhere."

He cocked his head. "So…you're saying that teaching at a community college might be easier than getting certified to teach in a high school."

"And you don't have to put up with as much attitude." She made a face. "Some, but not as much."

"Maybe I won't drop my English class."

"If you can pass that sucker, I wouldn't."

FINN ENDED UP missing his English class, which was better, he supposed, than dropping it, which was what he'd fully intended to do after leaving the administrative offices. But now, after spending close to an hour with Barney, going over requirements, he wondered why no one made it clear that it was possible to do something other than prepare for a regular education degree. After dealing with both Jonas and Denny, he figured he was a lot better prepared mentally to deal with the likes of them.

He stopped by Molly's office the next after-

noon to find out what he'd missed and to tell her
he was okay with his new grade—as long as it
didn't get any lower. He wasn't exactly proud of
a D, but it was passing and after talking to Barney, he realized that he could take the class again
and replace the grade if he needed to.

He knocked on the door frame and Molly
jumped, causing her glasses to slip down her
nose. She automatically pushed them up again
and he came into the room.

"I just want to tell you that I'm okay with my
grade being lowered."

"You can still get a C—"

"Yeah. I know. If I do well on the final term
paper." He didn't sit in the chair across from her
desk as usual. "I almost dropped your class after
talking to the dean yesterday."

Her mouth opened, but before she could
speak, he said, "I didn't. Instead I spent a long
time talking to the ag mechanics instructor.
She's an old friend. Remember Julia Barnes?"

Molly frowned, then her expression cleared.
"Barney. Never had real classes. Spent all of her
time in shop."

Finn smiled briefly in spite of himself. "That's
the one. There's a possibility that I can take a
two-year course and teach automotive or metal
fabrication here at EVCC. And if not here, then
at another community college. Two years," he

reiterated. "Not four. One English class. Not as many courses, not as much writing."

Molly's expression seemed frozen.

"You okay?" he asked.

"Finn...more than anything I want you to be successful in whatever you want to do."

How very formal. "I thought...look. This is me getting into something I can do. Something I can make a career out of. Something dependable." He gave her a long look. "That was the key word, right? *Dependable?*"

"There's more to it than that."

"Like what?"

Molly looked past him to the door as if hoping that someone would come in and save her. They didn't, so she drew in a long breath before saying, "Here's the problem, Finn. I care for you, okay? More than I can handle." She gritted the words out from between clenched teeth. "I care for you more than I want to."

"Then why can't we work this out? See if we have what it takes to make a relationship?"

"I don't want a relationship. I don't want to lose myself. I don't want to try to balance someone else's life with my own."

"So this had nothing to do with me not fitting your idea of the guy you need in your life. There isn't a perfect guy, because you don't want a guy."

"I'm *afraid* to want a guy, okay? I already spent my time as a doormat."

She could have smacked him and it would have startled him less. "You think that I would treat you as a doormat? Without giving me a chance?"

Molly's hands were clasped tightly in front of her and Finn wondered if they would be shaking if she wasn't holding on to them. "I like being on my own."

He didn't believe her. She liked having no waves in her life. She liked the aura of security that not taking chances gave her. But he knew that it was just an aura. Shit happened no matter what.

"No guts. No glory." The words dropped from his lips one by one.

Her chin came up. "I go with no glory."

"That's too bad, Molly. You're going to miss a lot of life."

"But I'll be my own boss. In control of my destiny."

Finn pressed a hand to his forehead and squeezed, then dropped it again. "You win." He smiled humorlessly. "I tried. I'm done."

Finn turned and walked out the door. What else could he do? He'd tried twice and that was it. With his frustration red-lining, he stalked down the hall and rounded a corner too fast, practically running over Jonas, who stepped back quickly and then snarled at him, "Watch where you're going."

Oh, yeah. He was going to take crap from this kid now on top of everything else.

"I have an issue with you." Finn closed the distance between them. "You've been spreading rumors about me."

"I have not…" An odd look crossed the kid's face as he realized that the accusations he'd lobbed at Molly also included Finn.

"That's right," Finn said softly. "I'm not involved with my instructor, and spreading the rumor has the potential to do me harm, for which I will have to seek redress." *Thank you,* Law & Order *reruns.*

"My father has lawyers on retainer."

"Who are going to prove what? That you lied? That you made unfounded accusations in an effort to do me harm?"

"Not you," the kid sneered.

"Then who?"

Jonah realized his mistake too late. "This conversation never happened." He settled his backpack higher on his shoulder and brushed past Finn.

Finn continued on to the parking lot, catching a glimpse of his reflection in his truck window before he opened the door. No wonder Jonas had given up so easily. Finn wouldn't have pushed around a guy who looked like him.

He got into his truck and then let his head fall back against the seat.

When had he fallen so hard for Molly?

And why couldn't she trust herself enough to love him back? This had nothing to do with him proving himself or getting a steady career that would last forever, or joining a bowling team, being generally sedate, predictable and boring. This was about Molly's inability to get over the scars of her past.

He jammed his key in the ignition and turned it.

And there wasn't a hell of a lot that he could do about that.

CHAPTER SIXTEEN

FINN WENT THROUGH the motions of life for almost a week. He ate, he drank, he attempted to sleep. He missed Molly. He was pissed at her and he missed her. Mostly he missed her.

He, who enjoyed meeting challenges head-on, who'd muscled through an English class that embarrassed him more times than he liked to think about, couldn't muscle his way through this challenge, and it gnawed at him.

There was literally nothing he could do. So he went to class, pretended everything was normal, as did Molly, and started working on his term project, which would take the last four weeks of the semester to complete. Jolie had already offered to give him some help in the organization, and the rest he was determined to do on his own.

And it was hell being in the room with Molly having things between them the way they were. He'd shoot her a look every now and again, try not to remember how he'd been so consumed with her when they'd slept together. How that husky voice of hers sounded whispering soft, almost-dirty things in his ear. Telling him what she wanted.

Well, now he knew what she didn't want. Something that involved any kind of permanence or commitment.

He stopped by Mike's house after math class on Thursday, having called first as Mike had asked. Elaine was there, sitting in the second recliner, looking as if she'd been part of Mike's life forever.

She smiled at him and apologized for being a little tired.

"She had her first radiation treatment," Mike said. "It went well." He reached out and took her hand, and she squeezed his fingers.

"They're very hopeful that I'll be cancer-free within a few months," Elaine said.

"Excellent."

Mike patted Elaine's hand, then got to his feet and motioned to the kitchen door with his head. Finn followed and as soon as they were out of sight of the living room, Mike asked, "What's going on?"

"What are you talking about?"

"You look like you're going to murder someone."

"I'm fine."

"You looked like you were going to murder

someone when you stopped by last Monday. That's a full week with no change of expression."

"Only five days," Finn muttered, shoving his thumbs in his back pockets. "And I'm fine. Nothing's wrong."

"Don't make me ask Georgina."

"What could she possibly know?" he asked coldly.

"Well, she knew that I'd better snap to my senses with Elaine because I was causing her stress."

Finn wrinkled his brow. "Georgina told you that?"

"No one else would."

"I think we tried to tell you that. Dylan, Jolie and I."

"She was pretty damned direct. And I'm grateful. Now what the hell is wrong with you?"

"Molly and I aren't seeing eye to eye."

"What are you going to do about it?"

"I wish I knew. She had a bad time with her last relationship and now I'm paying the price." He glanced up at his grandfather. "That guy has caused me no end of troubles."

Mike settled a hand on his shoulder. "You two need to get together and work this out."

"Thank you," Finn said darkly. "I never thought of that."

Mike's expression softened an iota. "Sorry.

Stupid advice." He let out a soft sigh. "You'd better take Buddy."

Finn gave him a perplexed look, but Mike just smiled. "Take him. You'll feel better."

Fifteen minutes later, Finn said his goodbyes and he and Buddy headed for his truck. As she closed the door behind him, he heard Elaine say, "Is he going to be all right?"

"Damn, I hope so," Mike replied.

So did Finn. And he hoped he still had kitty litter at his house. Otherwise, he and Buddy would be doing a late-night run to the grocery store.

But as the little guy wound around his neck and made bread on his shoulder, Finn found himself beginning to relax—at least to the point that his knuckles were no longer turning white on the steering wheel.

RAIN BEAT DOWN on the roof, but the garage drain that Finn and Chase had snaked was working well. No flood today. Georgina poured her cereal and they bought up the weather forecast for the coming weekend.

"It's supposed to stop today. Chase said that will probably be enough time for the trails to dry. One last hike before winter. Then he's going to teach me to ski." She scooped up a spoonful of raisin bran. "It's expensive, though, so it'll be more of a once-a-month thing. We've talked about cross-country skiing. That sounds kind of fun."

"How're things with his brother?" Georgina looked up. "The one caught drinking?"

Her sister gave a casual shrug. "Community service."

"Ah." Molly waited a few seconds, then said, "Are any of his other siblings in trouble?"

Georgina gave her a look. "I'll ask. Let you know tonight."

Molly continued to eat. *Well-played, little sister.* But then Molly's game was off of late. Very off. She blamed…herself.

Class with Finn wasn't as horrible as she'd thought it might be, if one didn't count the unrelenting unspoken tension. He did his work. She did her job. Denny always claimed her attention at the end of class and Finn left before Denny finished expounding.

It worked.

It also sucked.

Hell. Who was she trying to kid? She missed him.

She and Georgina drove to campus together. When they didn't talk about Chase, it was life as usual. She liked life as usual. It was what she was trying so hard to preserve. A life without bad surprises. There would be sacrifices, of course. Nothing came without a price, but these sacrifices paid off, unlike the sacrifices she'd made for Blake.

She had yet another Jonas meeting today. The follow-up to the previous meeting, in which they would see the big grade reveal. Waste of time, but the Simons had donated land…

"Are you okay?" Molly looked up to see Allie Brody peeking into her office.

"I'm fine." Molly worked up a smile.

Allie leaned her shoulder on the door frame, crossing her arms over her chest. "None of my business, of course, but you've seemed kind of preoccupied the last couple of times I've seen you. If there's anything I can do… Talk… Listen…"

Molly considered for a moment before saying, "We've only seen each other twice in the past couple days."

"Good point," Allie said with a small nod. "Rumor has it Finn is cranky and you're a million miles away and… I've been there. Not that long ago. I also know what it's like to have no one except for a protective sister to talk to, and your sister is pretty darned young."

"Thanks," Molly said. "I'm okay."

No, you're not. You need distraction.

"But I wouldn't mind coffee and general conversation." She felt almost as alone as she had after breaking it off with Blake, and Allie was right about Georgina being young. Molly discussed a lot of stuff with her little sister, but her sex life wasn't one of those things. Not that she was going to discuss it with Allie, but the idea of just talking, about anything, made her feel a little less alone.

"Sounds good," Allie said. "Let me get my purse."

They went to the student union, a place that was not all that conducive to private conversation. Who could talk about personal matters when surrounded by students? But as luck would have it, the place was nearly empty. Only a few students had claimed tables and they all had their heads down, studying.

"Quiet day," Allie murmured.

"Getting closer to finals."

"I get to teach two classes next semester. One evening. One day."

"This could work into full-time," Molly said as she stirred cream into her coffee.

"I don't know that I'd want full-time. There's still a lot to do on the ranch. We're rebuilding the main house and even though Jolie and Dylan are back in residence, they already have jobs elsewhere." Allie shook her head. "A couple days a week is good."

They discussed the ranch, the odd weather—

first so dry that fires ravaged the area, then so wet that there'd been a very real danger of flooding, and now somewhere in between—and then, after a short spell of silence, Molly said, "I really appreciate your checking in with me. I'm fine, but you're right—there are just some things you can't discuss with your little sister."

"Trust me. I know. I have three of them."

"And I'm curious...you said you've been through this yourself. Did it work out?" Or had it been some guy before Jason, who was responsible for the rock the size of Kansas on her left hand.

"Not without me giving a serious shot at keeping it from working. Fortunately, I have a guy with the patience of Job. He waited me out. Helped me see reason." Molly tilted her head curiously and Allie continued, "I had this thing about loss. And guess what? If you don't have anything, you don't lose anything."

Molly wasn't a big fan of loss, but she could deal. That wasn't her issue.

"I just don't want to get serious," she said. "I was in a long-term relationship and kind of lost myself in it. After that...well, I'm not looking for anything too deep. I've done deep." She gave her head a shake. "Too deep. No longer a fan." And then she abandoned her intention of not getting too personal because, damn it, she needed to vent. "All I wanted with Finn was a casual relationship. I made that clear before anything happened. Honest, I did."

"And how did you see this ending?"

Molly blinked at her. "I guess I didn't think about that." Who thought about things ending when they were just beginning?

"So the relationship was just going to peter out?"

"Yes?"

"Did it?"

Molly wasn't certain she liked this line of questioning, but Allie, being one of four sisters, was doing a pretty good job of sticking her nose into Molly's business in a way that Molly almost felt as if she had to hear the answers—even if they came out of her own mouth.

"No."

"Why do you think that is?" Allie set her chin on her folded hands, watching her carefully.

"Because I let it go too far," Molly said automatically.

Allie nodded thoughtfully, as if she were a doctor making a diagnosis. "Just one more question," she promised.

"Go ahead." What did she have to lose?

"Why did you let it go too far?"

"Because Finn is hot and I have no willpower."

"And that's all?"

"You said only one more question."

Allie smiled a little. "Well, maybe you can just think on that last one."

THE MEETING WITH the Simons showed every sign of being more of the same. The Simons were there to protect their son and to secure punishments for those who had wronged him. Molly pretty much being the major wrongdoer of the day.

After smiling at both Simons and forcing them to shake hands by offering hers and hoping aloud that they were well, Molly took her seat and waited for beleaguered Dean Stewart to start the meeting.

The office door opened and Molly looked back to see one of her colleagues come in.

"This is Mr. Cortez," the dean informed Mr. and Mrs. Simon.

Molly nodded a hello, taking care not to look too friendly, since Mrs. Simon was watching her carefully. She and Luis Cortez hadn't spoken often, because he was almost as shy as she'd once been, but she'd covered his classes while he'd had the family emergency. Of all the faculty, she was glad he had done the grading. She trusted him to be fair.

"I've had Mr. Cortez review Jonas's papers," the dean explained, bringing the attention back to him. Mrs. Simon sat a little taller. "In fact, I had copies typed of two of his problem papers and had Mr. Cortez grade them blind and then compared his results to those of Ms. Adamson's."

He set four papers on his desk. "Mr. Cortez marked in blue. Ms. Adamson in red."

Everyone leaned forward and it was all Molly could do not to smile. One grade was the same as hers and the other was two points lower.

Mrs. Simon sat back with an audible sniff. "Did Mr. Cortez know that Jonas is a high school student?"

"In this class he isn't."

The Simons didn't like that pronouncement. "So," Mr. Simon said slowly, as if he was in the process of making either a major realization or a major accusation, "you're saying that Jonas is a B student."

The guy appeared to be flabbergasted.

"It appears so," Dean Stewart replied. "Given the evidence before us."

"But this will ruin his GPA." Mrs. Simon sounded horrified.

"I'm sure he has time to fix this, if he chooses to apply himself." For the first time ever, Molly saw the dean's usually mild expression go stern. "He's not, you know. And I'm saying this with Jonas's best interests at heart. This is community college. If he goes to a four-year school next year with this same work ethic…"

The dean suddenly clammed up, as if realizing he may be screwing up the next campus land donation. He put a hand up to his mouth and gave a slight cough. "Transition is always a challenge and Jonas is young."

Molly kept her mouth shut, knowing they were looking for something, anything, to jump on, in order to remove the blame for Jonas's performance from Jonas himself.

"What about that other student?" Mr. Simon demanded. "The one getting the false marks?"

"Federal law prohibits me from discussing that matter with anyone other than the student and the instructors."

Mrs. Simon gathered her purse. "I suppose you also don't care that Jonas was threatened yesterday."

"Threatened? That's a serious accusation."

Mr. Simon gave his wife a nudge and Mrs. Simon lifted her chin. "I think we've received all the satisfaction we can expect." She got to her feet. "We will, of course, be discussing the matter with Dr. Womack."

The dean nodded. "Of course."

He waited until the door was closed behind the Simons before muttering, "Tell him I said hi."

Molly waited until Luis Cortez had left before rising to her feet and coming to stand in front of the dean's desk. "Will this incident affect my professional evaluation?"

"There will be a record, but no."

Relief made her knees feel a little wobbly. "Thank you."

"No," he said softly. "Thank you. Keep fighting the good fight."

Molly nodded and left his office, carrying with her the uncomfortable feeling that she was getting better at running away than fighting. And that didn't make her feel very proud.

Molly thanked her lucky stars that the hallway was now empty as she started for the entrance, so she didn't have to pretend to be unaffected by the meeting.

You wanted to teach.

Her head was throbbing by the time she made her way to her car—one of the few in the nearly empty lot. Most people, with the exception of Luis Cortez and Allie, whom she'd heard in the art studio, and the dean, were eating dinner with their families. Soon she'd be home deep into a bag of potato chips. Unless Georgina was there. Then it would be something healthy, chased by potato chips.

Parked next to her car was a low-slung sports car that had seen better days. A perfect student fixer-upper, not old enough to be classic, but not new enough to be cool. Molly had just noticed the Arizona plates when the door opened and the bane of her existence stepped out onto the pavement. Molly was so stunned that all she could do was think that this was perfect timing on Blake's part, because she'd just been wondering how her day could get worse.

Blake was still beautiful. Tall, very muscular, chiseled features. Pretty damned close to perfect. Even the strands of premature gray that threaded through his dark hair made him look hotter.

Molly was so very done with hot. Hot dulled her protective instincts.

"Good to see you, Blake. Did you bring the check for the house?"

He smiled at her and he was watching her closely, as he did when he was about to work things. "Not yet."

"How's Butte?" Other than too damned close.

"Not what I expected. There's, like, a copper mine in the middle of town."

"It's a pit, I believe." Molly closed her mouth then and waited—waited for Blake to explain why he was here in person, upsetting her life yet again. It was amazing how the guy who had once been the center of her world now made her feel so angry—more at herself than at him. Not that she wasn't still plenty pissed at him. It was as if he were the incarnation of all the mistakes she'd made after leaving home.

No—that was exactly what he was. Mistakes she would not repeat.

"I have to admit to being mystified as to why you're here. Why you sent me flowers."

"So you got the message?"

"Message received and denied," she said lightly, determined not to show him how much he could still upset her.

He let out breath and then pressed his lips together as he contemplated the ground near his expensive athletic shoes. "We were good together."

"You cheated on me."

He looked up at her then, his eyes so amazingly blue and dazzling that she thought it was a shame they were wasted on such a rat. "I was wrong to do that."

"For over two years."

"It was a mistake."

"It's also unforgiven." Molly paused. "No. It's forgiven, but for me, not for you." And then she couldn't help but add, "I did everything for you while you were out on the road disrespecting me."

"It wasn't disrespect. It was nothing. Those women meant nothing."

"Yet your teammates knew their names."

They'd had the groupie discussion before—several times—and it sickened her that he thought of these woman more as bed warmers and arm candy than as people. She was not having the discussion again. Not when her heart was pounding against her ribs out of sheer anger and her headache was getting worse. "You've made trust a hard thing for me, Blake. I'll never get back to where I was before I met you."

"We can go to counseling. I've looked into it."

Molly gaped at him. She'd suggested counseling once and he'd told her they could work things out alone. "Go to hell, Blake."

"You're a hard bitch, Molly."

She laughed and it felt good, if not a little hysterical. "I've worked hard to get there."

He reached into his shirt pocket and pulled out a folded piece of paper and thrust it toward her. Molly took it automatically and unfolded it. A personal check made out to her.

"I thought you said—"

"The boat. Not the house. It was supposed to be a peace offering."

"Then we'd get back together?" And she could embark on another journey of paranoia? She thought not.

"It's part of what you owe me, Blake. And that's it." And it wouldn't come close to paying for the damage he'd done her. She dug into her purse and pulled out one of her business cards. "Mail the next check if the house ever sells. And do not *ever* come see me in person again."

After Blake got into his sad sports car and ripped out of the lot, Molly got into her car and sat for several long minutes before finally putting the key in the ignition.

Something wasn't right.

As soon as she got home she dropped her bag on the sofa next to Georgina's laundry and booted up her laptop.

It didn't take too much of a search to bring up a sports gossip site and discover that Blake's newest woman had allegedly hated Butte. The picture with the article had a Photoshopped rip between Blake in his new uniform and his lady, who was a systems analyst—no surprise there, because Blake liked his women smart, yet docile. Apparently this one wasn't so docile and now he needed a replacement.

Molly was nearby...

She shut the lid to the laptop a little too hard, then quickly tested it to make certain she hadn't damaged it. Blake had screwed up enough things in her life.

The laptop was fine and Molly leaned back in her chair. She'd cash the check, put the money toward something useful yet not tangible. Like six months of rent. That way she wouldn't have to look at a new sofa, which she needed, and think of the scars Blake had left her with.

CHAPTER SEVENTEEN

SOMETIMES IT SEEMED to Molly that her sister was spending more time with Mike and Elaine than she was at home. And she knew why. Georgina didn't appreciate Molly's concerns over her relationship with Chase, so when she wasn't studying, she often slipped around the chain-link fence and went visiting. Molly missed her sister time, but she also had legitimate concerns. Her sister didn't have the experience she had and Molly would not see her make the same mistakes.

Things came to a head as Georgina was getting ready to go on her last fall hike. She finished lacing her boots, then leaned back in the chair and said, "Go ahead. I'm ready."

"For what?"

"A few strategic questions about my boyfriend."

Molly sat on the edge of the sofa on the opposite side of the small room from where Georgina sat. "You know I'm only asking out of concern."

"And I also know that you're not my mom."

Georgina got to her feet and picked up her day pack from where it was leaning against the chair. "You mean well. I get that. But Moll? You can't project what happened to you onto me."

"I'm not doing that."

"You are."

"Just the mistake parts."

"The perceived mistakes." Georgina's jaw was tight, a sure sign that she was holding her temper. "I like Chase for who he is. Not for who his dad was or what his brothers do. I like *him*."

"Those other things affect him and thereby affect you."

"He's dependable, Molly. He doesn't lie."

"That you know of."

Sudden anger flashed in her sister's eyes. "*Stop it*, Molly. Stop judging everyone on the merits on one washed-up asshole ballplayer who used his dick for reassurance that he was the best thing ever. Just…stop."

Molly opened her mouth to answer, but no words came out. Georgina hoisted her pack onto her shoulder. "I'm late. I'll see you tonight."

She strode to the door without another word and left the house. The door closed behind her with a careful *click*, leaving Molly staring at the oak panels, still with no words.

Slowly she sank down onto the sofa.

Georgina's words rang just a little too true. As did Finn's.

Was she damaged by the past? Yes. Was she working to get better?

In some ways and not others. In her professional and social life, yes. In her personal life… not really.

It was natural to avoid pain.

But not if it meant avoiding living.

Not when it meant letting a guy with a dick problem ruin your future.

Okay. She'd make peace with her sister when she got home. Try harder to not react to deep knee-jerk fears. Maybe work her way toward trust, as in trust in her own judgment and accept that sometimes she was going to be wrong and when she was, there would be consequences.

So damned scary, that.

FINN WAS IN the warehouse when the call came in that someone wanted to see him. If it had been Molly, he was pretty certain that Lola would have teased him rather than barking that he was wanted.

When he got into the store he could see why Lola had barked. The couple standing next to the counter looked distinctly out of place in a feed store—even one with a boutique.

"May I help you?"

"We would like to speak in private."

"Sure." He walked to the office and opened the door. For once Karl and Cal weren't there. He gestured to the couple and they walked inside.

"How can I help you?"

"We are Jonas Simon's parents," the woman said.

"You're kidding."

The woman blinked at him. "Why?"

Finn made a gesture. "Please. Go on."

"We're not certain if you realize how difficult it is for a high school student to tackle college."

"I know how hard it is for me," he said candidly.

Mr. Simon nodded. "I can imagine."

Finn's jaw muscles tightened, but he let the remark pass. "Why are you here?"

"Jonas said you threatened him."

"With legal action. Not fists or anything."

"Legal action?" The guy seemed thoroughly stunned. Apparently Jonas had left out that detail.

"He spread rumors about our instructor and me that were not true." At the time. But technicalities counted. He settled a hip on the desk. "Even if they were true, it would be none of his business. If he was made to feel uncomfortable, it's because he barged into Ms. Adamson's office hours whenever it suited him, whether another student was in there or not. At least one time that other student was me."

"Why would he make up such a rumor?" Mrs. Simon asked.

"My guess would be revenge." Finn lifted his eyebrows. "Anything else?"

"You can't prove this."

Finn gave a short, humorless laugh. "Guess what? I don't want to. I just wanted your kid to think before he attacked." And he didn't mind wiping the superior look off his face for all of a split second. He got back to his feet. "How did you find me?"

"Wasn't hard. Jonas knew your name."

Finn shook his head and led the way to the door. "Tell your kid that there are other people on the planet who matter."

Mrs. Simon looked as if she wanted to argue the fact, but her husband took her by the arm and propelled her forward toward the exit.

"I hope Jonas survives your parenting," Finn muttered as the door swung shut behind them. He headed out of the office toward the side door leading to the warehouse when Lola suddenly said, "What?"

Finn stopped and then moved toward the counter as Lola sent him a wild look before focusing back on the phone in her hand. "You're sure? Yes. I'll tell him."

She hung up the phone and her eyes were wide when she said, "That was Chase's mom. Can you give her a ride to the hospital? He rolled his truck off some mountain road. She just got word."

Finn was almost to his truck when his phone rang in his pocket. He pulled it out, answering as he opened the truck door.

"Finn…" Molly's voice cracked before she got his name out.

"I heard. Do you know anything?"

"No. I'm heading to the hospital now."

"Have Mike drive you."

"I—"

"Please."

A few seconds of tense silence passed, then she said, "Sure. Fine."

She hung up and Finn hoped she was really going to do as she said. He didn't want Molly driving around in a state of shock. He'd done that a time or two. Never good.

MOLLY HATED THE smell of hospitals, but she could see from the way Mike's body stiffened as he opened the door for her and Elaine that he hated it more. He had reason to, she knew. The first person she spotted in the waiting area next to the admitting area was Finn. He headed toward her the moment he spotted her, pulling her against him. She allowed her one brief moment of holding him close, drawing strength, before pulling back. She needed answers, not comfort.

"They're both okay," he said.

But Molly needed to hear it for herself. She eased back another half step and he let her go, gesturing with his head toward the ER waiting room. "The nurse should be back in a few minutes. Chase took the worst of it. Georgina just got bruised up. Has a concussion."

Molly's eyes widened. "What happened to Chase?"

"Broken arm for sure. Ribs. The air bag on his side didn't deploy."

"How did this happen?"

"Road gave way. Weakened by rain."

"Should he have been driving on it?" She hated the sound of blame in her voice and did her best to soften it when she added, "I mean, was it an obvious danger?"

"No. Lots of other people had driven on it."

Mike took her by the shoulders. "Come on over here and sit." Molly nodded and allowed him to lead her away from Finn, who went to sit beside a small woman who seemed drawn into herself.

Chase's mother. The resemblance was strong. She met Molly's eyes across the waiting room and then looked away. The nurse came out from the swinging doors then and headed straight for

Chase's mother. Molly got to her feet and crossed the room.

"You're the sister?"

"I am."

"Well, your sister will be released shortly. No internal injuries. Just a lot of bruising." She turned to Chase's mother. "Your son will spend at least a day with us. Precautionary. But rest assured, he'll be fine."

The woman closed her eyes as the nurse walked away and Molly saw her lips move in a clear prayer of thanks. When she opened her eyes again, she said, "I can't afford too many days in the hospital."

"The store will cover it," Finn said from behind Molly.

"His insurance only pays fifty percent."

"The store will cover it, Lilah." This time Mike spoke, in a voice that would brook no nonsense.

"Double-teamed," Lilah murmured. She looked up at Finn. "He'll be okay."

"That's what they said."

"And so will Georgie."

Georgie. Molly pressed her lips together. Her sister had never been a fan of that name, but somehow, hearing it on Chase's mother's lips, it sounded like an endearment. His mother liked Georgina.

Part of Molly instantly thought, of course she

does. What's not to like? Then another part shot back, and what's not to like about Chase?

"Yeah, she'll be fine, too," Molly said when she realized all eyes were on her.

"Chase carried her up the mountain."

Molly frowned at Lilah. She was in shock, obviously, and so was Molly because she didn't understand what the woman was saying.

"The truck rolled off the mountain and wedged against a tree. Georgina got knocked loopy," Mike explained. "The tree was unstable Chase wouldn't leave her in the truck. He hauled her out and up that bank."

"That's…amazing, what with injured ribs and a broken arm."

"That's the kind of man he is," his mother said softly.

Molly opened her mouth, but couldn't push any words past the thickness in her throat. She met Finn's gaze, then closed her eyes briefly as he settled a hand on her shoulder, then gently pulled her against him, slipping an arm around her waist.

"I really appreciate what he did today. It shows a lot of heroism."

Lilah smiled weakly and then focused on the floor once again. Elaine sat beside her and took her hand, speaking to her in a low voice as Finn loosened his hold and led Molly to a chair not far away. There they both sat, side by side, hand in hand.

No words.

None necessary.

CHAPTER EIGHTEEN

ONCE GEORGINA GOT HOME, her biggest concern was Chase, until he called her from his hospital bed in the early evening and she finally relaxed, as did Molly. Her sister was bruised up and sore, had a pretty decent shiner, but she was home. Safe.

"It was a crazy thing," she told Molly as they shared a cup of tea sitting side by side on the old sofa, Georgina surrounded by pillows to help support her bruised body. "One minute everything was cool. The road was clear. No sign of any kind of danger. We weren't even on a curve."

Molly hugged her cup with both hands, taking comfort in the warmth because she'd felt cold all day. Shaking nervous cold. Being near Finn had made her feel better, but he was gone, helping Chase's mom wrangle her three kids and doing the chores that Chase normally handled around their small acreage.

"It just happened with no warning. I saw Chase reach out for me, then the air bag hit me and that's all I remember until we somehow got to the road." She closed her eyes. Shuddered. Then she pulled in a deep breath.

"But we're okay. You know?"

Molly reached out to stroke her sister's long dark hair. "I know. I'm beyond grateful. Chase did something pretty awesome, too."

"Yeah." Georgina sipped her tea. Closed her eyes. A few seconds later her hands relaxed and Molly rescued the tea, setting it on the side table. She got to her feet and paced through the empty house.

You can't control everything in your life. Things happen.

Or as Finn had said, shit happens.

Finn was a good guy—one that she wanted to have in her life. Was it too late to try to convince him that she was working toward change? That she didn't want dull and boring and predictable? That she wanted him?

He'd said he'd tried twice and wouldn't try again. That meant that the ball was firmly in her court. Now she had to figure out how best to handle it without screwing up again.

He was there for you at the hospital. He held you, demanded nothing of you.

She went to the window, saw the light of the television through Mike's curtains. Elaine's car was still parked in front. She turned away from the window, then, before she did something stupid, like talk herself out of things, she went to the front door and let herself out into the cold night air.

A coat would have been lovely, but Molly ignored the cold and dialed her phone. When Finn answered, she said, "Are you busy?"

"Heading for Mike's place."

Now or never. Well maybe not never, but she wanted Finn now. "Could you stop here first?"

"That was kind of my plan."

Molly's throat went a little dry. Instead of asking why, she said, "Good to hear."

When Finn parked his car in front of Mike's house five minutes later, Molly was waiting at the window. He got out and she bit her lip when she saw that he had the kitten, who was approaching teenage-cat size, with him.

She went to the door and pulled it open. For a moment he stood on the cold porch, then moved past her into the warmth of her small living room. "I thought Georgina might enjoy a visit from Buddy. He's kind of a miracle worker, you know."

"In what way?" She took the kitten from Finn and curled him under her chin. His motor started and Molly closed her eyes for a moment, breathing in the comforting scent of his warm cat fur.

"Wherever he is, things seem to start working out."

Molly opened her eyes. "Maybe wherever you are things start working out."

Finn snorted. "Call me crazy, but it doesn't feel that way."

"What does it feel like, Finn?"

He gave her a long narrow-eyed look. "It feels as if I have to fight hard for everything I want."

"Do you keep fighting?"

"Well, I tried to drop this English class once, but the instructor wouldn't let me, so I fought on."

She gave a nod. "Anything else?"

"There was this woman…"

She couldn't help it. Her insides tightened at the mention of "this woman." "Yeah?"

"She gave me all kinds of hell."

"What did you do?"

"I tried to fight on, but eventually honored her request to be left alone…hardest thing I've ever done."

Molly stroked the kitten, who continued to purr close to her ear, drawing strength. "She needed you to do that."

"So I hear."

"I kind of fell in love with you, Finn."

He didn't move. "That doesn't matter unless you let yourself do something about it."

"Like telling you that I'm done huddling on the safe side of life? That I'm not looking for a guy who fits my cookie-cutter mold so that I'm not forced into taking a calculated risk?"

"Something like that."

"It scares me to love you."

"What are you going to do about it?"

What was she going to do? The only thing she could do. "Make the leap."

"Can you?"

She took a step toward him—it wasn't a leap, but it was a move in the right direction. "You aren't Blake. And I'm not the Molly who loved Blake and was taken in by him."

"You're honestly ready to take a chance?" His tone was still less than convinced. Well, she hadn't expected this to be easy. Not when she'd shot him down in so many ways. Not when she'd worked so hard to build the barrier between them that she now wanted to obliterate.

"Look at me," she said softly, setting Buddy on the sofa so that she could move closer, slide her arms up around his neck, press her lower body against his and feel his rather gratifying reaction. "I'm stepping right up to the edge."

A small smile started playing on his lips.

"Look at you," he murmured. His hands came to her waist. "You feel good up against the edge."

"I'd feel better underneath you."

His eyebrows lifted and she leaned back, keeping her hands around his neck. "More than that,

I want to be with you. Build with you. Believe that even though we're different we can tackle things together." She drew in a deep breath. "I want to take a chance on us."

His hands tightened on her waist. "I'd like that. I love you, you know. I have for a while now."

She rose up on her toes and kissed him, welcomed him. Into her life, into her heart. She jumped a little as something brushed her leg and she looked down as Buddy threw himself against her ankle. She laughed and reached down to pick him up, cuddling him between herself and Finn.

"Good job, Buddy."

The kitten butted his head against her chin and then Finn kissed her.

All was well.

EPILOGUE

"I DIDN'T SEE this one coming," Elaine said as she tucked her hand in the crook of Mike's arm.

"Neither did I," Mike muttered. His friend Cal had essentially cleared the dance floor at Dylan and Jolie's Lightning Creek Ranch wedding by requesting a tango.

Jolie had confided to Molly that she assumed that Cal's plus-one for her wedding would be Karl and vice versa. No one had dreamed that Cal had not only found a serious lady friend on his online dating site, but that the two of them shared a love of ballroom dancing.

"I wonder if Karl's jealous?" Finn said with a laugh as Cal executed a series of kicks in tandem with his lady friend. "I mean this whole online dating thing was his idea and he's now the odd man out."

"I don't think Karl is a tango kind of guy. Besides, he'll meet new women when he moves to Dillon," Mike said.

Molly knew that Mike would miss his friend, but he had Elaine in his life now and no longer spent most of his waking hours at the feed store. And neither did Finn, who was working on his second semester at EVCC, working toward his associate's degree so that he could teach metals there. Chase had been hired on full-time to do the warehouse work and Jolie had taken over Mike's job as manager.

Mike turned toward Elaine as Cal did another flamboyant turn. "I'm just glad you're sane."

Elaine laughed and put a light hand on his chest. "You say the sweetest things."

She looped her arm through his and they moved toward the buffet table where the new bride and groom stood holding hands and looking very satisfied with life.

"Do you think Mike and Elaine will get married?" Molly asked Finn as he took her hand and they walked together toward the trees that lined the driveway of the Lightning Creek Ranch. Mike had been a rock during Elaine's successful radiation treatments, and now they rarely spent time apart from one another.

"No telling. But I think we should get married."

Molly's gaze flashed up to his. He was dead serious. And even though she'd entertained thoughts of their relationship becoming permanent, her breath froze in her chest.

"I didn't mean to scare you," he said gruffly. "It doesn't have to be soon or anything."

"No. It's not that," Molly said, because being close to Finn didn't scare her. "It's…"

"What?"

She broke into a broad smile. "The best thing ever? Yes. I'll marry you."

A relieved look crossed Finn's face as he reached out for her. "I thought I was going to have to talk harder and longer. I wrote out a speech—used note cards and everything so that it would be well organized."

"Right," she said against his shoulder, before raising her lips to his.

"Hey now!" Chase called from the direction of the buffet table and then Molly heard her sister laugh. She smiled against Finn's mouth.

"Caught," she murmured.

"Don't care," he muttered back. He took her lips again in a quick kiss that held the promise of heat, then ran his hands over her bare shoulders. "I did have some convincing arguments ready."

"Unnecessary. I've been thinking about this, too."

"You might have given me a hint," he said as he laced his fingers with hers and they started walking again. "Saved me all the speech writing."

"I'd like to see this speech," she said as they slowly headed back to the party.

"No way. You'd either red-pen it to death or give me a higher mark than I deserve."

Molly stopped walking. "That red pen brought us together."

"As did my persistence in proving that I was the perfect guy for you."

She squeezed his fingers as she smiled up at him. "That, too." She raised her chin. "I love you, you know. For your persistence and steadiness and dependability." Characteristics she'd never dreamed he possessed when she'd graded that very first paper of his. She drew in a small breath, "But mostly I love you because you're you."

Mr. Wrong had been Mr. Right all along.

* * * * *

LARGER-PRINT BOOKS!
GET 2 FREE LARGER-PRINT NOVELS PLUS
2 FREE GIFTS!

HARLEQUIN®

Romance

From the Heart, For the Heart

YES! Please send me 2 FREE LARGER-PRINT Harlequin® Romance novels and my 2 FREE gifts (gifts are worth about $10). After receiving them, if I don't wish to receive any more books, I can return the shipping statement marked "cancel." If I don't cancel, I will receive 4 brand-new novels every month and be billed just $5.09 per book in the U.S. or $5.49 per book in Canada. That's a savings of at least 15% off the cover price! It's quite a bargain! Shipping and handling is just 50¢ per book in the U.S. and 75¢ per book in Canada.* I understand that accepting the 2 free books and gifts places me under no obligation to buy anything. I can always return a shipment and cancel at any time. Even if I never buy another book, the two free books and gifts are mine to keep forever.

119/319 HDN GHWC

Name	(PLEASE PRINT)	
Address		Apt. #
City	State/Prov.	Zip/Postal Code

Signature (if under 18, a parent or guardian must sign)

Mail to the **Reader Service:**
IN U.S.A.: P.O. Box 1867, Buffalo, NY 14240-1867
IN CANADA: P.O. Box 609, Fort Erie, Ontario L2A 5X3

Want to try two free books from another line?
Call 1-800-873-8635 or visit www.ReaderService.com.

* Terms and prices subject to change without notice. Prices do not include applicable taxes. Sales tax applicable in N.Y. Canadian residents will be charged applicable taxes. Offer not valid in Quebec. This offer is limited to one order per household. Not valid for current subscribers to Harlequin Romance Larger-Print books. All orders subject to credit approval. Credit or debit balances in a customer's account(s) may be offset by any other outstanding balance owed by or to the customer. Please allow 4 to 6 weeks for delivery. Offer available while quantities last.

Your Privacy—The Reader Service is committed to protecting your privacy. Our Privacy Policy is available online at www.ReaderService.com or upon request from the Reader Service.

We make a portion of our mailing list available to reputable third parties that offer products we believe may interest you. If you prefer that we not exchange your name with third parties, or if you wish to clarify or modify your communication preferences, please visit us at www.ReaderService.com/consumerschoice or write to us at Reader Service Preference Service, P.O. Box 9062, Buffalo, NY 14240-9062. Include your complete name and address.

HRLP15

LARGER-PRINT BOOKS!

HARLEQUIN

Presents®

PASSION GUARANTEED SEDUCTION

GET 2 FREE LARGER-PRINT NOVELS PLUS 2 FREE GIFTS!

YES! Please send me 2 FREE LARGER-PRINT Harlequin Presents® novels and my 2 FREE gifts (gifts are worth about $10). After receiving them, if I don't wish to receive any more books, I can return the shipping statement marked "cancel." If I don't cancel, I will receive 6 brand-new novels every month and be billed just $5.30 per book in the U.S. or $5.74 per book in Canada. That's a saving of at least 12% off the cover price! It's quite a bargain! Shipping and handling is just 50¢ per book in the U.S. and 75¢ per book in Canada.* I understand that accepting the 2 free books and gifts places me under no obligation to buy anything. I can always return a shipment and cancel at any time. Even if I never buy another book, the two free books and gifts are mine to keep forever.

176/376 HDN GHVY

Name	(PLEASE PRINT)	
Address		Apt. #
City	State/Prov.	Zip/Postal Code

Signature (if under 18, a parent or guardian must sign)

Mail to the **Reader Service:**
IN U.S.A.: P.O. Box 1867, Buffalo, NY 14240-1867
IN CANADA: P.O. Box 609, Fort Erie, Ontario L2A 5X3

Are you a subscriber to Harlequin Presents® books and want to receive the larger-print edition?
Call 1-800-873-8635 today or visit us at www.ReaderService.com.

* Terms and prices subject to change without notice. Prices do not include applicable taxes. Sales tax applicable in N.Y. Canadian residents will be charged applicable taxes. Offer not valid in Quebec. This offer is limited to one order per household. Not valid for current subscribers to Harlequin Presents Larger-Print books. All orders subject to credit approval. Credit or debit balances in a customer's account(s) may be offset by any other outstanding balance owed by or to the customer. Please allow 4 to 6 weeks for delivery. Offer available while quantities last.

Your Privacy—The Reader Service is committed to protecting your privacy. Our Privacy Policy is available online at www.ReaderService.com or upon request from the Reader Service.

We make a portion of our mailing list available to reputable third parties that offer products we believe may interest you. If you prefer that we not exchange your name with third parties, or if you wish to clarify or modify your communication preferences, please visit us at www.ReaderService.com/consumerschoice or write to us at Reader Service Preference Service, P.O. Box 9062, Buffalo, NY 14240-9062. Include your complete name and address.

HPLP15

REQUEST YOUR FREE BOOKS!
2 FREE WHOLESOME ROMANCE NOVELS
IN LARGER PRINT
PLUS 2
FREE
MYSTERY GIFTS

HEARTWARMING™

Wholesome, tender romances

YES! Please send me 2 FREE Harlequin® Heartwarming Larger-Print novels and my 2 FREE mystery gifts (gifts worth about $10). After receiving them, if I don't wish to receive any more books, I can return the shipping statement marked "cancel." If I don't cancel, I will receive 4 brand-new larger-print novels every month and be billed just $5.24 per book in the U.S. or $5.99 per book in Canada. That's a savings of at least 19% off the cover price. It's quite a bargain! Shipping and handling is just 50¢ per book in the U.S. and 75¢ per book in Canada.* I understand that accepting the 2 free books and gifts places me under no obligation to buy anything. I can always return a shipment and cancel at any time. Even if I never buy another book, the two free books and gifts are mine to keep forever.

161/361 IDN GHX2

Name	(PLEASE PRINT)

Address	Apt. #

City	State/Prov.	Zip/Postal Code

Signature (if under 18, a parent or guardian must sign)

Mail to the **Reader Service**:
IN U.S.A.: P.O. Box 1867, Buffalo, NY 14240-1867
IN CANADA: P.O. Box 609, Fort Erie, Ontario L2A 5X3

* Terms and prices subject to change without notice. Prices do not include applicable taxes. Sales tax applicable in N.Y. Canadian residents will be charged applicable taxes. Offer not valid in Quebec. This offer is limited to one order per household. Not valid for current subscribers to Harlequin Heartwarming larger-print books. All orders subject to credit approval. Credit or debit balances in a customer's account(s) may be offset by any other outstanding balance owed by or to the customer. Please allow 4 to 6 weeks for delivery. Offer available while quantities last.

Your Privacy—The Reader Service is committed to protecting your privacy. Our Privacy Policy is available online at www.ReaderService.com or upon request from the Reader Service.

We make a portion of our mailing list available to reputable third parties that offer products we believe may interest you. If you prefer that we not exchange your name with third parties, or if you wish to clarify or modify your communication preferences, please visit us at www.ReaderService.com/consumerschoice or write to us at Reader Service Preference Service, P.O. Box 9062, Buffalo, NY 14240-9062. Include your complete name and address.

HW15